Money Manager

CRYPTID BILLIONAIRES

LUNA CANTRIP

DEDICATION

*This book is for every weirdo who was
ever told their laugh was too loud.*

CONTENT NOTES

Moth Manager is an explicit monster romance. This book is a pretty light and easy read, but there are scenes of graphic sex, and some issues that could be triggering to some. Please keep yourself safe, I want everyone to have an enjoyable reading experience.

Content Considerations: *Stalking (lite), Pregnancy, Instalove/Instalust, Fated-mates, Parental Abandonment, Praise kink, Crazy-exs, First Act break-up, Strong language*

Mental health is important, if I missed anything that should have been included in the trigger warnings, please feel free to drop me an email: lunacantrip@gmail.com

BOOK PLAYLIST

"DISTURBIA".. RIHANNA

"TAMMY AND THE T-REX" .... COLD HART

"TELEPATÍA" .... KALI UCHIS

"NIGHT SHIFT" .... LUCY DACUS

"MAIN TITLE"..CHUCK CIRINO

"BREATH OF THE WILD - EPIC   L'ORCHESTRA
VERSION" ....CINEMATIQUE

"LET'S FALL IN LOVE FOR THE NIGHT" .... FINNEAS

"THE EDGE OF NIGHT"........................   CINESCORE

"STAR TREK: VOYAGER - MAIN TITLE"...... JERRY GOLDSMITH

"HALLOWEEN" ....   PHOEBE BRIDGERS

"TURN THE LIGHTS OFF"....................................TALLY HALL

"FIRE" .... BARNS COURTNEY

"FOREST INTERLUDE" ....BEN ZIMMERMANN

"FLY AWAY"... LENNY KRAVITZ

"NRRRD GRRRL"...MC CHRIS

"THE MOON"..BIT BRIGADE

"MOON & PRINCE" .... BANDAI NAMCO GAME MUSIC

"THE HOUSE AT SWAMP BOTTOM" .... JOE HISAISHI

"AT NIGHT" .... MAX LL

"PLANETARIUM"... ROBYN MILLER

"AFTER MIDNIGHT" .... CHAPPELL ROAN

TABLE OF CONTENTS

Prologue
PONTIUS

She's here. Somewhere. I can smell her. My fated-mate.

The night is early but Moonshine is already crowded. It's going to be difficult to pick her out from the other patrons. I know I smell her, even amongst all the other humans here tonight, her scent stands out. It's far more intoxicating than the liquor in my hand. Driving me to find her, protect her, steal her, fly her back to my nest, bury myself in her pussy, and convince her to be with me forever. Marry me. Bear my Mothlings.

She will be mine.

If I can figure out who she is before the noise of human nightlife drives me from the bar.

I unfurl my proboscis tongue, dip it into my glass and take a long sip of bourbon. Hopefully the alcohol will dull the throb building in my head.

I love watching humans. I love their culture, their music, their movies, their activities. They are fascinating, lively, entertaining, and completely exhausting. When I bought Moonshine I tried to create a place where humans and cryptids could interact. Even here, in a business I own, it still gets so loud it bothers my sensitive antennae.

Any other evening I'd finish my drink and head home, where I can decompress alone. I can't do that tonight. I have to manage my discomfort until I find the woman I am meant to spend the rest of my life with. She's here, somewhere. Her scent tells me she's human. Female. Perfect.

There are a couple dozen women spread through the room, and she could be any of them.

Any except the one sitting beside me.

"Don't drink like that, Pontius. It's gross." Tiffany, my date, and sometimes girlfriend, glances up from her phone to advise.

"Sorry, Tiffany," I say, pulling my tongue back into my mouth.

"No problem, babe." Tiffany's always tried to help me blend in with humans. She pats my arm gently. Usually I enjoy her company, tonight it feels wrong.

"No, I mean—" I pull away from her touch. "We have to end this." I gesture between us.

This has her full attention. Tiffany's eyes go wide.

"Are you serious?" Her brow furrows. We've dated, off-and-on, for almost two years. Before now, it was always her who initiated our splits. I knew she wasn't my fated-mate. Spending time with her was better than being completely alone.

"Is this because I went out with that gargoyle last week?" she asks. "I told you baby, he didn't mean anything."

My antennae curve down. "I can't see you again. I've found my mate."

"Your mate? Where?" Tiffany gestures skeptically to the empty seats at our table.

"She's...somewhere." I scan the room.

From my private booth in the corner, I can observe the entire bar; while I was talking to Tiffany more humans arrived and spread amongst the tables. Disguising her scent even further.

The crowd's attention is turned to a screen on one wall where we're projecting our monthly 'Monster Love Movie Night'.

"You're sure it's not me?" Tiffany leans her breasts into my arm. She's usually good at this sort of thing, flirting to make me feel more at ease, but now her touch feels wrong.

"It isn't you." I pull away from her again. It'd almost be easier if it were her. I've never had much luck with dating, human or otherwise.

Dating as a Mothman can be difficult. Most humans aren't willing to see me almost exclusively after sunset, and asking a stranger you match on an app to meet a monster in a dark quiet place isn't usually received well.

Tiffany sticks out her bottom lip in an exaggerated pout—the way she does when she's trying to get her way. It doesn't help tonight. She can't compare to the perfect woman waiting somewhere in this room. Now that I've found my real mate, even Tiffany's smell is artificially saccharine.

"You're serious? You are dropping me for someone you haven't met yet?"

"Yes," I hesitate before adding. "I'm sorry it's so abrupt—"

Tiffany interrupts me with a loud sigh and sinks back to her seat. "Am I still going to get the Burkin?"

"The bag? Sure." What do I care about a bag?

She smirks and begins scrolling through her phone at lightning speed. I might expect a different person to cry or yell. I know Tiffany better at this point.

"Will you text me when it comes in? The associate has my number. It's under your name on the list, so they might call you first." Her expression changes to pity and her voice drops to a breathy whisper. "You know this doesn't have to be the end, Pontius. You're a real peach. An awkward, hairy peach with a lot of weird quirks that are hard for most humans to accept."

"She'll like me," I protest. I know humans are put off by my odd features: my large red eyes, my fur, my mandibles, my wings. So many parts of my appearance have been called 'creepy'. My mate will be different. She has to be different.

"Of course she'll like you. But being with a Mothman isn't easy. Not everyone is as open-minded as I am. Don't be surprised if this new girl isn't willing to indulge you the way I do." She shifts her legs, drawing her skirt a little higher up her thigh. "You know, plenty of rich men don't limit themselves to only one woman. I'm okay if you want to keep our relationship—private."

"No!" I recoil instantly. Even if, like a lot of humans, she finds the idea of touching me appalling, I would never cheat on my mate.

"Well, if she rejects you, you know how to reach me." Tiffany mimes holding a phone up to her ear.

"She won't reject me," I say, more to convince myself than Tiffany.

"Promise to text me when the Burkin is available?" She leans over and presses a very light kiss to my cheek.

My antennae fold back defensively, I lean away from her and scan the crowd again. I hope my mate didn't see that; I don't want her to think I'm in a relationship.

Tiffany stands. "At least it's relatively early. My whole night isn't a complete waste." She's already typing on her phone again. "I'm sure I'll see you soon, Pontius."

I barely acknowledge her exit, returning my focus to the crowd.

I was excited when the Decrypting first happened, when cryptids stopped hiding in the shadows and joined human society. Between shrinking habitats and satellite imagery it'd become more difficult to stay hidden. Leaders amongst the various cryptid species got together and decided to expose ourselves. I was seventeen and ready to go out and join human society, but it proved harder than I expected. Even now, fifteen years later it can still be difficult to find places I feel comfortable. A lot of human infrastructure doesn't make it easy for cryptids to be ourselves. Things have been improving, and I've been using my own resources to make it better.

Fresh out of college, I started a tech company with my two best friends. We've been successful, really successful. More than enough for me to invest in local community improvements. Like buying a large share of the Moonshine, so I could focus on creating an all-species bar. Trying to make a space that's accessible to everyone.

Moonshine is doing well now too. There are a few obvious cryptids in tonight's crowd. No other Mothmen. We're rarer than a lot of species, and even amongst our own kind we're solitary creatures. Despite my best efforts, it's hard to imagine another Mothman choosing to hang out somewhere this loud and crowded.

Still, I'm pleased with the great turn out tonight. The audience is split into small tables, they chat quietly over the noise of the movie. The combinations of sounds is already grating on my nerves. Tonight's film is about a teenaged Denise Richards, falling in love with a robotic dinosaur.

My mate is watching.

Could I convince her to love a monster?

It's all I've ever wanted, someone who will accept me no matter what I look like. Someone who won't flinch away when they see my glowing red eyes, or my fur, or wings, or mandibles. I know Mothmen have taken human mates before, but I don't understand how. I would never force myself on someone, and even Tiffany—who was more accommodating than most—set hard limits in our physical relationship. There are many things I haven't had a chance to experience.

My mate will be different; she will understand me; she will let me touch her, hold her, be close to her. Marry her. Keep her in my nest. Fulfill every wish she's ever desired.

I will do anything to make her like me, to make her mine.

As soon as I figure out who she is.

I can't stay here much longer. I used to admire human nightlife from the outside, coveting their parties and social lives and music. It was disappointing to learn that, in person, these events are too much for me. I pay my tab and head into the cool September air.

I will wait.

My mate has to leave eventually. I'll watch the door until the bar closes if I need to. Mothmen are nocturnal, it will be easy to wait.

Hours pass. The night stretches so thin that I spread my wings and fly up to perch on the roof of the building, where I can comfortably sit as I watch the door. Each patron who leaves the building briefly spikes my hope, until their smell reaches me. Everyone of them is wrong.

I tuck my wings a little tighter around my shoulders. No one seems to notice me; it's easy to fade into the darkness when you are shaped like a large black shadow.

Finally, a perfect beauty steps onto the street. I

know, as soon as I lay eyes on a mess of red hair, that I've found her. I feel it in my nose, in my chest, in every atom of my body. The driving urge to swoop down and claim her for myself. Pluck her up and take her back to my nest.

It's her. My mate.

Her red hair is piled high on her head in a perfectly messy bun, a wide smile shows off perfectly crooked front teeth, a pair of thick glasses rest on her perfectly freckled nose, her mouth opens and produces a perfectly infectious laugh. Everything about her is perfect.

Except she's hanging onto a man. She's smiling, laughing, and touching someone else.

The bastard.

Jealousy roils in my stomach. That isn't fair. She should be with me. I'm sure I'd make her happier than he'll ever be able to.

I spent my adolescent years surreptitiously watching humans. Before the Decrypting, that was all I had. I coveted so many things humans had and I didn't.

Nothing has ever spiked this type of red-raw jealousy before.

She is meant for me. She is mine.

It's easy to follow her movements. Her red hair practically glows in the darkness. Like a flame drawing me closer. The couple turn left from the bar. Her bright yellow sneakers wobble on the uneven pavement, a hint of intoxication in her steps. Her drunken laugh echoes loudly into the night. The man shushes her before urging her forward with slight irritation in his voice.

My antennae flutter. My vision flashes red briefly. He had better not be forcing my mate to do anything against her will.

She doesn't seem concerned. She laughs and speeds

up, grabbing his wrist and tugging him along. I spread my wings and catch the wind. A small jump, and I'm airborne.

I follow my mate, and her date, through the neighborhood. His expression doesn't lighten the entire trip. He grumbles, and she giggles. I can't hear the whole conversation from above them, but I do catch her laugh again. Loud, light, and expressive. Like a mating call.

They don't walk far, maybe fifteen minutes. Turning down three or four side streets before they finally stop at a house.

My territory. My mate.

I land on the rooftop across the street from them. She pulls the man in close for a long kiss. His sour expression finally breaks and his shoulders relax. My hands clench tight into fists. It isn't fair that he has her.

I should be under her lips, receiving her kiss. This human man doesn't deserve to touch her, he doesn't deserve the smile she brings to his lips.

My mate says something I can't hear, making herself laugh again, before stumbling up the front stairs of a brownstone, pulling her date after her. She fumbles with the keys for a moment before the man pulls out his own set and unlocks the door. Her apartment. Or possibly their shared space.

I tighten my fist. That isn't right. She should be living with me. In our nest.

My mate is giggling as she pulls her date in for another kiss before leading him into the apartment.

How sad would she be if he disappeared? If she never heard from him again? If I snatched him from the street, flew three miles out to sea, and dropped him into the ocean.

The night air is chill so I tuck my wings around my

shoulder for extra warmth while I watch the windows. It's easy to track the couple's path as lights turn on and off throughout the apartment. Until finally, silhouettes are highlighted through sheer curtains on the second story. I can see enough to know it is their bedroom, and enough to know they are about to participate in bedroom activities.

It's wrong to watch. I know I shouldn't be here. I should leave now, go home alone, with only my memories of her.

I spread my wings and flit down to her front step.

Eventually she'll realize that human man is wrong for her. She will come to her senses and leave him.

A tiny peek through her front window won't hurt anyone.

The glass on the front door is textured, but there's a sliver of clear window that provides an unobstructed view into her home. A set of stairs leads up to the second story on the right side of a long narrow hallway. The left side is filled with moving boxes. In the rear the kitchen is cast in a warm homey glow.

Headlights pass on the street behind me and I flinch at the engine noise.

I can't get caught here. I shouldn't be spying into her house. But I need to be ready for her when it happens. I need to know everything I can about her. Learn what she likes, what she wants. I need to be waiting to give her... everything.

A flutter of movement catches my eye, a flier hanging from her mailbox catches the wind. I shouldn't look. It's illegal, and invasive. I pull it out, a piece of junk mail, it won't be missed. And now I know my mate's name.

Piper.

Piper Hamilton.

1

PIPER

Bars are always packed full of idiots on Halloween. I didn't expect my new favorite little cocktail joint, Moonshine, to be any different. I was so desperate to get my newly single ass out of the house that I didn't care.

"That's a great costume," a male voice near my ear says. The bar is crowded, so I don't judge him for standing close to me. He isn't actually touching me, just hovering near my shoulder while he waits his turn to order a drink.

"Thank you." I prepare a half smile before I turn around, ready to patiently accept yet another well intentioned compliment that's completely off the mark.

"You must not read from the book!" The voice quotes with a light chuckle, trying to match the cadence of the line from The Mummy.

"Oh! You know the movie!" I'm excited someone finally 'gets' my Halloween costume. A white button-down, long khaki skirt, and loosely tied black scarf. I was excited to think of something I could wear with my glasses. I can't see shit without them, and contacts have always bothered my eyes. The costume has turned out more obscure than I expected. I've already endured a half-dozen incorrect guesses about who I'm dressed as.[1] It's exciting to find someone who actually gets it. I spin in place, avoiding touching the other patrons, to find out what my new favorite person looks like.

Large red eyes examine me from a wholly inhuman face. He's tall, made taller by the skinny, curling, feather-like antennae rising from his head. His frame is slender, with narrow shoulders, and a thick fur collar around his neck. His skin is dark, covered in the softest looking fur I've ever seen. A strange urge flutters through me to reach out and stroke my fingers along his arm, curious if he feels as velvety as he looks. A pair of moth wings are folded neatly against his shoulders, out of the way of the crowd.

I'm taken aback when I realize, this is not a Halloween costume. He is a real-life Mothman.

Then I notice that, actually, he is wearing a Halloween costume. A blue shirt with a small insignia on the chest, and plastered to each side of his head is a pointy piece of plastic.

"Spock?" I ask.

"Yes!" One of the strange mandibles around his mouth tips up in an expression that could only be interpreted as a smile.

It's surprisingly endearing. I surprise myself by blushing in response. I'm not usually attracted to people this quickly. Most of the time, I have to feel a connection before I find someone hot. Being newly single might have opened my eyes to a world of possibilities.

"You're Rachel Weisz from The Mummy. Right?" He breaks the silence between us, and I realize I'm staring.

---

1 Female Indiana Jones, Female Steve Irwin, Female Ghostbuster, mostly just 'female' in front of any khaki colored pop culture figure.

"Oh, yeah! Yes!" My nervous fingers adjust my glasses and make sure my hair is secure in its bun.

"It's a great movie," he says.

"Right? It was something of a bi-awakening for me." An awkward laugh bubbles out of me. "I probably shouldn't say that to a stranger."

People, men in particular, get weird about the bi thing sometimes.[2]

"I get it. The same, basically. I had a little crush on Brendan and Rachel both," he says so smoothly that I instantly relax. A guy can't be too bad if he had a childhood crush on Brendan Fraser, right?

"What are you drinking?" His antennae point to the bar behind me. The movement is fascinating.

I've seen plenty of cryptids in public spaces since the Decrypting fifteen years ago, when mythical creatures stopped being myths and started joining human society. Passing a Kraken on the street is different than trying to flirt with a handsome Mothman who is clearly trying not to encroach on my personal space.

"Getting some Beetle Gin and Juice shots for me and my friends. Girls night." I nod to the table of women waiting for me in the corner. Crap. Was that a shut-down? Spending almost four years with the same man made me rusty at flirting. Not that I was ever very good. How do you imply you are newly single and potentially ready to mingle?

"How many?" He seems undeterred.

"Six?" When I hear the insecure rise of my tone that turns the word into a question, I correct. "Six. Two for each of us!" My voice is more decisive this time, like feigning confidence might get him to find me attractive.

---

2 Sometimes, in this case, means frequently.

The Mothman's antennae rise, and he catches the attention of the bartender behind me. "Six of the themed shots." He gestures toward me. The bartender nods and starts pouring from a premixed pitcher. "On my tab, please."

"Oh no, I can pay for my own drinks!" I blurt, sliding my at-ready credit card from my sleeve and holding it toward the Mothman using both hands, like it's some kind of placard to prove I'm a real adult, with real money. Not a lot of money, but I'm not here to scam free drinks out of people.

He glances down at the piece of plastic clenched between my fingers. Crap. That was the wrong thing to say. Flirting involves buying each other drinks. This is a sign he's interested. Isn't it? Or maybe I'm just taking too long at the bar, and the guy wants me out of the way. I should say something to encourage him to stay and talk to me. Something hot, or sexy, or funny. I've never been very good at hot, or sexy. I'd better stick with funny.

Crap. I'm still holding out my credit card like an idiot.

"Do you...Do you frequently find human behavior illogical?" I'm already cringing internally.

"Yes." His smile doesn't falter. Maybe I am reading his expression wrong. I am so far out of my element here.

I glance around his arm, to where my friends Anam and Kelly wait. Either one of them would know how to flirt with a Mothman. They're good at this kind of stuff, and by 'stuff' I mean talking to people. Anam catches my eye from across the room. I try to give her a pleading expression without actually moving any of the muscles in my face. She might be able to catch a glint in my eye that telepathically shouts, 'help me, I've forgotten how to flirt'.

When I look back, the Mothman is staring at me. Despite the packed bar, my ears are full of the silence lingering between us.

One antenna raises a few inches. "Come on, Piper, your money's no good here." A little purr in his voice sends a shiver down my spine.

"You know my name?"

He raises a hand, it's large. Like, really large. The skin dark like his fur, his nails long but dull. One long slender finger pokes at the clearly displayed name on my credit card. I wince.

"You didn't memorize the number too, did you?" I bark out a nervous laugh and then force myself to stop. Crap, the laugh is embarrassing.

"What if I did?" He's definitely interested in me; there's no other way to interpret the way he puts a little purr in his voice as he leans forward.

The bartender pushes my drinks forward and pours the Mothman something without asking.

"Do you come here often?" I let myself laugh this time. So he will know that I'm joking.

The Mothman shrugs. "Often enough to know you've been here before." He reaches around me slowly, his arm grazing mine as he collects his beverage. I feel a little heat creep up my cheeks.

I started coming here a lot when Colin and I moved into an apartment nearby a couple months ago. It can be tricky to find a good bar in a new neighborhood. Moonshine is a great place, with a perfectly cozy atmosphere. It's frequently crowded, but rarely packed. With plenty of seating for the nights they project movies on the large screen behind the stage, and plenty of floor space to dance when there is music, like tonight. It's their monthly silent disco. The tables are pushed to the side and in one corner a DJ spins a spooky Halloween mix through wireless headphones, so you can control the volume of your own music.

"You want some help with those?" The Mothman nods to my small tray of drinks. I begin to shake my head, change my mind, and open my mouth to say yes when Kelly pushes over to me.

"Hey, Piper! What's taking so long?" She steps between me and the Mothman, her expression reads she thinks she's doing me a favor.

The Mothman doesn't say anything else, giving me a tiny nod before he retreats into the crowd.

"Shit. Sorry, did I clam jam you? I mean, you weren't into the cryptid, were you?" Kelly asks.

"I'm not even sure if he was interested in me." I grab our drinks and push past her to head back to our table. I'm a little disappointed the Mothman gave up so quickly. Who wants to flirt with the woman wearing a shin length khaki skirt to the bar? I thought the outfit was cute at home, but standing here surrounded by gorgeous women in skimpy outfits, I feel a bit dowdy. No one is going to pick me when there's a sexy blonde devil in a bright red corset that pushes her boobs up to her neck available.

I should have shoved my boobs up to my neck.

Instead, I've got them squirreled away behind a starched white button-down. My boobs have always been my best feature. Colin loved them. Although, he didn't necessarily love when I wore tops showing them off.

I guess I'm allowed to show them to anyone I want now. Next year, I'll wear a fun, slutty costume and let everyone enjoy them. The Mothman wouldn't have walked away if I was wearing something he could see my boobs in.

Kelly and I make it all the way back to our table, where Anam waits, before I cave into my urge to check over my shoulder to see what the Mothman is doing.

I think he's staring in my direction. With his compound eyes, I can't tell exactly which direction he's looking, until he holds up his hand, clawed fingers separated into the Vulcan 'live long and prosper' salute. Classic Spock move. That makes me feel a little less like an idiot.

There was something between us; it wasn't entirely my imagination. I feel a satisfying heat creep up my cheeks. I can do this. I can be single. I can flirt.

"To Kelly's potential art show!" Anam interrupts my thoughts by holding up one of the shots for a toast.

"Here here!" Kelly agrees as she picks up a shot glass. "And to Anam's grant being awarded!"

Anam pumps her fist in the air. "And to Piper getting laid tonight!"

"I don't know about that." I laugh, and I clink my glass with theirs anyway.

"To Piper being single and finally having some fun!" Anam says.

I agree more enthusiastically to that suggestion before choking back the shot. Fun. Right. I thought I was having fun. I thought I had life neatly sorted. Good job, cute apartment, committed boyfriend. On my way to marriage and kids and home ownership.[3] I'm not sure what I did wrong to make Colin leave.

"Was he a real cryptid?" Kelly asks the second her empty shot glass hits the tabletop. She adjusts the hem of her short black cocktail dress. It highlights her running toned legs, and slim frame. Her long brown hair is pulled into a French twist. She looks elegant and sexy, because Kelly knows her strengths.

---

3 Or maybe not in this economy.

"Did he try to hit on you?" Anam yells, because once she gets drunk she begins speaking at twice the volume she thinks she is. She's wearing a low cut sexy bee costume, with letters cut out of construction paper taped all over her outfit. A 'Spelling Bee', because Anam also knows her strengths, humor and boobs.

"Yes? No? I don't know? He paid for these drinks," I admit.

"Ooo. Promising! You into him?" Anam asks very loudly.

"I don't know...do you guys think he's cute?" I twist my shot glass, making patterns with the rings of condensation on the tabletop. Kelly raises her eyebrows at me.

"I heard cryptids have huge monster dongs!" Anam holds her hands out to represent an impossibly long penis. "In the name of science, I'll need you to perform field research, and report your findings for peer review via text message tomorrow morning!"

"I don't really think he was into me," I say tentatively, hoping one of them will disagree with me.

"Don't be ridiculous, of course he was." Kelly always steps up to the plate. "I only intervened because you looked like a deer caught in headlights. I thought you needed rescuing. If you like him, go over there and talk to him!"

I risk a glance over my shoulder again. The Mothman isn't looking at me any more, he's talking to the busty devil, who actually knows what to do with her breasts.

"It looks like he found a better prospect." I tell my hot friends. They look equally cute and holiday themed. I'm the only nerd who decided to dress in a maxi skirt, long sleeves, and thick-rimmed glasses on what's supposed to be the sexiest adult holiday.

"Don't be an idiot," Anam scoffs. "You are hot shit, and we all know it! You've got a giant brain and big tits to match!"

My brain is the problem. I'm always trying to be so fucking clever. All I wanted was for Colin to do a cute couple's costume with me. He was never into cutesy couple stuff. He only agreed to be my Brendan Fraser because it was easy to do. By myself I'm borderline unrecognizable. Now I'm walking around the bar looking like a lonely dork, and feeling like my life is starting over at twenty-nine.

"It doesn't matter," I say. "I don't think I'm ready for another relationship this soon."

"Relationship?!" Anam laughs. "No baby girl! We are getting you laid tonight! No strings! No fuss! One night of sex!"

Beside her, Kelly shrugs. Kelly's been with her boyfriend almost as long as I'd been with Colin. Anam is our perpetually single friend. The one who feels actual joy when meeting new people. She loves that stuff, a new guy every weekend, hip restaurants, trendy bars, loud music, the kinds of things that make me exhausted just thinking about them.

I squirm a little. "It's only been a week."

"The best way to get over someone is to get under someone new!" Anam puts her hand over her heart like she is making a vow.

Kelly giggles. "Anam's right. Doesn't a one-night stand sound like it would hit the spot?"

"A bit of strange, after three years of the same bland thing?" Anam sticks her tongue out suggestively. "A new dick, or pussy, or whatever the Mothman is packing down there."

"I don't know, I've never done it before."

"What? A Mothman?" Anam blurts.

"A one-night stand," I mutter.

Anam gasps, clutching her chest in mock horror.

"Seriously?" Kelly's surprise sounds genuine.

I stare at the table, feeling a little embarrassed. "It never seemed like something I would enjoy. I didn't look for the opportunity."

"Girl. This is the perfect chance!" Anam wraps her hands around my shoulders to shake me gently.

"I don't know...Colin hasn't even moved out completely."

His boxes are still in our spare bedroom. *My* spare bedroom. The bedroom that, two months ago, on move-in day, Colin held my hand and said, 'maybe this could be a baby's room some day'.

Now, he's got a new job, he's moved across the country, and he doesn't even want to give long distance a try.

Crap, I gotta stop thinking about the guy who dumped me for a job.

"Screw him! He is an ass!" Anam announces. "You can do much better! You are smart and fun and sexy, and did I already mention smart? You are so smart! And you run your own business, and any guy would be lucky to snap you up! And you are so pretty and sexy and smart!" Anam tugs me into a hug, pulling me tight against her body, putting a little too much of her weight on me as she almost loses her footing.

The arrangement of empty glasses on our table imply she's taken more than her fair share of the shots. Which is fine. I'm too sad to drink tonight. Some sadness is complemented by alcohol, but tonight feels like it will end better if I go home sober.

Sober, and alone, to my big empty apartment.

"Come on! Let's dance your worries away." Anam pops her headphones on for the silent disco and immediately squeals. "Oh my god. This is our song! We have to dance!"

She points to the headphones and backs her way onto the dance floor, beckoning for us to join her as she shakes her ample booty.

I slip my own headphones on and turn the volume up. I don't remember ever declaring a remix of Rihanna's Disturbia was 'our song', but I don't argue with Anam's infectiously good mood. I let her coax me onto the crowded dance floor.

The room itself is relatively quiet, and the music is perfectly loud in my ears, so it's easy to forget that people can actually see us. My friends and I bump and grind around the dance floor, having fun as three women, just existing.

After a few songs dancing with my friends I've actually managed to banish Colin from my thoughts when I spot the Mothman again.

Staring right at me.

2

PIPER

The Mothman leans against the end of the bar, his arms folded across his chest making a strange and intriguing silhouette with his wings tucked in tight to his shoulders and his antennae high above the crowd. I wouldn't expect him to be interested in me when he clearly had the bustiered devil as an option. Although, she seems to have disappeared. Do I mind playing second fiddle to another woman? Or maybe I'm only imagining he's watching me?

Three more surreptitious glances in his direction prove he's definitely watching me.

The fourth glance over, he's disappointingly absent from the spot I've been making eye contact with.

Crap. I should have made my move.

And then he's standing directly in front of me, his antennae swaying slightly in the air. I stumble a step, surprised by his appearance.

"Holy shit." Kelly mouths at me from behind the Mothman's arm. "You good?" She's holding up her fist alternating between a thumbs up and a thumbs down.

I smile in her direction and give her a hesitant nod. Nervous as I am, it's not that the Mothman is going to do anything inappropriate.

Her cheeks stretch into a wide grin, and she tugs Anam in another direction so I'm actually alone with the Mothman.

His mouth arms quirk into a smile, and he taps the headphones he's wearing around his neck. I take the cue to lower my own, he leans close to my ear, his hand floats at my waist, not quite touching me, and his antennae barely brush against the top of my head.

"Would you like to dance with me?" There's something strangely formal about his question, the simplicity of it has my chest tightening. I've never really spoken to a cryptid before, let alone touched one. The strange curves of his body have my stomach twisting. It's more than wanting to replace Colin. There's beauty in the Mothman's alien form. I want to see what happens between us tonight. Not for the novelty, because something about this soft-spoken, gentle creature is exactly what I need in my life right now.

"Yes, please." I don't miss the way his wings flutter, just a little, when I answer. It's adorable.

We put our headphones back on, and his slender fingers find my waist. He tugs me a little closer, so our bodies barely graze. He sways strangely, not quite the way a human would dance, but he doesn't disrupt the crowd. When I catch his rhythm better, I let myself be pulled up against him, slipping his leg between mine, and following his lead. My hand creeps up to brush along the exposed fur on his arms. It's so soft and silky that I can't stop myself from trailing fingers through it a few more times. Velvet. It's like stroking the most luxurious velvet. I wonder if he's velvety soft everywhere. I wonder if I'm going to get a chance to find out.

When I look up, he's studying me, his antennae waving in time with the music. He's decidedly inhuman, and decidedly cute; with expressive antennae, a thick black fur collar around his neck, and wide red eyes that make me a little nervous as they study me. I avoid looking at his face, staring forward into his chest instead. My hand finds its way to the spot I'm admiring, enjoying the heat under his shirt and the pleasant hum emanating from beneath his ribs.

We spend long moments wrapped in each other's arms. As the music changes, so do his movements. He doesn't release me, and I don't feel a desire to leave. He doesn't say anything, he only sways and lets me feel safe in his easy grip. This close he smells amazing, like warm wool and vanilla.

When the music changes again, to something slower, his strong hands pull me closer. I don't stop myself from resting my cheek on his chest. He's soft and warm, strangely comforting, even though the purr rumbling through his chest is completely foreign to me. The vibration rumbles through my whole body, deep into my stomach, and between my legs. I wrap my arms around him and press our bodies a little bit tighter; I could melt completely into that gentle purr.

I'm startled when he pulls back suddenly, leaving my face cool and vacant.

I pull down my headphones and so does he.

"Sorry. Too much?" I ask.

His head shakes. "You're perfect."

My face feels warm at the casual compliment. His antennae swivel around, his hand still at my side, squeezes lightly. "Your friend... is she alright?"

"What?" I look around for Anam and Kelly.

The Mothman's head swivels, turning a full 180 on his neck to face behind him. I step to the side and I spot them at the bar.

Kelly is holding up a wobbling Anam who knocks a plastic cup from the bar. It smashes to the ground, splashing dark beer all over a stranger.

"What the hell, you stupid bitch!" a white woman in a witch costume, who is now also wearing most of an IPA, yells.

Kelly, always the guard dog, is already supporting Anam with one arm and shaking her other finger in the witch's face.

"Crap." I move past my Mothman toward my friends, putting myself between Kelly and the strange woman.

"So sorry, so sorry," I tell the witch. "She's just a little drunk."

The witch's mouth presses into a thin line, her eyes flicking to the space over my shoulder.

"It's fine." The witch is still scowling, but her tone calms surprisingly fast.

"Why don't I cover your tab for the night?" The Mothman's voice surprises me at my shoulder. I glance back at him and consider protesting, but if he wants to throw money at a problem that isn't his...well, I was already planning to sleep with him tonight.

I move to help Kelly wrangle Anam. "How are you feeling, sweetie?" I ask, putting a hand on my friend's shoulder. "Ready to go home?"

"I'm fine! Let's stay and party!" Anam rolls her eyes.

Kelly gives me a half-hearted smile, it's obvious she's already tried this approach.

"We should get some food in her." Kelly wraps her arm through Anam's elbow.

"Oh my gawd, yes! Let's go and get some french fries! Please!"

A large bouncer appears at their back. "I gotta ask you ladies to leave."

"I've got them," the soft male voice at my shoulder assures the bouncer. There's the faintest of touches as his hand moves to my hip.

The bouncer's eyes shift to the Mothman's hand before he nods. "Whatever you say, Ant."

I glance at my Mothman looking for some clue how he knows the man, but the Mothman says nothing as he leads us to the entrance. He holds the door while Kelly and I guide Anam outside into the chilly October air.

"Do you work here?" I ask him.

"Not exactly." He doesn't clarify further, just points down the block. "If you need to eat, there are a couple food trucks on the corner open late for bar goers. Tacos and cubanos."

"Yes! Oh my god!" Anam stumbles toward my Mothman a few steps and grasps one of his arms in her fingers. There's an unreasonable little curl of jealousy in my stomach when she touches him. "The only thing that sounds better than French fries is tacos! Piper! Kelly! Can we go and get some tacos? Please, please, please?!"

"Of course, sweetie." Kelly only sounds a little exhausted. "We'll get some food in your stomach before you go to bed."

"Yes! You are so smart!" Anam straightens her bee antennae with one hand and taps the Mothman's chest with the other. "You are a freaking genius, and he's kinda cute! Piper! Bring the cute genius with you!"

The Mothman's antennae twitch when Anam's hand meets his chest. He shifts away from her, steering her back into Kelly's waiting arms. I'm surprised how much comfort that brings me.

"Would you like to—" I run my tongue across my bottom lip feeling self-conscious before I actually get all the words out, "boldly go on this adventure with us?" I bark out a nervous laugh at the end of my question and wince at my own terrible joke.

His wings shift at his shoulders. "You want me to follow you?"

"If you want—I had a nice time—I am having a nice time—" I pause on the sidewalk a few steps past him, my friends attempting to forge ahead. "I wouldn't mind—"

His eyes dart from my friends to the food truck and back to the bar. I am being too pushy, asking too much of this stranger. He's not looking for some needy lonely woman to cling onto him all night.

"Hey! Mothman!" Kelly yells from halfway down the block, "Are you single?"

His antennae raise a fraction. "I definitely am."

"Cool! So is Piper! Come with us!" she announces. "Anam needs snacks! I am ready for bed! I do not have time for you two to navigate this shy nerdy bullshit."

I cringe, but the Mothman's antennae raise again as he steps toward me. I release a breath. Good, I haven't scared him off yet.

Kelly and I steer the stumbling Anam down the street, the Mothman follows at a reasonable distance.

I avoid turning around to watch him. There are a lot more nerves in my stomach now that we're away from the crowded bar. I don't realize how distracted I am until Anam and Kelly are laughing at some joke I missed and we arrive at the well-lit parking lot. A few folding picnic tables set up inside a half-circle of food trucks. We all order, and while I am collect condiments and Kelly wrangles Anam, the Mothman sneakily pays for our tacos and a big pile of nachos.

"That's sweet, but you don't need to keep buying us things," I say.

"I can afford it." His antennae curl back, I can't help staring at the movement. I wonder what they feel like.

"What's your deal? Are you rich? Why did everyone in the bar seem to know who you were but me?" I ask with a laugh.

"There aren't a lot of Mothmen in the city. I make a distinct impression."

"You'll certainly be hard for me to forget," I admit with another awkward laugh.

"Good memories I hope?" His wings flutter, almost like he's nervous to hear the answer.

"Planning on making some." I laugh, he smiles and sets his armful of food onto one of the picnic tables. His wings shift as he maneuvers himself into a chair.

He's so cute like this. Gosh it's nice. Not really knowing him, having the mystery, being able to project whatever I want onto him. I know if I learn more I'm going to develop feelings. I don't think I can handle that right now.

"What if we skip the getting to know you thing? I just got out of something serious and I need..." I lean on the table, keeping my voice low enough that only he can hear.

"Something not serious?" He nods. "That's what you're looking for?"

"Yes?" I bite my lip and focus on sounding decisive. "Yes. No strings. No fuss. One night of anonymous sex." I blurt out as heat climbs up my cheeks. Too much. I'm being too much again.

"Sex? Tonight? With me?" He sounds somewhere between confused and shocked. And here I thought I was being obvious.

"If you want to?"

"Of course I want to." The words come out so quickly that he stumbles over them.

"That isn't too weird?" I ask. "The sort of thing they do in the movies. It's always sexy and anonymous and exciting, right?" Maybe I shouldn't ask him, but I feel better as soon as the words are out of my mouth. "You know the kinds of movies I mean?" I laugh at the end of my sentence.

"I know those kinds of movies. If that's what you need tonight then I can provide it." His wings flutter as I slip into the picnic table beside him.

"Okay then, no full names. And no details. Nothing I can Google!" I say with another slightly embarrassing laugh. I let our legs graze before I lean over him to select a nacho.

His hand lifts, hesitates briefly and finally lands on my knee. His long fingers squeeze my leg gently. His mouth arms twist up, into his strange smile that looks nothing like a human expression. He's fascinating.

Crap, I need to be sure I keep this casual. Going home with a stranger–having sex with someone I hardly know–is the perfect way to celebrate this new single chapter in my life. As long as I don't start really caring about him.

"Fooooddddd!" Anam croons as she and Kelly dump a pile of salsa packets on the table. I feel the Mothman stiffen, but he leans toward me a little, letting our bodies touch.

"I'm Kelly, this is Anam, and what is your new friend's name?" Kelly asks me pointedly.

I nervously bite my lip. "This is, Ant?" I have to say it as a question, repeating the name that the bouncer gave.

"Is that your real name?" Kelly asks.

"Some people call me Ant." There's a quirk in the Mothman's smile. I think he would wink at me if he could.

"Well, Ant, Piper has people who are looking after her." Kelly eyes him suspiciously. Anam is already too busy with her tacos to follow the conversation properly, so she decides to do what she thinks is a good deed and attempts to talk me up.

"You know, Piper is one of the smartest people I know, and she's into all kinds of weird shit," Anam says.

"Weird shit?" Ant's antennae tilt forward, there's an amused lilt to his voice.

I vocally groan, but it doesn't deter Anam from continuing.

"Yeah, all of this." She waves a hand in Ant's general direction, and my stomach sinks. "This nerd shit," she finishes. "She's always watching some show, or raving about some movie I've never heard of. She knows about all the vintage video games and all that weird stuff."

"Is that stuff weird?" Ant asks. "I have a collection of vintage games."

"You do?" I lean toward him, unable to contain my excitement. "What kinds?"

"All the old consoles: Atari, NES, SNES, Sega Master System, the works."

"Duck Hunt!? With the Light Zappers?" I exclaim, real excitement rolling through me.

"Of course."

"I'll kick your ass at Duck Hunt," I threaten.

He shakes his head very seriously. "You couldn't."

"Maybe I should come over and prove it?" It would sound cool, but a nervous laugh pops out after. Loud and awkward.

There's a little purr in his chest. It radiates through the shoulder he has pressed against me. The reverberations calm my nerves, I shove another nacho in my mouth before I can say anything more embarrassing.

Soon we are loading a very drunk Anam into an Uber, so she can sleep on Kelly's couch.

Before Kelly follows Anam into the car, her eyes lock on Ant, but she's clearly talking to me. "Do you want to catch a ride with us? Or are you alright here?"

"I'm fine." I feel my cheeks heat, and glance at Ant, who is waiting for me under a street lamp, looking like a tall shadow from a storybook with his wings folded behind him. "I'll be fine."

"Good. Good. This will be good for you." Kelly bites her lip before she sucks in a deep breath and grabs my hand to pull me aside. Not far enough to have a truly private conversation, but she doesn't seem to give a rats ass if Ant hears everything she says.

"Give me your phone." Kelly waves her hand at me. "You are sharing your location with me. And I want you to text me all the addresses wherever he takes you, And I will be calling you in the morning to make sure you are okay, and I want you to use protection. And you can call me anytime, from anywhere. I'll come get you. Or I'll make Jeremy come and get you. You know we will. We both love you."

I roll my eyes as I let out a loud sigh. "Okay, okay, okay, thanks Mom." But I happily turn on location sharing. "And you text me when you get home safe."

"Have fun tonight." Kelly grins, tiara crooked on her head. "You deserve to enjoy yourself for once." Without any prompting, she wraps her arms around me in a tight hug, then climbs into the Uber with Anam.

I'm left standing on the sidewalk, alone, with the Mothman.

3

PIPER

He shifts on his feet, his wings whisper across each other, and all of my self-confidence melts like butter under Tatooine's twin suns.

Crap. What is next? I don't know how to do this. Take a guy home the same night that I meet him. I don't know anything about him. I'm not even sure what his real name is. When my girlfriends were here, I was so certain about what I wanted, now all I'm certain about is that I am a complete idiot.

He closes the distance between us.

"Piper?" He says my name quietly, like I'm an animal that might run. "Would you like to come home with me?"

"Now?" I squeak as the nachos in my stomach churn violently.

Crap. He's going to think I'm some idiot who can't do casual sex.

"Not if you don't want to." The Mothman's antennae raise a few important inches. He's absolutely adorable. The velvet of his fur shimmers in the streetlight. He reaches up to brush a strand of my hair out of my face, his fingers grazing the shell of my ear. I can't help tensing up.

What is wrong with me? This is good! I like this guy! I want to fuck him! I want to go home with him and let him do things to me. I want to—

His hand drops to his side.

Crap. I am ruining it.

"I do want to!" I clarify. "It's just, you know, meeting a stranger in a bar. Going home with someone I barely know, letting him do whatever wild thing he has in mind."

"What do you think I have in mind?" he muses.

I can't help grinning. I cover my mouth and shake my head, not willing to answer that open-ended question.

"You don't need to hide." His hand catches my chin, pulling my face up to look at him. "Your smile is beautiful. It lights up your whole face. I'd smile all the time if it made me half that beautiful."

Crap. That's sweet.

"You have a great smile," I protest. His antennae curve toward me.

"I could just walk you home?" he suggests. "We could call it an early night?"

"No!" I bite my tongue at the end of the word. I have to do this now. Tonight. I can't throw away this opportunity. This will be good for me. I can't imagine finding another person I'd feel comfortable doing this with so quickly. "Maybe we could go somewhere else for a while? It's still kind of early, right?"

"It's early for a Mothman, certainly."

"It's not even midnight yet. With my insomnia, I'll be up for another three hours regardless." I continue sheepishly. "There's still time to catch the showing of Chopping Mall at the Artemis Theater." I wince, it's a stupid suggestion.

"You want to go to a movie?"

"It's a special midnight showing. I mean, I've seen it before. Several times. Never in the theater, though. Have you? It's great, an absolute classic. And the Artemis isn't too far from here." I scrunch my nose. "If we walk over now, we'll only miss the first ten minutes or so."

"Or, I could fly us," he suggests tentatively.

"What? Seriously?" I ask with a loud laugh.

As an answer, his wings swoop out wide. Street detritus skitters away from him, and with a few powerful flaps, he is three feet off the ground.

It's awesome.

"Crap, you can like, really, fly," I murmur. Why is that hot?

"I could carry you."

"Really?" I bark out another loud excited laugh, and then choke it down. That's not sexy. I'm trying to be sexy tonight, not come off like a braying donkey.

The gust of wind tugs at my hair. I adjust my glasses so I can take him in. His wings are wide and dark, but they look so very soft. With a faint but intricate design that shimmers iridescent in the streetlight. He's absolutely beautiful.

"If you trust me." His toes lightly touch the ground as he returns to earth.

Trust a near stranger for the opportunity to fly? It's a little dangerous, for sure. But I'm already planning to fuck him. Is this more dangerous than that? Maybe. Probably.

"Have you carried anyone before?"

"A couple."

"How many did you drop?"

"None I didn't intend to drop."

I laugh again, loudly, before I manage to quiet myself. Colin used to tell me my laugh was too loud. Ant just smiles. "You wouldn't intentionally drop me, would you?"

"Not you. Never." His wings flutter around his shoulders, the movement is fascinating.

"Can I feel them?" I can't stop grinning. "Sorry if that was rude, you can say no. It's just, I've never seen anything like them."

"You really like them?" The hesitancy in his voice tugs at my chest.

I nod enthusiastically. "You're beautiful." My face feels very warm when I recognize my slip-up. "They are beautiful."

He shakes his head. "You are the one who is beautiful, Piper." He tucks a loose curl behind my ear. "Like a moth to a flame."

He turns quickly. For a brief moment, I worry I've offended him somehow, before his wings spread wide again. They fold neatly across his back, draping to ankle length when they are closed, and when he spreads them fully, he is easily wider than he is tall. A wingspan of at least seven or eight feet. There are four individual wings, a top pair with ragged edges, and a bottom that are a little rounder. They are nearly translucent, his silhouette visible through them. Swirling in dark browns and grays and black. Between the wings, along his spine, is a thick patch of dark hair, similar to the scarf that grows around his neck.

"You can touch them, if you like." His voice is very soft.

I raise a hand up to the wing, pausing just before my hand reaches him. "I won't hurt you, will I?"

"I trust you," he says.

I'm not sure I trust myself. I lower my open nervous palm to brush along his top wing. He twitches under my touch and then sighs and presses slightly harder into my hand. It's soft, but taunt, like touching an open umbrella covered in a fine silt of fuzz.

Sliding my hand across him I finally reach the fur between his wings and run my fingers down through the hair there.

He shudders under my touch and pulls away, turning and grabbing my hand before I can move.

"Sorry, too much?" I ask.

"No, you are wonderful. The center area is... sensitive," he says calmly. His hands circle mine, large enough to cover them completely, warm and gentle. I stare at our intertwined fingers for a long breath.

"The movies, then?" I ask, finally looking at his face.

His antennas perk up. His mouth arms lift. "May I?" He stretches his arms wide.

I give him an enthusiastic nod, then hesitate, not exactly sure what to do. He moves quickly, easily scooping me up like I weigh nothing at all. One arm beneath my knees, keeping my skirt in a modest position, one arm behind my shoulders in a bridal carry. It's almost like having my own personal superhero.

"Ready?" His breath is so close that it tickles my hair.

"Don't go too high." Fear and excitement spike through my veins.

"I've got you, my flame," he says so softly, I think I may have misunderstood him.

He crouches just a little before leaping in the air. There's one terrifying moment of free fall, and then his wings catch the air, and we are fucking flying.

I squeal. I don't care if I am twenty-nine. This is fucking exciting! Who gets to do things like this? Who has a hot sexy stranger literally carrying them through the air? It's exhilarating.

We aren't terribly high. He levels out above the three-story buildings, being mindful of wires and telephone poles. Ant cuts easily through the blocks, halving our travel time. With the wind in my hair and Ant's strong arms carrying me, I'm almost sad that it's going to be over quickly.

He's shockingly strong, the muscles corded in his biceps are like steel holding me firmly against his chest. My arms circle his neck instinctively, digging my fingers into the fur there. From this angle I can examine his face closely, his intense expression as he focuses on the path before us. He's covered in that sweet vanilla scent. I'm completely at his mercy. He could do anything to me right now, take me anywhere.

I wish that idea didn't turn me on quite so much.

I chew on my lip and press myself a little tighter against him, my body flooded with adrenaline and endorphins. He lands on the roof of the Artemis Theatre and sets me on my feet. I do an impromptu spin, my skirt twirling around my ankles. I'm practically buzzing with energy. We flew. I flew! It was exactly like every dream I've ever had of the experience.

"That was fantastic!" I adjust my glasses, cackling loudly, too excited to care if I am being over-the-top. "That was so cool! You're amazing, Ant! You can go anywhere? Any time you want? I have so many questions!"

He's smiling, but seems almost bashful.

"Sorry. Too much. I know." I roll my eyes and take a step back, but Ant catches me by the waist, stopping my retreat.

"No. Don't apologize," he says definitively. "I like seeing you happy."

His tone and touch are simultaneously sobering and exciting. I'm being appreciated, not scolded, for over-the-top behavior. It's so simple. I hadn't realized my expectations were set so low.

"If you have questions, I will answer as many as you can ask." He's staring at me with such intensity that, for a moment, I think he's going to kiss me. I want him to kiss me. I pull my limbs tighter to my body so I can get a little closer to him.

"Are there rules? Can you go wherever you want?" I'm a lot quieter this time, and gosh, he is very cute. How do I get him to kiss me? Just ask, or what?

"We do have a few rules in the community. Going much higher than we flew is frowned on, slower speeds at lower altitudes, avoid private airspace..." His voice trails off, but my curiosity doesn't.

"Do you do that sort of thing a lot?"

He nods. "It's hard to find modes of transportation with enough room for my wings to fit comfortably. You can't fit wings in airplane seats."

I sigh. "I would fly everywhere, all of the time, if I had the option."

"I'll fly you anywhere you want to go." His hands tighten slightly around my waist. It's sweet, and kind, and way too much for me right now. This kind of fore-play makes me feel all warm and fuzzy inside.

I'm going to get attached to him if I'm not careful. That's such a bad idea, I know I'm not going to see him after I fuck him.

I pull away so I can peek over the edge of the building. "The only other question I have right now is how do we get down?"

Ant waves me toward an unmarked door, leading me down a set of stairs and into a dark narrow hallway above the theater.

"We can't just sneak in!" I say in a hushed whisper.

"It's fine." His long warm fingers slip between mine and I let myself be pulled into the building.

I whisper to Ant. "It's fine? What do you mean it's fine?"

"I promise." His grin, even with his inhuman features, feels mischievous.

We pass a theater employee, a reptilian male, pushing a mop and bucket. My heart leaps into my throat that we might be caught sneaking in, but he just nods at Ant.

"Evening, Ant," the lizardman says, "Ma'am." He tilts his head in my direction as well.

"Evening," I mumble hurriedly to the reptilian. "Who are you?" I hiss at Ant as soon as we're alone again.

"Nothing you can Google, remember?" he replies, somewhat mysteriously. And, oh no, I think that is sexy too.

We step through another door into the dark open balcony of the movie theater. I've always known it existed and I always wondered what was up here.

It's an old building, converted years ago from a more traditional stage, back when they still built balconies for theaters. The ceiling is painted like a night sky, twinkle lights installed for stars. Every time I've been to an event here the balcony has been cordoned off, and now I see why.

There are rows of seating up here, but a lot of them have been removed or modified. The balcony is half full of figures. Even in the dim light, I can tell they are mostly cryptids. A pair of Bigfoots share an enormous bucket of popcorn sitting on a couch that would swallow a human-sized person. In another pair of seats, a chupacabra hangs upside down from the ceiling, while her human date occasionally tosses her M&Ms. Other odd shapes occupy the darkness, their silhouettes aren't clear enough to discern their species.

I peek over the railing at the crowd below us. An almost entirely human crowd fills all of the available seats.

"Is this...special Cryptid seating?" I ask. That would explain why I've never been up here.

Ant tugs me over to an odd-looking padded bench, when he folds himself into the chair I see that careful holes have been cut into the back to accommodate a pair of wings. "Some of us require different seating than humans do. They're available here."

"That's great!" I whisper as I slip onto the bench next to him. "Wait, we aren't just going to watch without paying for tickets, are we?"

His antennae twist in opposite directions. He seems to be trying to decide something as the previews start.

"Wait here," he says. "I'll get us tickets."

"Alright," I answer tentatively, as Ant disappears toward the lobby.

I settle into my chair, pull out my phone, and fire off a quick text to my friends about the situation. Kelly said she wanted updates, so I send the group my location.

KellBell: So excited for you!

DamnAnam: luuuuuvvvvvv!!!!

I'm smirking at the messages when Ant settles back down beside me, just as the titular mall appears on screen, with its teenaged cast ready to be chopped.

He passes me a large bucket of popcorn and a box of Swedish Fish.

"Oh my goodness, these are my favorite!" I whisper, clutching the candy to my chest. "Are these for me?"

"Of course," he says, pulling out a pair of earplugs which he slides into the sides of his head.

"Everything okay?" I ask.

"I just have sensitive ears," he explains quietly. "Movies can be a little loud."

"Oh! We don't have to stay!"

"It's okay," he says firmly, but he smiles. "I want to enjoy this with you."

"Alright, if you're sure." I pop the box of candy open and curl into the seat beside him, ready to watch some robots explode people's heads.

There's no armrest between our seats and it's easy to take advantage of that, letting myself lean a little closer to him. His knuckles graze against mine on the bench between us.

I glance at Ant's face to check his expression. His features are so strange. It can be hard to tell if he's nervous, irritated, or happy. It's kind of nice not being sure. Colin never wanted to hold hands in public. He wasn't a fan of PDA. He preferred to stay home, and he preferred it when I stayed in with him. Far to many nights I let him talk me into sitting on the couch instead of going to the event I wanted to attend.

It's easy to project those same expectations onto Ant. But fuck it. I barely know this guy. What do I care if he doesn't have 'physical touch' listed as a love language? I know what I want.

I slip my fingers into Ant's, and turn back to the screen. His hand shifts in mine slightly, my heart pounds loudly in my chest, waiting for him to pull away, but he just gently squeezes my hand.

The simple action has my heart skipping a beat. Crap. Am I this desperate for someone to show me this casual affection?

Who cares? I adjust the box of candy between my knees and inch toward him.

Ant's hand leaves my grasp.

I'm too eager, yet again.

And then, his arm lifts behind me, curls around my shoulder and tucks me against him. The heat of his arm sinks into my body. Warm and cozy and comfortable. I smirk in the dark at my success.

4

PIPER

The movie contains just as many head explosions, robot lasers, and cameltoes as I remember. By the finale, I've managed to scoot much further into Ant's personal space. My shoulder against his chest, our thighs pressed together, his fingers gently grazing up and down my arm, sending little chills across my skin. It's so supremely warm and comfortable that I'm disappointed when the credits start to roll. I'm not ready to move.

Ant doesn't budge an inch, except for his thumb still sliding up and down my arm.

When the overhead lights switch on, he winces, and lifts a wing to gently shield his face.

"Oh crap. Does that hurt your eyes?" I ask.

"It's fine," he says.

"No, it's not. Let's get out of here. Okay?" I slip my hand into his and tug him toward the clearly marked 'exit' door that leads down a flight of stairs and into the alley behind the movie theater.

His shoulders visibly relax when we step into the darkness. The cool night air hits me, highlighting that any traces of alcohol in my blood are gone. All that's left is the two of us.

"Better?" I squeeze his hand once.

"Much, yes. Bright lights can give me headaches." He looks down at our still intertwined fingers and then at my face.

It's really, properly late now. The bars are closed; there are no more movies, or tacos, or excuses. Just me and the Mothman, alone in a dark alleyway.

"Thank you for coming with me."

"Thank you. For spending the evening with me." He leans in. This is it. I nervously shove my glasses up my nose even though they haven't slipped.

The best way to get over someone is getting under someone else. I step toward him, hoping he will take the hint. It's now or never, and I really need him to make the first move. I don't think I can do it.

"The evening isn't over yet, is it?" I slip my spare hand into his empty one. Letting all of our fingers intertwine casually, enjoying the feel of him, and looking forward to feeling more of him.

"It doesn't have to be." He smiles. Expectant butterflies battle in my stomach.

When was the last time I felt this nervous, this excited or enthusiastic about kissing someone? The last time I felt like if someone didn't put their mouth on mine in the next three seconds that I would explode?

"Can I kiss you?" He asks.

"Fuck, yes. Please." I can't get the words out fast enough.

He dips down and tentatively presses his mouth to mine. Light, tender, gentle. His mouth arms graze my cheek. He pauses, like he's waiting for something. I drop his hands so I can loop my arms around his neck. This encourages him. There's a small press at the seam of my mouth, my lips part instinctively. His tongue slips into my mouth. It's long and slender, slippery, like a curling tube. It's odd, nothing like a human tongue. He tastes sweet almost like honey and bourbon. I suck on his tongue experimentally and he grunts in excitement. His hands move to my waist, a possessive grip holds me still while his mouth toys with me, using playful easy movements that build a heat deep in my stomach. He's absolutely perfect.

My hands find their way to his chest, broad and defined. There's that quiet vibrating purr again, reverberating deep beneath his ribcage. It shoots straight to my stomach and sinks lower, lighting up every inch of my pussy this time. He doesn't have to pull me closer. I'm already drawn toward the heavy purr in his chest.

I push into the kiss, encouraging him, and the hum in his chest grows louder. His tongue delves a little deeper, the tip latches onto my mouth there's suction, from just his long tongue. Precision attachment. A little moan erupts from my mouth.

There is a warning grumble in his body. His wings flare and move us until my back hits the wall and we are making out like lovesick teens. It isn't funny at all, but a nervous snicker still sneaks between my lips.

He pulls back as I try to silence my giggles, watching me with shining eyes. "Something funny?"

"No. Sorry, sorry," I shake my head, and try to hold him close. "I'm just enjoying myself."

"Do not apologize for your laugh, Piper Hamilton. I find it utterly intoxicating." The purr in his voice is almost a growl and his hands circle my ass. I squeal as he easily lifts me, my legs naturally wrap around his hips. Cool fall air hits my legs as my skirt rides up. His body slips neatly between my thighs. I shift so I can push my pelvis into him, there's something boney and decidedly not erection-shaped between my legs, but the friction still sends delicious sparks through me.

He presses light licks and kisses into my neck while I giggle and clutch at him. His hips move to grind into mine, the pressure on my clit is so good that I moan.

"You make such beautiful noises." His breath brushes my neck and my whole body heats. "It's been a wonderful night. You are like a perfect dangerous flame, Piper. I—" He stops himself mid-syllable and releases a sigh so ragged that it sounds painful. "I'm not going to let you go home alone tonight."

"I don't want to go home alone tonight." I laugh with one breath, but feel myself hesitating in the next. I need to do this. I can't back down now. "You could take me back to your place."

He twitches, his hands tightening around my ass briefly. I fist my hand into the fur around his neck.

"Was that too forward?" I shake my head. Colin was never a fan of what he called my 'too-much gene'.

Ant stops my head moving with a light touch to my chin. "My flame, I would love to bring you back to my nest." His wings flutter behind him when he says the weird little nickname he's chosen.

I bite my lip before asking, "It isn't a literal nest, is it?"

"It's an apartment." He's grinning. "On the waterfront."

"With a Super Nintendo?" I joke.

"With every video game console you can imagine."

"Perfect. I am going to kick your ass at Duck Hunt." I tug gently on his furry cowl and he growls.

"You could try," he challenges.

I laugh.

His grip shifts and suddenly he's supporting my weight away from the wall. "Ready?"

I nod enthusiastically, wrap my arms a little tighter around his neck, with a little jump, we are airborne again. This time we're pressed front to front. I squeal when we leave the ground behind, tightening my arms around his neck, and there's a satisfying laugh from him in return.

His home is in the industrial area of the waterfront. The outside looks like every other warehouse on the block, except for a large cement fire flower sculpture in the minuscule patch of grass that constitutes his front yard.

The inside of the building is wide open, with concrete floors and ceilings so high they disappear into the darkness above us. The space is dim, I assume to accommodate his eyes, with moody colorful lighting scattered around; as my vision adjusts I notice twinkling fairy lights strung high toward the ceiling, almost like stars.

Even with the massive open space, there are neatly cordoned-off living areas. Cabinets stretch along one wall, with a large butcher-block island for food prep designating the kitchen. The boundaries of the living room and bedroom are indicated with layered carpets. There's a huge couch, and an even bigger bed, all visible from where we are standing near the front door. The plush furniture makes everything feel cozy and lived in.

"Wow..." I admire. "Lots of space."

"I like to spread my wings." They unfold as he says it, stretching out slowly. Watching the movement makes my stomach swoop. He gives me room to explore, leaning against his kitchen island while he watches me circle his home. All the little nerves in my body flare.

I shouldn't have let him set me down. I shouldn't have stopped touching him.

"This is like… a whole warehouse?" I ask. "Are you rich?"

He shrugs. "I got a good deal on it."

He shifts on his feet, his heavy gaze follows me as I give his bed a wide berth and pause beside his desk to admire his computer. It's a custom build, with multiple monitors, LED backlighting, and an adjustable height desk. It's one of the largest and most impressive setups I've seen in real life.

"Oh, sweet machine!" I lean in to investigate, but the screens are all turned off. "Gamer? Programmer?"

"You really want to know?" There's trepidation in the question, his antennae curl toward each other. Cute.

I shake my head. I would love to know, but at this point I think it's better if I can't get more attached to him. "No, never mind, no details."

"Whatever you want, Piper." He reaches up to his head, pulls the plastic Spock ears from his face, and tosses them to his counter. He doesn't actually have ears, just feathery protrusions on the sides of his head. "Would you like something to drink?"

"No, thanks," I murmur.

"A snack?"

"Maybe some water?" My throat feels slightly sticky.

He crosses to his fridge, and I can't bring myself to speak while he pulls out a pitcher of chilled water and pours it into a glass. His antennae sway above his red glowing eyes, his wings open as he stalks toward me. He hasn't looked quite so wonderfully inhuman as he does now. It feels like I'm being hunted. Is this what it felt like to be a prehistoric human a millennia ago? Huddled around a campfire and wondering about the things stalking them in the dark? How did they not constantly cream their jeans?

When he is close enough to tower over me, he hands me the cup. I'm embarrassed to see my hands trembling slightly as I reach for it.

"Are you alright?" His warm fingers brush mine as I take the cool glass.

"I'm great!" I chew on my lip, knowing that's not making me seem more at ease. I quickly down the drink, the cold water is harsh contrast to my hot nervous throat.

He's staring down at me, all tall, and mysterious, and sexy. How did I manage to get this far? Every step of this journey has been completely out of my element. And now he's just staring at me. What's he even looking at? Do I have a booger? What's he waiting for? Why doesn't he make a move? Kiss me again? Grab a boob? Men usually just go straight for the boobs.

He can't possibly have changed his mind this fast. I never should have let him stop touching me. I should have taken off all my clothes the second we walked into his home, and thrown myself at him. I should have taken off all his clothes.

His hands flex at his sides, and I realize neither of us has spoken for several moments. This is my chance to seduce him with something sexy or smart or funny.

I take a deep breath before blurting, "Where's your bathroom?"

He points to a door near the kitchen.

"I just need to freshen up." I cringe saying it, and force a smile as I flee to lock myself in his bathroom.

I stare into the mirror above the sink for a long moment. What am I so nervous about? I've had sex before. Not really casually, not in a huge expensive loft, and not with a Mothman. Surely the mechanics are mostly the same.

I think I might be nervous because I actually really like him?

Which is silly. This was supposed to be low stakes, no fuss sex. I'm only here to get over my ex. It's not going to be anything more than that. We just met tonight. It's ridiculous to be thinking about a new relationship already. Even if it's with someone who seems really sweet and kind and into the same things I am.

I clean off my glasses with his towel. Clean hand towels? Does he secretly have a girlfriend? Single guys don't do that.

I open and close all of his bathroom cabinets. Not looking for anything in particular, just hoping they might offer me some form of clarity. All I find are neatly organized toiletries. No signs of a second person living here. It seems like we use a lot of the same brands, but there are a few things that I don't recognize. I pull one bottle out of his shower and sniff it. Yep, there is his vanilla scent. The smell has me slightly calmer. I carefully return it to its spot on the shelf, memorizing the label, just for future information.

I came here for a reason. Casual sex will be good for me. Even if my stomach flips excitedly every time Ant looks at me for too long.

I slip off my kerchief and undo the buttons until the front of my shirt hangs open completely. I'm just wearing my classic, practical, nude bra. It's not fun sexy lacy underwear. When I left the house I wasn't expecting to show it to a stranger today. I drop the shirt to the ground and turn to the side to examine myself in the mirror.

It's a level of nudity no one except Colin has seen from me in a long time. I know my breasts are good. They are large and full, and even if my middle has always had some squish, and my butt has some cellulite, I've never had any complaints about the ladies.[1] If they don't get me laid, then I don't know what will.

I rearrange my hair, piling it on my head in different ways, until I am satisfied that it looks acceptable. There's not much else I can do. Not enough time to do a million crunches. Or suddenly develop body confidence. He'll have to take me as I am.

I take a deep breath before I open the bathroom door.

---

1   Except from my back muscles.

5

PONTIUS

This isn't how I expected the evening to go. I didn't think she would be here, in my home, tonight. I just wanted to speak with her, just once. Introduce myself, that's all. So she'd know I existed. So she could get used to the idea of me.

She was just so beautiful, so kind, so fragrant. My flame. I was stupid to think I could refuse the draw I feel to her.

Then I heard the plan she and her friends discussed.

Casual sex.

No strings. No attachments. Just sex.

I shouldn't have eavesdropped. But once I saw her, smelled her again, there was no reasonable way I could stop myself from listening to her conversation.

She is mine. My mate. My flame.

I couldn't let her go home with another male. I just couldn't. Not again. If she wants a one-night stand then I will be the one to give her that.

Now she's here, in my home, my nest, touching my things, spreading her glorious scent everywhere.

And hiding in my bathroom.

Sometimes she trembles when we touch.

She's scared of me.

I've done something wrong. Maybe I shouldn't have brought her here this quickly. I could have given her more time to get used to me. I am only trying to give her what she said she wanted. Casual sex.

I grimace. Nothing about this is casual for me.

I cross the room to my collection of gaming consoles. I can wait as long as she needs. I'll wait forever if I have to. I'll make sure she has the space, and time that she needs to feel comfortable around me.

I can't lose her now, when I am so close to having her.

Behind me, the bathroom door creaks open.

"What are you doing?" Piper asks.

"You threatened to kick my ass at Duck Hunt." I gesture to the Super Nintendo in front of me.

"Oh, right... I did didn't I?" There's a smile in her voice as she suppresses a laugh. The beautiful sound twists in my chest every time. I would give anything to hear her laugh every day.

I glance over my shoulder and freeze at the sight of her. She's shirtless. Her breasts are on display. The soft ambiance in my home highlights every beautiful curve of her body.

"I thought you might want to continue our conversation from the movie theater?"

"Our conversation?" I ask. There's nothing in my brain except the slope of her breasts and the naked skin between her bra and her skirt. My cock strains at my seam, making its desire to emerge known. How could anyone have a single thought with this perfection in front of them? I've wanted her for so many weeks, and longed for a mate much longer than that.

"You know," she laughs nervously and takes a step toward where I am kneeling on the floor of my living room, "our conversation in the alley. Against the wall."

"Right...that conversation." I finally breathe out as she reaches me, still barely comprehending her words. Her breasts at my eye level. My hand goes to her waist instinctively, drawn like a moth to her gorgeous flame. Her skin, I am finally touching her naked skin. She's smooth and soft beneath my fingers.

"Or you know. We can play Duck Hunt, whatever you want to do." She laughs and dips down to press a kiss to my forehead. So sweet.

"I know exactly what I want," I say. Her, in my arms, in my nest, forever.

She reaches for me, her hands shaking slightly. I catch her fingers in my hand.

"Are you alright?" I ask her again.

"I'm fine!" Her voice jumps up an octave.

"Are you scared of me?" My voice is quieter this time, and I selfishly do not remove my hands from her person.

"No. No!" she insists. "I'm not scared! Just nervous. Excited. Jittery? Ugh. I feel like I just had three shots of espresso." She laughs loudly, then closes her mouth with a wince. "Sorry. Nervous habit, the laughing."

"Don't apologize." I tug her closer, letting myself put both hands on her waist. A purr rumbles through my chest and she leans toward me.

"I've never been with a Mothman." She adjusts her glasses.

"Few people have. We aren't common."

"Is there anything...off limits?" She rests a tentative hand on my cheek, and I can't help leaning into her touch, a mandible stroking along her palm. I've never felt so...wanted before.

"The antennae," I say, quietly.

"Don't touch the antennae," she agrees.

"Just be gentle, please." The idea of her not touching any part of me is anathema.

Her hand moves toward the top of my head, she pauses a few inches away. I dip my head slightly to give her better access. Her fingers are gentle as they briefly run across the feathers. The sensation sends a shiver up my spine, pleasant and ticklish. I can't wait for her to touch other parts of me.

"Okay?" she asks.

I purr in response. She grins.

"And this?" Her hand moves to cup my mandible.

I purr again.

"And here?" Her hands wander to the thick collar encircling my neck.

"Piper, you can touch me anywhere. Touch me everywhere. Please." I murmur. Her fingers dig deep in, letting the fur settle between her digits. Her touch pulls a deeper purr from my chest. Having her here, in my home, I couldn't be happier.

"Are you going to return the favor?" She laughs quietly.

"You want me to touch you?" It's a simple request, and still, my heart flutters.

"It's why I'm here." She giggles.

I stroke my hand along the slope of her waist, wanting to explore more of her, and learn more about her body.

"What parts of you are off limits?" I ask.

Her cheeks darken a little. "I'm not sure? Maybe we can find out together?"

A possessive growl rumbles up my throat and I pull her into my lap. She settles against me with a light squeal, her thighs straddling one of mine. The scent of her is everywhere. The smell of her desire pools between her legs. She wants me. She enjoys being with me. There's no stopping the smell from invading my nose; invading my life.

Her palms rest against my chest, smoothing the fabric of my shirt. She leans in to kiss me lightly. She initiates the touch. Like it isn't a big deal. Like she actually wants to touch me. She is warm and sweet and giving. I'm vibrating with excitement. I kiss her back, slipping my tongue between her lips and sucking lightly at her mouth, until she gives me a pleasant moan. The noise has my cock straining against my seam.

That noise is intoxicating. I need more. I need to draw more sounds from her. I need to hear how she sounds when she comes for me. I need her to explode for me.

I dip down, to taste her neck, her shoulders, her chest. Letting my tongue dance across the top of her breasts. Purring as I revel in her salty taste. She shifts her hips, her skirt fanning around her legs. She drags herself up my thigh. The air getting heavy with the scent of her arousal as she moves. The tip of my cock slips from my seam, starting to travel down my pant leg, seeking the heat she presses to me.

"Piper," I whisper her name against her skin and she shifts in response, her broad thigh pressing up against my crotch. Her hips tilt as she drags her pussy across me again, her warm legs stroking my cock. My hands tunnel beneath her skirt and climb her legs until they find purchase just below her ass. I groan at the feel of her curves. Fingers tracing along the edge of her underwear,

I encourage her to move again, to slip her body up and down my leg. She makes a needy little whine, guiding my face to her chest.

I press my tongue deeper into her breast to find a nipple and suck on it.

She makes a soft noise as she moves her thighs across me again, and again. A tiny exhale of pleasure as she drags herself up my leg. Her eyes closed, her face scrunched in concentration. There's wetness in her underwear, seeping into my pants. My glorious mate, using me for her pleasure, coating me in her sweet nectar. I am the only thing she needs in the world, I am going to give her everything.

"Yes, Piper. Take what you need," I murmur, keeping my hands busy at her thighs, and my mouth on her chest, sucking and licking each nipple in turn. She tastes divine, like citrus and cream. Sweet with a tang.

I'm completely lost in her. Her warmth, her wetness, the noises she makes, the smell she exudes everywhere. Her thighs wrapped around my leg, trapping my cock, stroking its length as she shamelessly humps me. I want to be inside her, I want to feel her surrounding me completely. Her fingers grip my shirt like I am the only thing anchoring her to the earth.

A tightness forms behind my seam. I need to hold back, I have to be here for her.

Her fingers tug tight on my collar, as I clench my hands into her supple ass, her thighs squeeze my cock into my leg in response. She whimpers my name directly into my ear.

It's all too fucking much.

"Piper." Unable to hold back any longer, I press my face into her neck as I spill my release into my pants.

She goes still in my lap.

Shit. I'm ruining everything.

6

PIPER

Did he just come in his pants?

"Did you just—?" I cut myself off before I start laughing.

I cannot laugh. He will not think it's funny.

Sure, the situation is hilarious. Humping his leg on the ground like overeager teens. We're fifteen feet from a bed. Three feet from a couch.

We're idiots. We're ridiculous.

He will only get mad if I laugh. I bite my lower lip to try to stop the smile.

He shakes his head against my neck. "That wasn't supposed to happen. This was supposed to be about you, Piper."

My shoulders are shaking now from holding back my giggle.

Ant pulls back to watch me with bright glistening eyes. I throw my hand in front of my mouth, which doesn't make my expression any less obvious.

"I didn't mean to—" he starts.

I open my mouth to reassure him it's alright. That's a mistake because the laugh falls out. I slap my hand back over my mouth to cover it up.

He smiles at me. "You aren't mad?" His whole body seems to relax.

Relief floods through me. "Of course not! It's okay, Ant. I was—" My face feels burning hot. His hands grip my legs, and he pulls me toward him, dragging my still-swollen clit across his thigh, "close, too." I gasp.

Ant presses his face against my neck again, the fuzz tickling my skin as he takes a deep breath. "It should have been about you."

"Ant, it's okay. We have all night."

"All night?"

"Don't we? I mean, I'll leave if you—" My sentence ends with a squeal as he scoops me into his arms and stands.

"I'm not done with you." He's grinning widely, but his voice hits a serious note that sends a butterfly fluttering through my stomach. He deposits me on the couch. "You are going to stay right here. I am going to clean up, and when I come back, we will see who is laughing and who is coming in their pants." His voice is almost a threat as he presses a light kiss to my forehead.

I nod, watching him cross to the bathroom. I giggle, just a little. Have I ever made a guy come in his pants? Is it weird to feel a little proud? Maybe this is a regular thing for Ant. I don't really know the guy.

I kinda wish I knew him a little better.

I leave the couch to circle his apartment. Checking the spines of his books and the titles in his game collection. He seems to have a bit of everything. I'm not sure what I'm looking for. A reason to dislike him, maybe? To cross him off my list of potential paramours, so this one-night stand will feel like a better idea.

My hand hovers at a drawer while I weigh the pros and cons of opening it.

"What are you doing?" A voice comes from directly behind me.

"Yeesh!" I spin to find him directly at my back, tall and sexy and looming. "You move so quietly."

He's wearing a loose pair of sweatpants now. My eyes flick to his crotch and then back to his face, hoping he hasn't noticed. I felt him between my thighs. Hot and pulsing and huge. I want to know what his cock looks like. I hope I get a chance to find out.

He grins. "Looking for something?" His hands move for my waist, pulling me toward him.

"Just being nosy." I wince. "Is that a problem?"

"Depends on what you found," he murmurs. Returning his nose into the crook of my neck, he breathes me in, like smelling me is his whole reason for living. A low purr emanates from his body, like a pleased cat.

I press my hands to him, trying to get closer to the noise. The purr in his ribcage feels like it touches every inch of my body. It would be calming if it wasn't so incredibly arousing. The buzz simultaneously makes me want to melt and climb him like a tree.

"What is that?" I ask, adjusting my glasses so I can press my cheek into his chest. I close my eyes and feel it.

"Hmm?" The purr changes when he talks, my whole body squeezes on the low 'm' sound.

"Are you purring?" I ask.

He chuckles, and the way it echoes through his chest and into my ear gives me a full-body shiver. "It's like a mating call. To attract a mate."

"A mate?" I laugh. "Well, it's working."

"I can tell." He chuckles again, his hand moves up and down my spine in long soothing strokes that light up every nerve on my back, until he finally stops at my nape. His palm covers the back of my neck, the heat of him hitting every inch of skin. I can't hold back the little moan building in my chest, my body is still primed from our floor humping session.

He tips my face up for a kiss. I'm ready for the strangeness now. His mandible caress my cheeks and his long curious tongue flicks through my mouth, delicate and slippery. I lean into him, pressing my torso against his chest as his hand cards deep into my hair.

My hair tie snaps, and my locks falls loose, his fingers getting hopelessly tangled in the newly freed curls. I stifle a giggle around his tongue.

I pull away to detangle his hands, he just continues kissing me. Tasting my chin and neck, and tickling my body all the way down to my breasts. When his tongue dips into my cleavage, I laugh so hard I have to hold onto him for support.

"There, that is your mating call." He doesn't give me time to protest before his newly freed hands scoop me up. I squeal as my feet leave the ground. He kisses me again, while I am all curled against his chest. Just when I'm relaxing into him he tosses me gently. I land on his bed, my hair blossoming around my head.

I laugh even louder than before and stop myself. "Sorry, sorry, for laughing."

"Don't be sorry." Ant stands at the foot of the bed, staring at me. "I like your laugh."

I can't help rolling my eyes, I know who I am. Big tits and loud obnoxious laugh. Boyfriends like some parts and put up with other parts. Not that Ant is a boyfriend—

"Don't do that." He cuts off my thoughts by gripping my ankles and tugging me down the bed toward him. I make an unsexy squeal as his strength surprises me.

"Do what?" I ask, distracted as his thumb brushes across the top of my foot, he begins removing my shoes.

"Don't roll your eyes, like you think I'm lying. When I say something, I mean it." He smooths a hand up my shin, and his voice drops to an octave that is dangerous to my libido. "I don't want to see an eye roll from you again."

"Right." I squirm, something in his expression stops me from arguing.

His bed is huge, plush, and covered in pillows. When was the last time I met a single man with real bedsheets? Who even is this guy? I spread my arms out across the soft fabrics. He stays at the foot of the bed, watching me with a heated expression. He's probably had hundreds of girls in these sheets. No reason to think I am special. I'm just another notch.

There will be no strings tonight, no attachments. One night of fun.

I prop myself onto my elbows, fighting the urge to cover my squishy middle. Who cares if he sees some rolls, or the little stretch marks that squiggle up my stomach? I'm never going to see this guy again.

"Nice bed. Are we going to put it to good use?" I try to maintain a casual tone, but I'm just excited for his hands to continue their path up my leg.

"Piper, you are..." He pauses.

"Ridiculous?" I suggest with a grin. "Outrageous? Silly?"

"Soul-shatteringly, breath-catchingly, word-stealingly, gorgeous," he finally finishes.

"Ugh." My stomach drops, and I let myself fall back from my elbows with an eye roll. I don't have the mental capacity to accept his compliments right now.

"Hey." His voice drops an octave again. "What did I tell you about rolling your eyes?" He leans forward, his arms landing on the mattress on either side of my legs.

"What are you gonna do, Ant? Punish me?"

"Yes." He pauses like he doesn't have any idea what to threaten me with. "Give me your bra," he finally demands.

I laugh again. "That's my punishment?"

"Yes."

"Isn't the goal here to get both of us naked?"

"Yes." He crawls up the mattress until his arms are caging me in. "Now, hand it over." He dips in for another kiss. I wrap my hands around wiry, muscular arms. Really nice arms.

"Give me the bra," he announces. "I want to see them."

"You first." I laugh.

"I am not wearing a bra."

"Your shirt." I sit up, pulling my knees to my chest. "Your shirt for my bra, an even trade."

"That's your punishment? Seeing me naked?"

"Cross my heart. I promise not to enjoy it!" I say solemnly, putting my palm on my breast.

He pulls back, there's a moment of hesitation before he pulls off his shirt. A set of snaps keeps it closed around his wings. I lose all interest in those mechanics when he reveals his body. Sucking in a breath as his shirt lands on the floor. He's slender and muscular, with a narrow torso and broad chest. The fur is thicker around his neck, like a scarf, a fine short fuzz covers the rest of him. He's simultaneously strong and soft, and I want to burrow myself into him.

"Oh no!" I quickly cover my eyes.

"What?" There's a spike of nervousness in his tone.

"I'm enjoying it! I promised I wouldn't!" I laugh through the words. He catches my wrists and moves them, pressing me back into the bed and pinning my hands to the mattress above my head. The swift movement shoots a warm surge of desire through me. His wings spread wide over us, shielding some of the lights and throwing his silhouette into sharp relief.

"You're saying that you like looking at me?"

I squirm and nod. "You're gorgeous."

His dark wings shimmer with an opalescent spectrum when they catch the light.

"You are gorgeous. Every inch of you is absolute temptation." He releases my wrists to stroke gentle fingers down my side. I huff out a breath, barely managing not to roll my eyes this time.

The purr in his chest gets louder, and he lowers himself to kiss me again, tracing his long strange tongue over my lips and down my neck, heating up my body until it feels like every part of me is tingling. I explore him with my fingers in return. He is mostly human-shaped below the neck. His rib cage that doesn't quite end where I expect it to. His heartbeat a little lower in his chest and a little faster than a human's. Tracing further down, his stomach is a little more concave, and when my fingers finally reach the waistband of his sweats, I'm practically purring with excitement.

"What about these?" I ask playfully, running a hand around his waistband.

His body stills. I pull my hands away, feeling I've crossed some unspoken line.

"You should know, I don't look like humans do." He breathes out an exhausted sigh. Like he knew this conversation would happen.

67

"How so?" I ask, my brain intrigued, and my pussy straight up excited by this announcement. Everything felt reasonably as expected before.

"I just want to prepare you," he says. "You probably won't like it."

My heart melts a little. "Hard to imagine disliking part of you." I clench my fist into the sheets as soon as the words come out of my mouth. This is supposed to be no strings. I think I'm already developing strings. I'm so stupid.

His antennae twist a little. I want to make him happy. I want him to have a good time. I should have known nothing about this would be easy for me. I stifle a giggle and it ends up coming out as a whole loud laugh. I cover my mouth, trying in vain, to pull myself back together.

"What?" Ant asks. I expect anger or irritation, but there's just bright curiosity in his voice.

"I just expected to be the only one with body image issues here," I admit, folding a hand across my stomach rolls.

"Your body is perfect." He shakes his head.

"And I'm not allowed to roll my eyes when you say things like that." I poke him gently in the chest.

"When you roll your eyes, it makes me feel like you don't believe me. I am deadly serious," he says. "You are perfect. A bright beautiful flame."

"Right, sure, okay." I bite my lip. "I want to see you naked. I don't want you to do anything that makes you uncomfortable. But if you think I can't handle it, then—"

"I didn't mean it like that, Piper." His voice speaking my name tightens my chest slightly. "You really want to see me naked?"

"Yes!" I bite my lip. Was that too eager? "Please?"

He moves back, the aching cold where his body was pressed to me makes me whine. "I don't want to scare you."

"That deserves an eye-roll." I point a finger in his direction. "I let you carry me thirty feet in the air. You think this is scarier than that?"

He smirks, his antennae lift and then drop. Almost like a shrug.

Crap. I really like him, and I am going to make a fool of myself to prove it.

"I'll trade you," I announce. "Your shirt for my bra. My skirt, your pants?"

He sucks in a short breath. I don't really wait for him to agree. Scared I will lose my nerve, I scoot back so I can sit up for better access.

I slip my arms out of my bra straps, holding the cups in place with one hand while the other reaches around my back to unhook the bra.

He is stone still, unmoving, unspeaking, just waiting.

My skin feels hot, I'm probably flushed red all over. When I finally drop the bra, I can't look at him, letting that heavy self-conscious weight of my breasts fall against my body. Ugh. I wish it was a different time of the month. They are always perkier when I am ovulating. Even on the days when I like them, it's nerve-wracking to sit and be examined like this.

"Good girl." Ant growls low in his throat.

My eyes shoot to his. Crap. I enjoyed that. Am I going to let myself enjoy that?

Ant is grinning, his hands flexing against the mattress like he can't wait to touch me.

"Good girl. Show them to me." His voice is so raspy and low that it's difficult to hear. Yeah. I'm definitely going to let him call me that.

I giggle lightly and sit up straighter, rolling my shoulders back to give them all the advantages I can.

"Yes. My gorgeous, Piper." He inches forward and stops himself. "Put your hair on your head."

"What? Like this?" I pile my loose curls up.

"Both hands," he insists.

I get another 'good girl' when I put both hands above my head. The last one finally uncovers a nervous laugh that's been building in my chest. I don't have the mental fortitude to sit up any longer. I collapse back onto the mattress.

"Touch them," he insists. "For me."

Staring at the ceiling, I swallow hard, sending my protests back into the back of my throat. I am ready to lose myself for a moment, let all of my thoughts disappear, and be told what to do.

So I close my eyes and slip my hands up the sides of my breasts until I reach my nipples, squeezing them gently. Fondling myself, for him, for myself. Who knows anymore.

"Yes," he hisses, before a shadow falls over my closed eyes, as the weight on the mattress changes. "My beautiful flame." He grumbles low, the purr in his chest returning. "May I touch them?"

The question is so easy, light. I nod, but don't open my eyes as I lower my hands to let him take control of the situation. His hands replace mine and he purrs low in his throat before his long tongue snakes across my breasts until he reaches my nipple, there's carefully placed suction. I gasp, my back arches off the bed toward him. I need him other places; I need him everywhere.

"Ant," I say desperately, not even sure if it's really his name.

He's already obliging me, like he can read my thoughts. One hand moves to grip my thigh with strong insistent fingers. I'm all too ready to spread my legs for him, until my knees get tangled in the fabric of my skirt. I hiss in irritation.

"Crap. Just take it off, please," I insist, helping him find the zipper and wiggling to pull the skirt, and my underwear completely off. I am nearly breathless when I'm finally free. We aren't touching anymore, he's just staring at me with those predator-like eyes. He makes an animalistic noise in his throat that sends a shiver straight to my pussy.

I adjust my glasses to see him better. "Fair is fair." I point to his legs. "Pants."

He makes a noise of protest, but I stubbornly cross my arms over my chest. Finally, his fingers move to his waistband, and he lowers his sweats.

It's obvious that he's not human, still finally seeing him without any clothing on, it suddenly becomes very real. There's no sign of the dick I clearly felt earlier. The area between his legs has a strange bumpy texture. It starts to move. I lean forward, intrigued, as two long hard-looking protrusions fold out from his body, gently flexing in the air. Each is as big as my forearm and shaped similarly. That's not what I felt between my thighs earlier.

"Ant— is that supposed to go—inside me?" There was a dick earlier. I definitely felt a dick.

"No." He sighs, like the weight of explaining is too great. "These are my claspers. They will—hold you in place while we mate."

I have to put a hand to my mouth to cover my smile at the word mate. "And your dick?"

He shakes his head with another short sigh. "Aedeagus—stays inside me, until it's—needed."

I sit up, eager to learn more. He hesitates, but I'm not going to stop unless he tells me to.

"Can I?" I hold a hand close to one of his claspers.

He gives a curt nod, and I stroke a finger along one. He shudders.

"Okay?" I ask.

He nods. The clasper is thick, boney, hard, and covered in something like peach fuzz. I wrap a hand around the sides. It flexes slightly in my hand, like the two pieces would hold onto something, onto me. That sends a little shiver of excitement through me. I run my hand up, across his flat stomach, the velvety fuzz that covers his abs, and then down, to the mound where a dick should be. He groans, thrusting slightly into my hand, as a vertical slit opens along his body, and something emerges.

I gasp, but don't pull back as a thick dark tube appears and prods at my fingers, prehensile, almost like it has a mind of its own. It slips itself between my fingers and I wrap a loose grip around it. He's wet, pre-lubricated.

"Piper." He moans above me.

"Okay?" I ask tentatively as my hand continues to explore him. "Good?" I repeat when I don't get an answer.

He grunts an affirmative and seems to be trying his hardest to hold still while I touch him.

His skin is soft and pliable in my grip. I stroke him gently, letting myself explore him. Enjoying the way his prehensile dick follows me. It pulses against my palm a fascinating gentle vibration.

"Amazing." I lean forward and squeeze him slightly and giggle with glee.

"Piper." He pulls back and, with a small shudder, his aedeagus sucks back into his body, the claspers folding neatly over his torso. Disappointment at its disappearance overwhelms me.

"Sorry. Sorry, for laughing."

"Don't be sorry for enjoying yourself." His face seems impossibly sad.

I can't believe I'm ruining this. "I didn't mean to laugh."

"You aren't bothered by it?" He cuts me off.

7

PIPER

"**B**othered?" I laugh. "No way! It's not exactly what I expected, but I think we'll make it work."

His face warps. "Humans haven't always... responded well."

"Those humans were dickheads," I say without thinking, running my hands over his fuzzy thighs.

He leans forward to kiss me again. This time he is sweet and soft, real gratitude coming through in the kiss. There's patience and compassion. He takes his time, not moving his attention from my mouth for a long moment. Until I am finally squirming and eager for something more. I wrap my arms around his neck, trying to pull him closer, until he finally breaks the contact of our mouths.

"Where have you been all my life?" he murmurs.

I laugh and, without thinking, roll my eyes.

"What did I say about rolling your eyes?" he menaces.

"Well, I'm naked now. What are you going to do to me?" I stick my tongue out at him.

"Whatever I want." He moves to straddle my thighs and snatches my glasses from my nose.

"Hey!" I yelp.

He dips his face into my neck, and nuzzles until I am giggling and writhing under him. He switches to gentle kisses, then moves to light licking and sucking until I am breathless and writhing. His hands return to my breasts making me gasp and lean into him. I reach up, tracing a hand along his cheek, and running my fingers through the soft fuzz on his face. Nothing I do hurries him. He explores me slowly and thoroughly like he needs to memorize every part of me. Lighting little fires on every inch of skin that he touches. The sides of my breasts, the curve of my stomach, all the way down to the strip of skin where my thighs touch.

"Be a good girl, and spread your legs for me." His voice is low and dangerous again.

Embarrassment washes through me briefly.

"Show me that perfect pussy." He growls.

I couldn't possibly disobey that order. Cool air hits me when I let my thighs fall apart. It's a level of vulnerability that I'm not used to.

"Good girl," he says without taking his eyes off of me.

The words take the edge off of how exposed I feel. His hands stroke up and down the inside of my thighs reverently, like he cannot believe his luck. I giggle when the fur of his cheek tickles along my inner thigh, and he doubles down on the movement, pulling a gasp from my lips when his tongue traces the same sensitive spot. A single finger strokes up and down my folds, finding the wetness in the center and dragging it all over me until his finger reaches my clit and he circles it over and over.

I groan loudly, and then his tongue latches onto my clit and he sucks.

I nearly fly off the bed, the pressure intense and sudden, he keeps going, gently sucking the whole thing.

I wail into his sheets, my inner walls fluttering around nothing, desperate for slightly more, desperate for the tightness of being filled, of having something inside me.

"I need, Ant, you—"

I don't have to finish my sentence. He presses two long digits inside me, and my body and my walls clench around him flexing as I come around him.

He makes a satisfied noise when I finally pull his head away from my sensitive bud of nerves.

"Fuck." I pull him up to my face to kiss him. His fur is wet from my juices, and I don't even care as I put my mouth against his. "You are very good at that."

He moans against me, his breathing heavy and strained. He shifts on the bed, holding himself above me with slightly shaky arms. Between us his claspers have unfolded. I reach down to press a palm against his seam and feel the slithering head of his aedeagus pressing toward me.

"Piper. It needs to be inside you," he mutters, almost like it is a separate part of his body.

Inside me.

My whole body flushes at the thought of that writhing thing, moving, and prodding, and filling me. Ant strokes a long finger under my chin. "Or we can go play Duck Hunt," he says breathless. "Whatever you like."

I laugh loudly. Fuck, of course I want this. It's completely unfathomable, leaving here without feeling him inside me.

He grins when I laugh, and I grip his arms and pull him closer.

"You. I want you. I want to feel you inside me," I say between kisses that reach every part of his body available to me. His face, his strong arms, his wiry chest, the thick mess of hair around his neck.

He grips my hips, tilting them up so the hard press of his claspers can wrap around the inside of my thighs. They cup just under my ass, tugging our bodies flush together. I can barely move, we're completely locked together. Fuck, this is hot.

He groans against my neck, his hip shifting forward, grinding his slit against my clit just hard enough to shoot a spark of pleasure through me. I yelp.

And then I feel him protruding. Slipping into me, inch by glorious inch, while our bodies stay locked together.

He's breathing loud and heavy in my ear, like this is the most difficult thing he's done in his life.

"Piper. You feel so good."

I dig my fingers tight into his fur. Desperate for something to anchor me while his aedeagus thrusts deeper, although neither of us move. Its strange head probing and exploring me.

It twists inside me, shooting bright sparks through every nerve. I whimper, I don't know how much more of this I can handle.

"Piper," a voice whispers in my ear. "You are doing so well, such a good girl. You can take all of me." He moans, and another inch slips into me, the fullness stretching as it moves.

The probing tip returns to that spark inside me again. I cry out and wrap my legs around his hips. Pressing our bodies even tighter together, needing more of him, more of this stretching invasion. His wings beat through the air around us, his arms wrapping around my back, pulling me into his chest, as a low purr rumbles through his torso, straight into my clit.

The press of him is too much, too tight, until he twists again, and my back arches in pleasure as the sparks shoot bright and hot through my body.

"Good girl, letting me use that tight little hole. Just a little more. Fuck, you feel so good." Ant's voice is harried in my ear.

"More?" I can barely get the word out.

"You can take it," he whispers. "I know you can. Your pussy is perfect. You are perfect. Perfect for me. My good, perfect girl."

There's another push, as the thick base of his aedeagus presses into me. Tight and hot, stretching me to a point that feels impossible. It finally stops. I push my face into his neck, and focus on breathing. The stretch, the tightness, the fullness, every part of it perfect. I don't think I could handle anything else. He doesn't move, but something inside me pulses. A hot vibration that seems to travel down his length, flexing against my inner walls. I almost scream.

"Fuck, baby girl. You are doing so well. You feel so, so good. Your perfect pussy wrapped around me."

The heat from his aedeagus races through me again and again, like a rhythmic stretching. He holds me still, tight and captive, against his body. There's nothing I can do but cling to him through the overwhelming sensation.

"You are such a good girl, taking all of me. Letting me use that tight little pussy. Letting me fill you up." He's muttering into my ear, half of it just coming out as pleasant noise and praise. The intensity of the pulses grows harder and faster, vibrating me from the inside.

And then, with my name between his lips, he groans against me. One last large pulse that breaks me. I cry out, my whole body seems to snap around the strange appendage inside me. It's the hardest I've ever come, darkness and sparks fly across my vision.

He shudders and, with a primal groan, finishes. Splashing heat fills me, his wings beating and his body clenching around mine. "Yes, baby girl, take everything I have to give."

I'm still trying to catch my breath when the wind moves my hair, flinging it past my back, I realize there's nothing but air behind me. When I look backward we are several feet above the bed.

His wings suspended us as we fucked. I was too busy getting railed to even notice that he'd lifted us from the ground.

8

PIPER

He floats us gently back to the bed and unwraps his arms from my body. His aedeagus draws from me with a wet slurp, disappearing into his body, before his claspers release their grip on my thighs. I'm still trying to catch my breath as I sink into the sheets. My entire body feels limp and sensitive at the same time. I can feel his cum dripping out of me, cooling against my thighs. Crap. It's a good thing I'm on the pill. We didn't even talk about birth control. Is there even a condom that would cover him?

He doesn't move from above me. His fingers comb through my hair and graze across my cheeks, his antennae waving gently.

My breath is still heavy, I press my face into his hand, nuzzling his palm.

"Are you okay?" he asks, his voice heavy with concern.

"I'm great, phenomenal, amazing." I say. If anything, I'm mildly irritated by him inundating me with questions when I'm trying to revel in my post orgasm high.

He doesn't seem convinced. "You are sure?" he asks again, his finger brushes gently across my cheek. That's when I feel the wetness. I reach up to wipe my own face.

Tears.

I'm crying.

This is new. I've never had a crygasm before. How embarrassing.

I pull away from his touch, swiping at my own face. The tears are flowing freely now, like my relaxed muscles released something pent up inside me.

"Please, tell me if I hurt you."

"I'm okay, I promise," I repeat and turn away from him, wiping more wetness from my face.

"It isn't normal for humans to cry after sex." He says it like a fact he learned on the back of a cereal box. "It is usually when they are hurt or sad. Is it one of those? Have I hurt you?"

"I'm not hurt or sad." I glance at him, trying to see if he is making an odd joke. He sits on his heels, watching me earnestly, his antennae tilting forward, his wings fluttering.

"Can I do anything? Call someone? Should I get a doctor?" he asks.

"No." I laugh, but his concern is endearing. "I just—had a really intense orgasm and I think it unblocked some kind of emotional dam."

How long has it been since I came from anything other than my own hand?

Colin and I were together for three years, but the past couple months have been—dry, and even before that, the orgasms weren't super common, not that he was bad at sex.[1] Maybe we just weren't compatible. Maybe I am compatible with...a Mothman.

"Do you need anything? I will get whatever you want. Food, drink, medicine—" He leans away from me,

---

1 Maybe he was bad at sex.

his hands hovering in the air like he is ready to fetch anything I ask for.

"Maybe you could just hold me?" I ask.

"Hold you?" He repeats the phrase like my words don't make sense.

"Don't worry about it. It's silly—" I start to roll from the bed but then he's there lying beside me, tugging me in close to his warm body. One hand wraps around my shoulder, pressing my face to his chest, and the other pulls a blanket up and tucks it around me. It's comforting, safe, cozy. Like a cocoon.

With one shuddering breath, I allow myself to melt into him, burying my face in his furry mane, breathing in the slightly dusty scent of him, and digging my hand into his fur, our legs intertwining.

There are more tears now. It's intensely intimate, even compared to him coming inside me. I'm not normally a crier. It makes me feel vulnerable, which is terrifying. But, since I never plan to see this Mothman again, I can let go. I can express whatever emotion I feel. It doesn't matter if I embarrass myself.

I wrap a hand around his narrow waist, needing to feel a little more of him.

He doesn't speak, like he knows I need a moment of silence. His gentle breath brushes my hair, his arm strokes up and down my spine. He continues even after my tears have dried up.

"Are you sure I didn't hurt you?" he finally asks. "Is there any pain?"

"Just the right amount of pain. I promise."

"It was good?" There's a long pause after his question, like he has more to say, so I wait for the eventual follow-up. "I've never done that with a human before."

I sob out a laugh, and he stiffens under me.

"Wait. Are you serious?" I pull back enough to see his face. His antennae manage to look sheepish. "You were really good."

"I made you cry."

I choke back another laugh. "You made me come so hard that I cried. It's very different."

We are quiet for another long moment.

"Did you enjoy it?" I ask tentatively. "The uh…sex."

A soft tittering laugh echoes from his chest. "I liked it very much, Piper. You are also very good at it."

"That might mean more if you had something to compare me to," I tease, although the brief thought of him with someone else irks me.

"I don't need anyone to compare you to," he says quietly. Crap. Can Mothmen read minds? "I'm glad I could make you happy."

"Very happy." I rearrange slightly, and I don't stop touching him. "Crying isn't a normal human reaction after sex. If you decide to have sex with more humans after me." Which I don't want to think about right now.

"You may have ruined me for other humans." He purrs and I lean into the sound.

I laugh. "Sorry for crying on you."

"You can cry more, if you want. I don't mind."

"I think I got it all out." I trace a hand across his ribbed stomach, just enjoying touching him, before a wave of embarrassment washes over me.

It's well past 2am, but the endorphins of the night are still rolling through me. I've always been a night owl, two is a regular bedtime for me. This is barely pushing my limit. I probably should go. That's how one-night stands are supposed to work, right? I should've clarified with Anam. I should be leaving, or he should be kicking me out. Right?

"Sorry, you are probably sick of cuddling an almost complete stranger." I start to pull away, his arms don't release me.

"Stay. Please. I want to hold you as long as you let me." His words are very quiet and I'm grateful for that because I want to ignore the way they make my stomach sink.

9
PONTIUS

She's staying. My beautiful perfect mate is staying. She is mine. Truly. She relaxes into my embrace, like it is the easiest thing in the world. I could hold her like this forever. I love the way she smells, the way she tastes, the way she holds onto me.

I love her.

I can't tell her that, not yet. Every piece of human media has told me humans need more time to fall in love. They don't know after a few hours. I don't like keeping the truth from her, but I don't want to scare her when things are so perfect. When she's so relaxed, curled in my arms, and staring at the ceiling.

"Do you want to watch a movie or something?" I ask quietly.

"Sure." She sighs. "I'm not really tired yet."

She starts to get up, but I squeeze my arm to stop her.

"Don't worry, we don't have to move." I reach into my nightstand for the tablet I programmed for days I want to stay in bed. With a few button presses the projector turns on, throwing light onto the screen that hangs from the ceiling at the perfect angle to view while lying in bed.

"Oh crap! That's so cool!" she yells. "What a genius idea!"

I chuckle. Her joy is so infectious. Her hand splays across my chest, warm, gentle. She likes me, and the simple touch has me purring. She shifts her position slightly and I know why. Every time I purr, her scent changes, tinting with arousal. I turn her on. Me.

"Sorry, I'm a bit of a tech nerd," she interrupts my thoughts.

She's so sexy.

"Same." I squeeze her shoulder.

"So, what are we watching?" she asks.

"Well, I think there's only one choice." I move my tablet so that my movie selection will be a surprise. I receive a satisfying gasp when the opening credits of The Mummy starts playing.

"Absolutely!" she announces settling into the crook of my arm. She rearranges to see the screen slightly better and ends up with her head on my chest. I selfishly let loose small purrs enjoying the way her body reacts to me. My fingers trace little circles along the naked skin of her shoulder. I can't stop touching her. Being together feels so surprisingly easy. I knew having a mate would feel good, but I never imagined quiet moments of bliss like this.

By the time Rachel Weisz is knocking over bookcases, which are inexplicably placed in a perfect circle, Piper has rolled over and stuck her tongue down my throat.

By the time Imhotep is stealing tongues, I have my tongue between her legs again, attaching myself to that perfect spot that has her screaming and flying from the bed. I could do this forever. Please my mate. Feed on her nectar. Live off the beautiful noises that she makes and the perfect way she smells.

She eventually has to pull my face away from her pussy and catch her breath. "Don't you ever get tired of that?"

"Mothmen have a lot of stamina." I grin, wiping her juices from my face. I would do this for her every day if she would let me.

"Well, you are really, really good at it." She swipes a hand across my cheek and I nuzzle her palm. Her casual touches are like a drug I didn't know I needed. I purr into her grip.

"Are you sure it was enough? There aren't any tears this time," I tease.

She releases my face and rolls from the bed with a laugh.

"Let me get a glass of water and we can get to your part." She picks up a random shirt from the floor and pulls it on. It's my shirt. My specially fitted Spock costume. The fasteners that kept it around my wings mean it neither fits her well, nor covers much. Not that I'm complaining. She looks good in my clothing. She belongs in it.

"That's alright." I wave a dismissive hand, hungrily tracking her movements across the room. If I watch closely I can see the way her ass jiggles with every step she takes.

"Are you sure?" Her eyebrow raises. "You don't want to fuck again? You took care of me several times. I'm happy to return the favor."

My aedeagus is straining at my seam. I want to take her again. I would love to fill her with my cum, to fuck her on every surface of my apartment. It's unfortunately impossible, I know how humans work.

"I know humans aren't a big fan of—it." I gesture vaguely toward the space between my legs.

She laughs as she opens a cupboard looking for a glass, and pauses when I don't respond the same. "You aren't joking?"

I shrug. "It's okay if you don't want to do it again."

She shakes her head. "Well, I was definitely a fan. You are good at sex. Like really, really, good at it. Like the best I've ever had." Her words make my heart swell. Her face slowly turning red as she opens more cupboard doors at random, circling the kitchen aimlessly.

I enjoy watching her reach for the higher shelves, the way that my shirt raises up to show a couple extra inches of her ass every time. "I'm glad you enjoyed yourself."

"You are shockingly good for someone who claims to have never—" She stops herself from talking. "You've dated humans? But no sex?"

My wings flutter nervously, my antennae folding back to my head.

"Sorry. I shouldn't have asked. I'm just a nosy person." She sighs loudly. "None of my business what your body count is."

"I've dated a few humans. We didn't participate in penetrative sex." I say quickly so I can't stop myself. The truth is difficult to speak. I pull myself from the bed, needing to be near her again.

"Oh, sure. Nothing wrong with that. There's lots of types of sex," she mutters, having opened every cabinet in my kitchen multiple times she stops and stands completely still.

I put one gentle hand at my mate's waist and reach over her head to open a cabinet, pulling a glass from its shelf. As I give it to her I catch her hands to hold her still.

Bowing my antennae I emit a low purr for her. "I am grateful to you for indulging me, but the woman I dated before you explained it—" I pause waiting for her sigh of relief. I don't want her to do anything for me that she doesn't want to do.

"Explained what?" Her eyes search my face.

"They explained, I'm not attractive..." I say gently, knowing it will relieve her that I'm already aware.

"Someone fucking said that to you?!" Piper exclaims.

"It's alright. I understand." I give her my best approximation of a human smile. "Humans don't like the way I look. They don't enjoy touching me, particularly not that part of me."

"That's not a nice or correct thing to say, to anyone." She shakes her head, furious. "You have a great body, and an amazing dick. Who put those ridiculous thoughts into your brain?"

I feel my smile falter and turn toward the fridge to disguise my discomfort. "I'm happy to fill our time with other activities. Eating you out is very nice. Women have allowed this before."

Piper takes a deep breath. "This helps explain your skillset. But it seems impossible to me, that anyone could know you that well and not want to fuck you."

I pull the water jug out of my refrigerator and turn back to her with some surprise. She is marvelous, my mate. A truly kind and empathetic person. I pour the water into the glass for her. She watches my movements silently, her body language still full of anger. My Spock costume dangles open around her front, the glimpse of the space between her full breasts is enough to drive anyone wild. I purr without meaning to. I know she hears it because the smell of her desire forming between her legs fills the air.

"You are good at the other stuff. It's nice of you to— the oral sex. Don't stop doing that for—for people." She pauses as my purr deepens, and she smells even more strongly now. "There are definitely humans who will touch you. People who will enjoy touching you. I like touching you. I want to do it again, if that makes you happy."

My cock is straining, ready to be loose. I cannot help myself. When she talks like this it makes me happy, and I purr, and when I smell my mate turned on, I want to be inside her. Now that I know how good and perfect sex can be.

"It made me very happy to put my dick inside you." I wrap my hand around her waist.

She takes several large swigs of her water and sets the glass on the counter before speaking again. "You should be with someone who likes your body the way that it is."

"Before tonight I wasn't sure it was possible." My fingers gently toy with the ends of her shirt until her perfect breasts are fully on display again. Her nipples tighten when the cool air hits them.

"Of course it is." Her voice catches slightly as I run my thumbs across her bare skin and up to the bottom of her breasts. I could look at her like this all day, if looking at her didn't make me want to fuck her senseless.

"Yes, it appears so." I back her against the cabinet just roughly enough to make her gasp, and bend down to kiss her. Toying with her breasts until she's moaning against me, smelling so ready and wet for me. Her hands travel over my body. She isn't shy about enjoying every part of me, until her hands come to rest very purposefully on my claspers. I am having a hard time controlling my breathing as they unfold.

"Spread your legs for me and let me feel how wet you are."

She releases a breathy laugh. "Really? No penetration before tonight? Where'd you learn to talk like that?"

"I know what I want, and I know how to ask for it." I growl. "I want to fuck you on top of this counter. Now be a good girl and spread your legs."

Her obedient thighs drift apart, exposing more of her heady aroma to the air, primed and positioned, my claspers grip her hips, and pull her close enough that I can grind my slit along her. She's putty for me, easy and pliant and perfectly enthusiastic as the head of my cock emerges to slide up and down her pussy. She feels perfect, ready, warm and wet. I already know how deep she is, how she will easily take every inch of me. I drag my aedeagus over her clit, slippery and hot. She moans as I move along her lips several times, and gasps when I finally let just the first inch penetrate her. Pumping slowly in and out, increasing the speed as my body gets more used to the action. She's clutching me the way she did the first time, when she was right on the edge, when I held her in space and she came around me. My perfect mate, we are already in sync, and I hold our bodies flush and firm while she moans into my chest. I am her pleasure, and she is mine.

"Please. Ant." She's squirming against me. "Please. I need—"

Her words break, but I already know what she needs. Me.

"Good girl. Take all of me, beg me to fuck you. Beg me to fill you."

"Please. Please. Yes. Please. Fill me. Fuck me. Please. I need all of you." The words in her throat become garbled as my hips tilt and press my full length into her, pulsing hot vibrations as I do. She whispers my name when she comes around me.

I am only a few moments behind her, purring in her ear. Stroking and petting her hair as I empty myself into her, soothing away her nervous energy. She shudders through her aftershocks and clings to my chest. No tears this time. Just a long string of gratitude as I carry her back to my bed.

She is mine now. My mate. In my nest. I will find a way to make her love me. I will find a way to make her stay.

10
PIPER

Eventually, between fucking and napping in each other's arms, it becomes morning. I know I shouldn't let myself fall asleep in his apartment.

I do it anyway.

Curled up against his warm chest, his semen still leaking between my legs. He purrs while we cuddle, it's the nicest I've felt in a long time.

I text my friends that I am alive. They congratulate me on an evening well spent.

Ant offers me coffee, and we finally end up playing naked Duck Hunt on his vintage Nintendo. I make a joke about doggy-style, and we put that position into practice.

We play Smash Bros for a couple hours, before we smash again. I come with his dick deep inside me and his fingers working my clit.

How is this all so deeply satisfying? I don't think this is what one-night stands are usually like, or people would do them all the time.

Ant lets me use his shower. When I get out, I snoop a bit more. Searching through his cabinets for a blow dryer. Maybe it's silly to expect a single male to have one, but he is covered in fur. I find the mother load—a fancy Dyson, with all the attachments, in a basket under his sink. I can't just turn it on, that'd be tantamount to admitting I was snooping.

"You don't happen to have a blow dryer, do you?" I poke my head into the living room.

"Look under the sink," he says. "I'm going to order lunch. If you want to stay for it?"

"Alright." I can't keep from grinning. I'm still drying my hair when it's delivered, and he spreads half of the menu of a Thai restaurant across his coffee table.

"Oh shit! Is this from Thai Me Down?" I pull a floor pillow up to the coffee table. I know I should leave, but it's a free lunch, and he's clearly ordered more food than one Mothman could eat.

"It is." He grins.

"How did you know?" I ask with a laugh.

"Know?"

"That their green curry is my absolute favorite food in the world?"

"Is it?" he asks quietly.

"Ugh, it's been ages since I had Thai food!" I exclaim.

"Why's that?"

"I'm not sure," I lie, not willing to admit that Colin didn't really like eating out many places. He was a steak guy. We didn't go anywhere that didn't serve a decent fillet. It was easier not to argue every time we ate out.

I pile rice and chicken high on my plate and change the subject to which Star Trek captain was the best. Then we make out while we watch Picard be hot in First Contact.

It's all frankly wonderful, and even though I know I should be headed home, I find myself idly perusing a

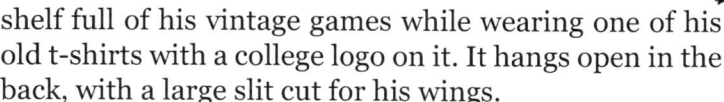

shelf full of his vintage games while wearing one of his old t-shirts with a college logo on it. It hangs open in the back, with a large slit cut for his wings.

"Super Mario Bros is the first game I remember playing." I'm talking mostly to myself as I flip over a cartridge of the game that is older than I am.

"Where did you get a copy of that?" he asks.

"My parents loved video games. They had a big collection of consoles." When I turn to Ant he's smiling, but his antennae droop.

"You played together? With your whole family?" Ant asks.

"Of course! Me and my siblings used to fight over who got to be Player 1. I was the oldest daughter so I only got the Player 1 controller if Paul wasn't around. I'm still sore about it." I grin at Ant, who's lounging on the floor nearby while he watches me almost wistfully. Cute. He looks so fucking cute all of the time. "You played a lot growing up?"

He shakes his head.

"When my little sister started to lose her eyesight, she couldn't play video games quite the same, but I'd read all the instructions and storylines out loud to her so she could still enjoy them with us." I pull out a copy of Legend of Zelda, one of my favorites.

"How many siblings do you have?" he asks.

"Well, Paul's the oldest, he's married, with two kids. Rachel, his oldest, has a birthday tomorrow. Then it's me. Then Paget, she's in New Orleans finishing a graduate program for creative writing. Penny is the youngest, she's training to become a physical therapist. We all used to love playing games together."

"There's four of you?" He sounds almost jealous.

"Yeah. Penny is the one who started losing her eyesight in the fourth grade. She still loves playing games, but there aren't many with visual accessibility adaptations. We still enjoy MUDs together, and there are modifications that make some games usable for her—" A small gust of wind hits my shoulders.

When I glance up Ant has moved across the room, almost silently. His wings flex, and the wind brushes me gently.

"Sorry, I know this isn't interesting." I laugh a little.

"I could listen to you talk all day."

I look at the ground, trying to stop myself from laughing at his sincerity. He isn't funny, but sometimes all of those serious emotions get turned into awkward laughter. It's easier to laugh than it is to express my real feelings.

"Don't you dare roll your eyes." He menaces lightly. His hand cards into my hair and tugs my face up to look him in the eye, sending pleasant little tingles through my scalp. "I am being serious."

"I believe you! I believe you!" I laugh and hold up my hands in surrender. His grip loosens, but his fingers stay loosely combing through my curls.

"I hadn't really considered making gaming more accessible, until recently." Ant's voice is quiet enough to make me want to continue.

"It's gotten more popular since the Decrypting too. Some things just aren't built with tentacles or claws in mind. That's what the company I founded, Penpoint Assist, focused on when we started, making gaming more accessible. We've expanded to other types of usability advice and improvements since then. There's lots of little things companies and developers can do to expand usability," I say.

"That sounds like it could be useful for everyone." His looming presence makes me slightly self conscious, there's a long moment of silence before he speaks again. "Would you like to play it?" He gestures to the game still clutched in my fingers.

"No thanks. I already have it at home, on a couple different platforms. You know they have it on other consoles now," I tease. His fingers still in my hair. It's strangely comforting. I gesture to his collection. "You don't have to keep all these dusty old consoles around."

"Nah. I like the dusty stuff. I like old, forgotten things." His antennae shrug.

"Are these left over from childhood?"

He shakes his head. "I collected most of them over the past decade. I loved watching other kids play. I never got much of a chance myself."

"You came into gaming later in life?"

"I just like getting to know more about the stuff I missed."

"Why'd you miss out?" I let myself lean against his leg, just a little, not willing to move when he's stroking my hair like this.

"Well, I grew up without a console, or a TV, or electricity." He smiles while he says it, even though he is clearly sad.

I know I must not be hiding the shock from my face very well because he sighs loudly before he continues talking.

"I grew up under a bridge in West Virginia. It was a big bridge, a nice one. It used to have trains on it, although it was abandoned when I moved in. I built a cute little nest up under the tracks."

"Right." My stomach sinks for him. "Before the

Decrypting, you wouldn't have been allowed to talk to humans." What a very lonely life that must have been.

He shrugs his antennae. "I got a chance to play games occasionally. I'd find an old Gameboy, or a lost DS. I usually managed to return them to their owners, but I always ran them out of batteries first."

I giggle at the image of a small Mothman playing with his purloined handheld console. "Your whole family lived there?"

"No." He shakes his head again, his fingers moving idly through my hair. "Mothmen fend for themselves from birth, the eggs hatch alone, I grew up alone."

The idea is unbearably sad to me. I'm still close with my parents, and my brother and sisters. I see them most weekends. We still sometimes game together.

"So that's what your life was before the Decrypting? Just...solitude?"

"I traveled sometimes. Visited other bridges, met another cryptid here or there, no one stuck around. If Mothmen are lucky, we find a mate, and pair off for life."

"Lucky lady to get you for life," I tease lightly. His fingers tighten in my hair, and my breath hitches.

"You really think so?" His wings flutter. He's so cute. I do think he'll make someone happy. With his gentle heart and the great sex, of course. Can you say that out loud to a one-night stand?

"Wait, then who did you watch play video games?" I ask to avoid answering his question.

"Humans. At night. Through their windows," he admits sheepishly.

"Oh geez." I grimace. "You spied on people?"

He fidgets. "Only sometimes. When I was really lonely."

His voice soft and sad. He doesn't deserve that. He deserves good things.

I trace a hand up his naked thigh, enjoying the velvet texture of his skin. The urge to make him feel better inches through me. He's naked. Somehow it feels less aggressive than human nudity when his cock has sunk back into his body. I slip a hand up to his abdomen. I want to take care of him. Make him feel appreciated, at least in this small moment.

"Piper?" His voice is quiet.

"Can I make you feel good?" I ask. "The way you do for me?"

He nods, it's hesitant, small, and adorable.

I grin, and lean in to press a kiss against his leg, while my hands slide up stroking along his claspers. They tremble a little under my touch, but don't unfold.

This close, I can see the small slit that hides his dick. I trace a finger down it. It pulses under my touch, like there's something that wants to break through.

I slip a finger inside him, it's warm and wet inside. I trace along the narrow walls and can feel the shaft of his cock, writhing just behind his outer covering.

I manage to hook a finger around him, squeezing lightly, and above me, Ant groans. Then his cock slides out—the whole long, glorious thing. Dark, thick, and slick. I loosely wrap my fingers around him, and he responds almost in turn. The prehensile member slipping through my hand and down to wrap partially around my wrist.

"Piper," he whispers my name again, needy and low. His fingers combing through my hair.

I lean forward and kiss him on the tip. It practically leaps toward my mouth. I bite back a laugh. When I look up to catch his eyes, Ant is smiling at me.

"Is this okay?" I ask.

"Fuck. Piper. Are you going to—"

His words cut off as I lean forward and lick him. The texture is smoother than expected, slick and soft but not slimy. The cock moves of it's own accord in my grip, letting me know what it likes as I explore him with my tongue and lips, kissing and licking along him as he makes strange groaning noises above me. The tip is slightly bulbous, when my breath glances across it, the head moves toward me. Pressing against my lips, like it is seeking my wet heat.

"Good girl." His voice is raspy. "You treat my cock so well."

I lick my tongue along the bottom edge of the shaft, watching his expression through my lashes as I open my lips and let the head of his dick slip into my mouth. His eyes are locked on me, completely enrapt. His hand fisted just tight enough in my hair to let me know he's there. Not pushing, or trying to move me, just letting me take control, as I hum around him, swirling my tongue. I cannot nearly take all of him in my mouth, I let my hands do the rest of the work, pulling and slipping around him.

"Shit. Piper. You feel so good. Letting me use your sweet, hot little mouth."

My eyes water from the strain of my full mouth. His dick seeks to go deeper, to slip all the way down my throat. I gag a little. I have to hold his straining length back with both hands while it tries to go further than I can handle. Ant starts to pull back, but I lean forward, encouraging his head to tunnel until I find my own limit.

"Fuck. You are so good at that. My beautiful girl. You take me so well, so deep down that tight little throat." His fingers tighten in my hair.

I can feel the purr in his chest; it affects me even sitting on the ground in front of him. I move to press my thighs together, enjoying a little bit of friction on my clit as I bob my head along his length. I grip the base of him, holding him back, and enjoying the way he strains toward me. Groaning and shuddering like I'm everything he's ever wanted.

"Wait. Piper. I'm going to—"

Before he can finish the words he comes down my throat. Hot, wet, sticky. There's so much of it. Too much for my unprepared throat.

I pull back with a sputtering cough. Still gripping his cock tight in my fingers. He continues coming and splashes my face, hands, and chest with hot semen.

I laugh, which it doesn't help with the choking feeling. I cough more, trying to clear my throat so I can take a deep breath. I'm covered in sticky cum. I was trying so hard to look cool and sexy. Only to end up nearly doubled over, hacking out a lung, and completely unable to stop laughing.

"Piper! I'm so sorry!"

I shake my head, barely able to breathe through the laughter. It's mostly my own fault. I give him a thumbs up so he knows I'm alright.

"I'm sorry, I should have warned you." He crouches beside me, one hand moves to my back. "I didn't mean to surprise you like that."

"It's okay," I say, finally sucking in a full breath of air. It's a little flattering, and a little embarrassing. "If I were better at this, there wouldn't be a mess."

"Piper. You were fantastic. No one has ever—I didn't realize it would feel so good."

"Did I just give you your first blow-job?" I suddenly realize.

His antennae curl toward each other, and he sheepishly avoids eye contact. "It was. Let me get you a washcloth. Please. I'm so, so sorry." He hurries to his kitchen area. I do believe it was unintentional. Some men might have lied—done it on purpose—but Ant's honesty shines through in everything he's said to me since we met. I'm going to choose to believe him. The Mothman's wings flutter behind him while he fiddles in his kitchen. He's fully naked still, and through my semen-splattered glasses, I get a glimpse of a tight fur-covered ass. I unconsciously lick my lip, catching a drop of his semen.

The sweet taste dances across my tongue. It doesn't taste like human cum, it's still a little salty, but sweet instead of bitter. Like honey, or salted caramel. Curious, I dip another finger into the white goo covering my cheek and slip it into my mouth. It's pleasant, easy, and kind of...good?[1]

Ant makes an odd noise. When I look over, he's watching me.

"Do that again. Please?" He adds the final word as a question.

"Did you like it?" I laugh, enjoying how intrigued he is.

He nods expressively, clear effort going into the human movement.

I fight a giggle and slip another finger of his cum into my mouth. The sweet and salty flavor dances across my tongue. He groans watching me.

"You are amazing. You know that?" He's standing in front of me now.

"I'm a mess." I start to roll my eyes, realize my mistake, and try to turn away from him. His hand

---

1 I'd give so much more head if semen tasted better.

catches my chin to face him and gently swipes my cheek with a washcloth. It's warm. He's taken the time to let the water heat up, to make me more comfortable.

"I love the way you look, all messy, your face covered in my cum." His eyes are somewhere else for a moment, and in a quick movement, he's lifted me up into his arms so my legs wrap around his waist. "In my arms, in my shirt, with my cum on you."

"Maybe I could use your shower? In your bathroom. To clean your cum, off my face?" I smile, still feeling sheepish when I slip my arms around his neck.

"Let me clean you up," he murmurs as he carries me to his bed. I lose his shirt somewhere along the way. He drops me fully naked into his sheets and continues wiping, cleaning off delicate parts of me that don't even need to be cleaned. The nape of my neck, over my chest, down to the soft skin on my inner thighs, leaving little goosebumps in its wake as it cools. He dips his face into my neck, his breath hot where the skin is still damp. A gentle lick, a kiss.

"You taste almost as good as you smell," he says in a breath.

"I smell good?"

"So very, very good." He grunts a response. I reach up unconsciously, to trace fingers along his cheek. One of his mandibles grips at my hand. Then the sides of my breasts, the curve of my hip, the strip of thigh between my legs, until I am wet, not just from the washcloth, and he puts his mouth between my legs. It doesn't take long until I am the one coming all over his face, and he is preening, pleased with his actions.

I've never had a one-night stand before. I don't think it's common for them to last for nearly thirty-six hours straight, but Ant easily convinces me to stay the night again by fucking me into oblivion, then curling around me purring. It's easy to sleep pressed against his chest. So much easier than in my own empty bed.

When Sunday morning rolls around, I really have to leave what I'm certain has been the most enjoyable one-night stand in existence. I know it's illogical that part of me wants to stay here in our little sex nest forever. Ignoring the entire world, and the fact that I don't have any clean underwear.

The idea of never seeing him again, walking away from him forever, has my heart twisting in my chest. I know what our arrangement was, still my stupid heart can't help wondering if he might entertain a different agreement.

11

PONTIUS

'm pouring a cup of coffee when she walks out of my bathroom, freshly showered and wrapped in a towel. My towel.

She's beautiful. Her skin is still slightly pink from the hot water. I can't believe she's here. My mate. Covering everything in her scent. Getting more of her smells embedded in my house, in my linens, in every part of my nest. Her damp hair tumbles over the slope of her bare shoulder. She bends over to sort through her pile of dirty clothing, the towel gaping open at the side providing a view of the perfect sliver of skin leading up her thigh.

"Can I lend you something to wear?" I ask selfishly. I want her in my clothing. I want her marked with my stuff, and my stuff to be marked by her. I want to pull her back into my bed and never let her leave.

"I need to go. It's my niece's birthday," she says simply.

"You can't miss that," I tell her. I know it's unrealistic to keep her here forever. She said she needed a one-night stand. A night of no-strings-attached sex. I want her to have everything in the world that she could ever desire. So that's what she'll get. I'll see her again, even if it's from across the street, and I never get to hold her in my arms. My fingers tighten around the handle of my coffee mug. I push the second mug in her direction: almond creamer and two Splenda. Exactly the way I've watched her prepare it through several coffee shop windows. "I had an amazing weekend, Piper."

"Me too." Her eyes are focused on the ground, seeming suddenly shy. "I wondered if maybe...we might...do this again..."

Again. I would do anything to be with her again. I hold back for a moment before I speak, scared I'll come off too eager for her company. "You said you wanted no strings."

"I know what I said." She's smiling at the floor. "Ugh, let me put clothes on or something. I can't think, standing in front of you, with both of us mostly naked."

I glance down at my body. Right, nudity. I never really wore anything before the Decrypting. Somehow being with her brings me back to that level of comfort. I grab a pair of pants from my pile of clean laundry and hold my breath as she fumbles with her own clothing.

It feels like hours later that her head finally emerges from inside her shirt, with a wide beautiful grin on her face. "I just got out of a long term relationship—"

Me too. I don't cut in.

"And I know that can make things complicated—"

It doesn't have to. I don't say it out loud.

"My ex hasn't even moved all of his stuff out of our apartment—"

I will fix that. I will remove him from her life. I feel myself scowl, and her expression falls.

"Doesn't it feel like we should do this again?" She finishes with a wince.

"I think we should do this as often as possible. I'd really like to see you again, soon," I say quickly, adding a smile at the end. Soon, she will not be going home to her empty apartment with her ex-boyfriend's things. She will be here, with me, every day. If she can handle my presence for a weekend, then we can find a way to manage forever. She let me touch her, hold her, fuck her.

"Okay." She's all smiles. My heart sings. I've done it. I may have actually convinced someone to like me. Found a woman, a mate, who will spend time with me. All of it was worth it—every minute I waited for her, every time I followed her, every little morsel of information I learned about her. It all led to this, led us here, helped her fall for me.

"Okay?" I reach for her hands, pulling her toward me. She steps easily into my embrace. I purr and she giggles, putting one hand against my bare chest. I never want to let her go, never let her out of my sight, never let her leave my home. "You'll see me again?" My voice is quiet.

"If you'll let me." Her voice is quiet too.

"Of course," I say simply, while my brain screams yes, yes, yes. I dip down and kiss her, taking my time, indulging in her taste, and memorizing the feel of her beneath my hands. She's mine. She's going to be mine forever. She lets a little sigh into my mouth and pulls away.

"I have to go," she reiterates.

"Can I call you later?" I ask, even though I want to insist.

"I will be disappointed if you don't." She grins.

I'll have a hard time waiting to call her. I can barely stand to let her out of my sight now.

"Do you need a ride home?" I ask. "I would fly you except the sun can make it difficult for me to go outside. But I can order you a car."

"You don't need to do that." She shakes her head.

"I know I don't need to. I want to." I know I'm grinning wildly. "You live near Moonshine, right?"

"How did you guess?" she asks with a small bright laugh.

I can't admit the answer to that, so I turn my back. "Let me find my phone." I've barely looked at it for the past day and a half, completely consumed with her.

She fidgets beside the door. Adjusting a knickknack, moving a book. Touching my things, and getting her lovely smell all over them. I hear her open a drawer in the side table.

"Funny," she says. "I had a hair clip just like this, dragon wings, with red with gold flecks, to match my hair." She laughs. "I broke mine last week, lost it at the movies."

I freeze. Not the drawer. I should have gotten rid of the drawer.

"Who does this belong to?" She continues rifling.

"Don't worry about that—" I stop speaking when I see her face, horror stricken.

She's moving things around. "These are the same cherry chapstick I use, and—" She picks up a scrap of paper to examines it more closely. "This movie stub from the last Artemis midnight movie? From two weeks ago? And this a receipt from a late-night Walgreens snack run?"

"Please." I start, not sure how to finish the sentence.

"Is this my trash?" She catches my gaze, her brows knitted together.

"It's not what you think," I try to tell her.

"I think you have a piece of junk mail addressed to 'Piper Hamilton or Current Resident'." She's holding items up now. "You have a pile of my stuff in here." It's not a question.

"Piper." I reach for her. She backs away from me. "I didn't mean for you to see this—"

"How do you have this? Why do you have this?"

"Piper—" I hunt for any explanation that might make it seem alright. "I don't want to lie to you—"

"You recognized me at the bar. You didn't get my name off my credit card at all, did you?" She's throwing things from the drawer onto the floor. "Have you been following me?"

"Piper, I don't—"

"FUCK!" she yells as her fingers hit the wooden bottom. "I am such an idiot!"

"No, you aren't—"

"This is my mail, Ant. My stuff! You need to explain this. You need to tell me this is some kind of joke."

She's still here, she hasn't run yet. Maybe I can still fix this. "It's a Mothman's nature. It's in our very make-up," I start. "The urge to follow and protect the ones we love. To warn them of danger to keep our fated-mates safe—"

"Fated-mate?" She cuts me off.

"We belong together, Piper. You feel it too. I know you do—"

Shaking her head back and forth, she interrupts me again. "You think I'm really stupid, don't you?"

"No!" I continue. "I knew you were meant to be mine the first time I saw you. When you came into my bar—"

She takes another step back. "You saw me weeks ago and decided I'm your mate?"

"I didn't decide. Fate did. Pheromones. Science. Magic. Whatever you want to call it—"

"It wasn't fate that we ran into each other on Halloween. You planned it, you waited, and watched me, and schemed."

"I wanted to approach you. I knew it was pointless when you had the human man—"

"You were waiting to hit on me until I was single?"

"I saw him moving out of your apartment. You spend your nights alone now, but you don't have to. You can be with me. We can be together—"

"You think that's what I need? Some male to come along and fix me?"

"I think you need me, Piper. Just like I need you. You came back to my bar, Moonshine, several times. You think that was an accident?"

"I don't need anyone, I—" She interrupts herself to put even more space between us. "Oh god. Your bar? You own it?"

"It's full of me. Of my smell. Some part of you knew I was there, sensed that I was perfect for you. It's why you enjoy my company so much. It's why you like me when other humans can barely stand to look at me. It's why you took my dick—all of me—so easily."

"No. No. Please. Please." Her voice is so different than when she was begging me to fuck her. "You didn't do those things. You didn't follow me home. You haven't been stealing my mail. Collecting things that I dropped or lost. I need you to tell me this is a joke, Ant."

"It's not a joke. We've found each other. Now we can be together. My true mate—"

"Shut up!" She cuts me off. "I was so flattered by your attention. But you—you're a stalker—you're a

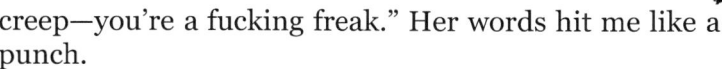

creep—you're a fucking freak." Her words hit me like a punch.

"Piper, I love you."

"You don't even know me," she insists.

"I know you better than I know myself." I can't help it. I reach for her again.

"No. Don't. Stop talking." She jerks back. "Do not follow me. Do not try to find me. Do not contact me. I never want to see you ever again. Just leave me alone."

And then she literally runs from me. The way I knew that she would. The very thing I was afraid would happen.

Through the door and into the bright daylight.

And it's all my fault.

I want to go after her. Grab her, drag her back here. Spread her across my bed and make her come until she agrees to be with me forever, but I can't.

So I curl up in my empty bed, where the sheets still smell like my mate, my everything—and let myself mourn.

12

PIPER

Crap. Crap. Crap, crap, crap.

The brightness of daylight shocks me when I walk outside. After spending so many hours in his dim apartment, the light is almost blinding. I have been such an idiot.

I might throw up. I have a stalker, and I slept with him. I spent a whole day, fucking him and cuddling him and coming for him.

I cried in front of him. I don't remember if I ever cried like that in front of Colin.

Ant was nice and kind and funny and cute, and my heart squeezes while I literally run from his condo. Crap. This is what I deserve for trying to be casual. Trying to enjoy one night of fun. Letting my hopes raise, just so I can fuck a guy who has apparently been following me for weeks.

Crap, crap, crap.

I walk at least ten blocks in a blind rage before I calm down enough to take in my surroundings and realize I have no idea where I am. It's a beautiful fall day. Quiet. Chilly. Crisp. The hairs on the back of my neck stand up as a shadow passes overhead. My stomach leaps into my throat. I duck under a building's awning and search the sky for a Mothman-shaped figure. It's just a flock of geese.

He wouldn't follow me again, right? Not in the daylight. Not after we fought.

I don't know anymore. He seemed so nice, trustworthy, not like the kind of person who stalks you. Under the safety of the awning, I pull out my phone and order a lift home. During the ride, I text my squad.

> Me: I have so much I need to tell you.

> Me: Stuff got crazy.

> Me: Ant isn't who I thought he is.

I stare at my phone, waiting for a response. Nothing comes. They must be busy, I know they'd answer if they saw my text. It's still early on a Sunday and my friends have lives. Anam is probably sleeping late after a wild night out. Kelly and Jeremy are probably having brunch together like the adorable couple that they are. I hate the idea of interrupting either of their mornings to complain about my ridiculous mistake.

The car is pulling up outside my apartment before I realize this might be a terrible idea. Ant knows where I live. He has my address. This might not be the safest place.

Another wrench in the matrix—a familiar car waits in front of my apartment. My Mom is here.

Crap. It's still my niece's birthday. Mom was going to give me a ride to the birthday party. She wanted to make sure that I actually left the house. What am I going to do? I cannot say out loud, to my flesh and blood mother, that I spent a weekend fucking and sucking a potentially dangerous stranger.

"Where have you been?" Mom exits her car when she sees me on the sidewalk.

"Good morning, Mom! How are you?" I announce pointedly, while tucking my wrinkled shirttails into my wrinkled skirt, hoping to make my disheveled appearance less obvious.

She purses her lips. "You're late."

I push past her toward my door. "I just need a couple minutes to change, and then we can leave." I fumble with my key, finally jerking them from my pocket and jamming it into the lock.

"You need to hurry," she says as my door swings open.

"You can just take the present and go without me." I point to the nicely wrapped gift that I left sitting on the front table, so I wouldn't forget to bring it.

"You aren't going to wear that are you?" She ignores my suggestion.

"No, Mom. I just need to change. It'll be quick."

"Let me come upstairs! I'll fix your hair while you do your makeup."

"It's fine." I smooth the loose bun I have my curls piled into. Still damp. I washed it at Ant's. At the time, I thought it was really convenient that he had all my favorite products. He said he'd been experimenting with his fur, and now I'm realizing he must have known which brands I used. Has anyone I've dated paid that much attention to what I like? It'd be sweet if it weren't so creepy. Crap. I'm such an idiot. "I just want to put on a clean change of clothes."

Mom follows me into the apartment and up the stairs to my bedroom. "Oh, this is such a nice apartment, Piper. Shame you'll have to move now."

"I'm not moving," I tell her. "I like it here."

It's a great location—two bedrooms, two bathrooms, a perfect little backyard, lots of cute details, hardwood floors, central air, and decent-sized closets. Everything you could want in an apartment. Except that a deranged Mothman knows I live here, and has been watching me closely enough to know what kind of shampoo I buy. Maybe I should move.

"You can't stay here, darling," Mom casually insists.

"Wait, why do you think I can't stay here?" I ask.

"Men don't like it when you have a nicer place than them."

I freeze in the middle of my bedroom. I'm definitely not getting a new apartment now. "Men?"

"You know what I mean, dear." Mom's voice pitches higher. "I know you make plenty of money on your own. You are so gosh-danged accomplished. I'm so proud of you! But whoever you're with, they'll want to feel needed. And you've got less time, now that you're single and—"

"Getting older?" I ask, knowing exactly where my mother is going.

"I didn't make the rules! It's a timing issue for women. I know you want a family. Kids and a husband—" Her voice comes from my bathroom.

"A husband?" My exhausted sigh is covered by the distinctive sound of her rummaging through my bathroom drawers.

"You know what I mean—" She stops herself mid sentence. She tries to be understanding of my sexuality, but never quite gets it right. "A spouse!"

I poke my head around the corner to see that she's plugging in the curling iron she's pulled from my vanity.

I slip a 'Bookmarks are for Quitters' shirt out of my dresser, and move to the bathroom to unplug the curling iron.

Mom looks at the shirt clutched in my hand. "Maybe, wear the yellow dress? The one you wore for Easter last year."

"I don't need to wear a dress like that to a child's birthday party." It's one of the few Mom approved outfits in my closet because she bought it for me for family photos. I do look really good in it, but it's much fancier than this event calls for.

"Never hurts to look your best, dear." She's already moving to my closet.

"It's dirty, Mom. It needs to be dry cleaned.[1]" I discard my dirty Halloween costume on top of my overflowing hamper, and pull the clean shirt over my head.

"Are you sure that you don't want help with your hair?"

"I don't need help, Mom."

"Alright darling, alright."

I reach for my favorite sitting down jeans, pausing briefly when I catch sight of Colin's side of the closet fully cleaned out. At least I get more storage space now. I change into clean underwear and slip the jeans on.

Mom makes a face that expresses her clear disapproval for my outfit.

"It's such a shame about the breakup, sweetie. I know you two loved each other. You definitely won't be getting back together, right?"

"Mom! No!" I grumble.

"I'm just making sure, dear!" She smiles. "I just want you to be happy."

"I know." I sigh.

"No make up?" she asks with a wince.

"Seriously?"

---

1 I know I'll never take it to the dry cleaner, but my mom still seems to think that's a possibility too.

"You never know when you might meet the right man!" she says. "Person!" She corrects herself quickly. "The right person!"

"Who am I going to meet at a seven-year-old's birthday party?" I snark.

This shuts her up.

She's tried to be supportive since I came out as bi in high school. With three other (mostly) straight children, two of them happily married, sometimes she still defaults to the heteronormative. I know she means well, but she's had over a decade to get used to the idea.

I glance in the mirror. My hair is a bit of a mess. I resist the urge to fix it. After all her fuss, I'm not going to mess with it now and let my Mom think she was right about that. I apply some mascara, smudge a little blush into the apples of my cheeks, and grab my favorite neutral lip color. Normally, I might have taken a little extra time for my face, but with my Mom here, I'm ready to stand my ground and leave the house looking low effort. I straighten my glasses and declare I'm ready.

"You are beautiful, dear." Mom smiles. "I hope you know that."

"Thanks, mom," I reply on reflex, grabbing my bag from the pile by my front door. It can be hard to truly acknowledge her compliments. I know she loves and supports me, sometimes she just picks the worst ways to show it.

Unsurprisingly, we end up at a cat cafe. My newly seven-year-old niece is completely obsessed with cats at the moment. Cat Rhapsody's is a new addition to the neighborhood, an adorable little building, freshly painted, all pink and purple and white. With a counter of human snacks for sale and a whole room full of cats and their toys.

"Welcome!" the pretty white lady behind the counter exclaims. She has a heart-shaped face and bright pink hair in a pixie cut. "Can I get you anything? Coffee? Bagel?" She is practically buzzing with excitement.

I snag a latte, grateful to finally get a bit of caffeine into my system, and settle into a seat beside my youngest sister.

"Penny." My exhausted brain gives the simplest greeting possible, to be sure my sister knows who is sitting beside her. Her visual impairment means she can't exactly make out facial features, even sitting this close.

"Running late?" Penny asks. She lounges on a long bench, her little pregnancy belly bumping her sweater out. She's four years my junior, with similar red curls, although hers have always been a bit more tamable.

"Mmph," I respond.

"Having a tough morning?"

"Mom is in a mood today," I mutter.

"Be on the look out," Penny says. "I think she's got someone special for you to meet."

"What? Why do you think that?" I ask with a laugh.

"Oh, because she told me she invited her spin instructor here for you to meet."

"Penny. No. No. Right? You're joking with me?" I ask.

She laughs in response.

"No! Pen! Penny! I can't tell if you are teasing or not!"

She shrugs, a mischievous smile on her face.

"Michael! Come over here and tell your wife she has to tell me the truth."

"I know better than to get into an argument between the sisters!" he calls from across the room, where he and our niece are playing with a pair of calico kittens while our oldest brother, Paul, and his wife entertain our parents.

"You are a menace," I groan and my sister laughs again.

Pen fills me in on the details of her life and I don't miss that she carefully avoids the topic of my relationship status. I'm glad not to talk about Colin for the billionth time, and even more glad not to talk about how I spent the whole weekend with a stranger and didn't realize what a creep he was.

It's only a few minutes before a large orange cat decides that my lap is the most comfortable place to settle down for a nap.

Petting a purring fuzzball does make me feel better. I don't have any pets, I always loved animals. Colin was allergic to cats, but the new apartment does allow them. Maybe I could take advantage of that. Find a fuzzy friend who would keep me company.

I scratch the big guy behind the ears. He purrs loudly.

It'd be nice to have this kind of unconditional approval.

"We found out the sex today." Penny's tone is almost conspiratorial.

"What? Really?" I ask excitedly.

"Yeah—" she pauses.

"You want to tell me what it is?"

"Well, I wondered if I could use—you know—the name." Her face is slowly turning beet red.

"The name? Oh? Oh, right!" I laugh a little. "Of course you can!"

"It's silly to still think about it," she says.

"No it's not!"

"I just always assumed you would be the one who used it—" Her words fumble to a stop.

"We always agreed whoever got there first." I laugh but put an encouraging hand into hers, since she can't see the sincerity in my features. "Of course you can name the baby 'Presley'."

She grins.

"Are you sure?" Penny asks. When we were kids Penny, Paget and I found a baby naming book. We spent an entire summer vacation picking out the 'best baby name'. There was a pros and cons table, a double elimination bracket, we even took a full family vote. Of course once we picked the 'perfect name' the three of us immediately started to fight over who'd get to use it. We rehashed that fight all throughout adolescence. Sometimes jokingly, other times more seriously. We settled on 'whoever gets there first'. As the oldest I always kind of assumed I'd be the one using it.

"Yes, of course I'm sure! I'm so very happy for you." It's not a lie, my sister deserves every ounce of happiness she's ever received, and so much more. "At this point, who knows if I will ever get a chance to pick out a baby name!" I bark out a laugh and it sounds so much more strained than I intend for it to.

Penny's been married for over a year. Her husband Michael is fantastic. Of course I'm excited they are starting a family, still a little twinge of jealousy forms in my stomach. Penny has a husband, and a kid on the way. I just had a one-night stand with a dude I met in a bar who turned out to be my stalker. I just thought I was a lot closer to the status of 'wife and mother' myself.

Penny smiles. We've always been close. For a long time, she felt like the one person in my life who really understood me. Our parents are great and have always been supportive, but four kids is a lot, and we never had tons of money. So when Penny started needing more help at school and care around the house a lot of it fell on me. The oldest daughter.

"Are you sure it's alright?" she asks, unable to ignore the strain in my laugh. Across the room, our niece, Rachel, squeals.

"Yes! Yes, absolutely. I just had a rough weekend." I admit.

"What kind of rough?" She waggles her eyebrows.

I wish I could laugh.

"Seriously, are you alright?" She presses her shoulder to mine.

I make eye contact with my mother across the room. I just can't tell the story right now, not with my whole family here.

"Can I tell you later?" I ask my sister. "How is your nursery coming along?"

Penny smirks at my change of topic. "It's alright so far."

The door of the cafe opens, and a man walks in. I know it isn't anyone we are related to because he is tall and lean. He's at least six inches taller than anyone in my family, with floppy golden hair and the thick toned thighs of someone who bikes, or even—spins.

Maybe even someone who instructs others how to spin?

"Oh no," I whisper. "Oh no. I think the spin instructor just walked in."

My little sister snickers behind her hand.

13

PIPER

"**P**enny. I cannot believe you were serious."

She outright laughs at me.

"Pen, oh no, what am I going to do?"

She shrugs.

"Hi. I'm Alex." The tall stranger holds out his hand for me to shake. "You're Piper, right?"

Crap. Across the room my Mom smiles widely and gives me the largest thumbs-up possible. Now I know exactly why she wanted me to 'look my best'.

"I think I need another cup of decaf." Penny grins, shoving herself to her feet.

"Penny!" I protest through gritted teeth, Alex is already slipping into her vacant seat. "Hi." I briefly consider leaving, but that would be rude to Alex, annoy my mother, and worst of all, upset the orange tabby who's settled in my lap.

"Your Mom says you're a programmer?" Alex asks. Mom does know how to pick them. He's undeniably handsome, in a slightly odd way, with a nose that is slightly too large for his face, striking light brown eyes, but no fur at all around his neck. Nothing I could really sink my fingers into. And he obviously can't fly.

"Yeah, I run a small company that focuses on technological accessibility. We're non-profit so there's not a lot of money, but we've gotten a lot of really good press lately. Do you work in tech?" I ask, trying to ignore the strange physical standards I seem to be comparing a potential date too.

He shrugs. "No."

"Do you game?" I ask, awkwardly trying to find some common ground. The topic of video games tend to get people talking, then I can relax and pretend to listen. "We've consulted with some really cool big developers!"

"Not really." He leans against the wall and then there are no more words in his part of the conversation.

"No board games, or video games, or tabletop? Maybe roleplaying?"

He shakes his head.

"I actually watched a really interesting documentary about Scream Queens and women in horror recently."

A blank stare in return.

"Seen any good TV recently? Or movies?" This is like pulling teeth.

"I don't have time to watch much."

I wait a moment longer. He doesn't provide any other information. Across the room Mom is boring holes in my head with her stare. I'm not out of the water yet.

"What kinds of hobbies do you have, Alex?" I make another attempt to pull more than one sentence from the man.

"I love working out. Obviously," he says with a straight face.

"Obviously," I repeat with a full-throated laugh, thinking he's making a joke. I wait for him to continue. He is silent in response. I close my mouth. "Anything else?"

"I'm a personal trainer." He flexes his arms, I don't think he can help himself.

I snicker. He does not. I re-sober my expression. I'm trying very hard to maintain a polite demeanor, but quickly loosing my motivation. "Sorry." I try to cover for my faux-pas.

"It's a good job." His brows furrow.

"Oh, yeah! Of course, it is!" My nervous laugh bubbles up a third time. "I mean, obviously you are doing great! Just look at you!"

He leans back with a small frown. "We can't all be computer geniuses."

Another brief chuckle escapes my lips.

"Is that funny?" He raises an eyebrow.

"Sorry."

His face doesn't change with my apology.

"It's just that, please believe me, I'm not a computer genius."

"That's not how your mother tells it," he crosses his arms. "She said you were top of your class in college."

"Really? I never would've expected that!" I joke with another little laugh, because of just how expected that is. Mom loves bragging about her kids accomplishments. Alex twists his head slightly to the side, like he is examining a particularly difficult to decipher work of art. So I continue the joke to make it more obvious. "Because that's so totally unlike her!"

"You laugh a lot, huh?" he finally asks.

"Oh. Sorry," I apologize again, a little taken aback. I feel my grin become awkward. I don't think I've had a really awkward smile all weekend. "It's just a bit of a nervous tick."

He's still looking at me like my face is a cubist portrait. "You're nervous?"

"Well yeah, you know?" I manage to squash the awkward feeling into a less invasive chuckle this time. "Just like, a little bit, all of the time."

"Hmph." He shrugs. "So you are always like this?"

Every part of me deflates, my energy completely gone. I can hear in his voice that he's trying to be polite, or that he thinks he's being polite. It's absolutely brutal. After two full days feeling like I was allowed to be myself, with a person who immediately understood me.

I might hate Alex. I definitely resent him.

I feel like leaving, but I just don't have the heart to upset the cat in my lap.

"It can be a lot louder." I roll my shoulders back. "That's all I really am. Just big tits, and a loud laugh."

"Oh, I'm sure there's more than that. Once people get to know you." He sounds strangely earnest.

I chuckle. "Not really. And I only plan on getting fatter and happier from here on out."

"Hmph." It's the only noise that he makes for a long moment.

"What would you do?" I barely care anymore. "If I laughed when you took your pants off?"

"Laughed?" he asks slowly.

"You know. When I got a good look at your dick." I keep my voice light and peppy. "If I just laughed real loud? Because that's what you have to look forward to."

"Is that some kind of joke?" he asks.

I shrug, but don't even stop myself from making a loud embarrassing bark of a laugh. One that takes two full lungs of air.

The man cringes.

I shake my head. "I don't think we'd be a good fit, Alex. Maybe not even physically." I chuckle again, just for myself. I let it be the annoying kind because it doesn't matter anymore. How could this guy stand up to Mothman dick? After the weekend I had, I might be ruined for regular human penis. I'm certainly ruined for men who don't let me have fun in the bedroom.

"Oh, too bad Alex, that you have to leave so soon!" I say loud enough for my mother to hear from across the room. My family members turn to look at me. Mom's mouth is a thin line of irritation.

Alex looks confused, so I lean in close to whisper conspiratorially, "It isn't going to work, between us. We both know it. Just take the easy out, it's all good. You won't offend me."

Alex agrees with my statement easily although he is still looking at me like I am abstract sculpture called 'Untitled'.

"It was really nice to meet you, Piper. I think at least." He cracks his first smile since he sat down, it's so handsome that it almost makes me regret suggesting he leave. Almost.

"Back, atcha, my guy." I shoot a finger gun at him, and watch the rest of his ego dissipate like he's been struck by a sniper rifle of awkwardness.

He says a polite goodbye to my Mom on his way out the door. Her face is bright red when he's gone, and she doesn't speak to me for the next forty-five minutes.

"So, Mom is really pissed." Penny gives a little laugh as she sidles up next to me.

"Yeah. I may have gone a little overboard," I admit. "I'll give her a couple days to cool down and then apologize."

"It was impressive how fast he got out of here. What did you say to the guy?"

"Ugh, told him I would laugh at his dick." I sigh, putting my head back against the wall.

"Really?" Penny asks appalled.

"Yes?" I say with a little question in my voice.

"Piper! You can't do that!"

"What? Laugh at his dick? Or tell him I'm going to laugh at his dick." I giggle.

"Both! Neither!" Penny giggles too. "We're leaving soon. Do you want a ride home?"

"Are you driving?" We both snicker.

"Michael won't mind. Honestly," she says. "And I don't think you want to ride with Mom."

"No, no. Thank you, I think I'm going to sit here for a little bit longer."

Ant doesn't know I'm here. He knows to look for me at home, if I just stay away from there a little longer, maybe I can decipher how I feel about the situation.

"Just let me know if you need anything." Penny waves as she leaves and the rest of my family follow suit shortly afterward.

I scratch behind the ears of my soft orange friend. He's still keeping me company, occasionally raising an ear when I laugh. I've got a nice soft pillow, a cozy footstool, and a 98% on my phone battery. I'm not sure I'm ready to go home to my empty apartment and be completely alone, just waiting for a Mothman to possibly show up.

I double check my phone. There's nothing there. No texts from my friends, and also no apology message from a certain Mothman. Not that I want to hear from him.

Crap. What am I doing? Maybe I would be better off with a personal trainer who thinks my laugh is too loud.

14

PONTIUS

I thought things would be different with Piper. She's my mate, she was supposed to understand me. I planned to do everything right. I wanted to give her everything she could ever desire. Anything she asked for. Finally, I'd have someone to really connect with.

Instead, I upset her. Just like I upset every other human. Now I'm alone. Again.

I can't even watch her like I did before. She asked me to stop, and even though I only want to keep her safe, I have to do as she asked. I already love her. Of course I do. She's perfect. And she thinks I'm a freak.

If I can't focus on her, then I'll move my focus to the only other thing I know. Work.

I power up my computer and log into my work account, pull up code, and start debugging.

This is what I'm good at, being alone, just me and the computer screens.

I already had a little bit of experience with technology before the Decrypting. I was a teenager, living alone. Sneaking into empty school buildings or houses when families were away on vacation. I could socialize on a computer: chat rooms, forums, social media. All of it was accessible, even if you couldn't show your face in public. For years it was my only real form of social interaction. When the Decrypting happened I was so excited for the chance to properly enter human society. Only to discover so many of the things that I loved to watch humans do and wanted to try myself, weren't very accessible to many cryptids. Particularly me.

Bars are crowded and noisy, regular movie theaters are cramped and uncomfortable, shopping centers, malls—all the places I wanted to walk freely—are too loud and bright for Mothman eyes.

Nearly everything I was interested in was difficult for me to enjoy. Except for technology. That was available 24/7. I could navigate it easily and in quiet, dark isolation. Computers, the internet, coding, video games—all of it was accessible and came to me easily.

So that's what I threw myself into.

And I thrived.

In college, I started a crypto security business with my two best friends. Magnes Loch, and Sacha Kwatch, a Lake Monster and a Bigfoot, respectively. They run the business and financial aspects of Cryptech. I contributed most of the tech portion. Sure, my part is important, but I never would have had a chance without them. They probably could have turned any half-decent idea into a thriving business.

They take care of expenses and customers and let me stay in my cave and do what I am best at—writing code. I wouldn't be anywhere without them. They are my best friends and have been looking out for me for the past decade of our friendship.

It's only a few minutes before Magnes Loch's name pops up in the video chat window my screen. It's not uncommon for either of us to be working on a Sunday afternoon. I assume he wants to ask me some work related question as I press the accept call button and adjust a little so he can see me on the camera.

"So, where is she?" Ness asks the second his green scaly face appears in the video call window.

"Where is who?"

"You know, the new woman. The one you met a couple weeks ago."

I swallow. I may have misled Ness about the situation. I didn't want him to know I'd found my mate. Not when his brutally rejected him four years ago.

"Is that why you video called me?" I frown. "To try and get a peek at her?"

"You've been MIA all weekend, I figured you must be with her. Nothing else could pull you away from work for this long," Loch says, his smooth green brows flexing in the middle. He's completely hairless and covered in green scales, the way every Lake Monster is. "I'm just glad you aren't with that Tiffany chick anymore."

I roll my eyes. "I thought you said she was hot."

"She was hot. She wasn't nice."

"She was nice enough."

"Not nice enough for you," Ness says. "I could help you meet dozens of hot women, nice ones, who would be happy to date a wealthy cryptid."

"It doesn't matter. They won't be Piper."

"Well then, where's the babe? Is she there with you?"

"Don't call her a 'babe'."

Ness huffs an annoyed breath. "The dame! The hottie. The woman who isn't Tiffany! The one who has been monopolizing all your spare time!"

"Piper Hamilton," I correct him. "She has a name. I don't want to talk about her."

"You've only wanted to talk about Piper Hamilton for the last three weeks." He smirks.

I stare at my keyboard. It's backlit and mechanical. It makes the most satisfying click noises when I press the keys and—

"She's your mate, isn't she?" Ness cuts through the silence.

I don't answer him.

"It's alright, lad, you can talk about it," he says in his soft Scottish brogue.

"She doesn't want to talk to me anymore," I blurt out.

"She rejected you?" His voice rises a terrifying octave. "Pontius?"

"No. Not rejected," I admit, still not looking at the camera. "She just...left. She's gone. She doesn't want me. I fucked up."

"Pontius," Ness repeats, his tone clearly intended to calm.

"She'll forget about me soon enough. She doesn't even know my real name," I tell him.

"Doesn't know your real name?"

"She just wanted a weekend of anonymous fun."

"Sounds hot." He smirks.

"Shut it, Ness," I grumble. "It doesn't matter, she doesn't want to see me again."

"It does matter," he says. "If she didn't reject you, then you still have a shot. There's still hope, you know?"

"I don't know."

"She's the one with that little business, right?" He asks. "We could buy it. She'll have to talk to you then."

"Ness. No."

"You have to do something, Pontius."

"Or I could leave her alone, like she asked me to."

"Do you want to end up like me?" Ness smirks, but there's sadness behind his question.

Even Loch doesn't want me to end up like Loch. He's the only guy I know whose mate rejected him. He's been fucking around ever since. With a new date on his arm every week, he's clearly still heartbroken. What do you do when the one person you are supposed to be truly compatible with leaves you?

I don't know how to help him. He threw himself into his job when Caddy rejected him. Our company wouldn't be anywhere near what it is today if it weren't for his dedication for the last four years. His days are full of nothing but work and random sex.

I don't want to end up like that.

Sacha, our other business partner, used to be similar, before he met his mate. Less of a balanced like and more work for him. And then he met Bailey, and now he's engaged. He's gone a bit soft, he doesn't spend long hours in the office anymore. He takes days off, and is in a much better mood than he used to be. With hobbies, and more friendships and a life outside the office.

They are like my two potential futures. A gentle male in love finding new meaning in life, or a broken-hearted idiot who throws himself into one quick and dirty relationship after another. Only one of those things is appealing to me. The future that has Piper in it. I can't stand the idea of going through the rest of my life all alone, without anyone to love, no family.

"I got an email," I tell Ness.

"From Piper?" he asks, thrown by my change of subject.

"No, from the agency that reunites families." It's not the same as having a mate who loves me, but it's almost as good. The idea that I might have other connections out there is exciting. Growing up alone was difficult for me. I never met my relatives. Never had family dinners or played video games together. "I'm going to go meet a Mothwoman who might be my sister, I'm not sure. She's the right age, we grew up a state apart but I've never met her before. She's living with her mate on the east coast of Canada." I let my voice trail off.

"Seriously? Pontius, that's great!" Ness sounds genuinely happy for me.

"I don't want to get my hopes up too high." There have never been as many Mothmen as there are some of the cryptid species. Lake monsters and Bigfoots had spread all over the world; there was some version on every continent. And the Decrypting broadened opportunities for those species. Families could travel and reunite after years spent apart.

Mothmen weren't quite as lucky. Our entry into society was hindered by lower species numbers, our love of solitude, and our incompatibility with humans. Plenty of Mothmen have decided to continue living off the grid, in the shadows and under bridges. It's made finding any form of family difficult through social media or any of the apps currently designed for this. Instead, I turned to a private investigation company to help me find any living family members. This is the most promising link we've found so far.

"How long will you be gone?" Ness asks.

"I don't know. I'll have to fly myself up there. That will take a while." Mothman wings don't really fit on planes. "We chatted a bit in email, and then on the phone. She said I could stay a couple months if I wanted."

"A couple months!" Ness exclaims. "And you're staying the whole time?"

"Absolutely," I say. "Maybe I should just move there? Where I'll be close to family?" If I stay here, where Piper is, I know I won't be able to stop myself from following her and trying to make her mine again. I was so close, I held her in my fingers so briefly. But I ruined it, and she ran from me. The way all humans do.

"I'm all for you meeting her. But moving? Don't you think that's a little extreme? What about your work? What about your mate? Don't you want to try and reconnect with her?"

I shake my head. "No. Piper doesn't want to see me."

"Are you sure, lad? She spent the whole weekend with you, right? That sounds like there was a connection." He sounds almost desperate.

"I'm not even sure she's over her ex. I moved too fast, Ness. It's my fault."

"What did you do?"

I shake my head. "It doesn't matter."

"Have you apologized?" Loch drums his fingers across his desk so violently that I can hear them through his speaker. Then he waves a hand, dismissing any response I might have. "You should go to Canada. You deserve a break."

"We both deserve a break, Loch."

He ignores that. "Go and spend some time with your family. But don't move yet! Maybe when you get back you'll have a change of heart?"

"Maybe." I mutter.

"Or I could speak to her for you?" Loch says.

"Don't you dare," I growl.

"Alright." He laughs lightly. "Just go. We'll survive without you Pontius, take your time, enjoy your holiday."

"I'll talk to you later." I'm already reaching for the 'end call' button. He's my best and closest friend. The one person I've been able to talk to about these things, and I can't even tell him the truth about how badly I really fucked up.

Leaving is my best option. I'll visit Canada, for a couple months at least. Maybe things will be different when I get back. There's just one thing I have to arrange before that.

15

PIPER

I'm honestly not sure how long it is between when my family leaves and the owner of the cafe comes over to check on me. I've completely disassociated, staring at a blank space on the wall, waiting for Anam or Kelly to message me back. I don't even know who else to turn to.

"How are we doing?" The cute woman from behind the counter steps into my line of vision.

I startle, jostling my lap. The cat makes a noise of irritation before he resettles himself. I scratch him behind the ears.

"Pretty crappy, actually," I say automatically, the cat purrs under my fingers. "I mean—he's great. I feel better having him around."

The woman gives me a bright smile that lights up her whole face. "Mercutio's always good at knowing when people need a little comfort."

"Well, he really picked the right lap today," I mutter. Mercutio blinks up at me slowly with bright yellow eyes. "Is he up for adoption?"

"Absolutely. All our cats are." The woman waits a brief moment before speaking again, clearly full of nervous energy. "Are you interested?" she finally blurts, her enthusiasm is infectious.

"I really, really am." Maybe it will help, not being completely alone in my house. Mercutio isn't exactly a watchdog, but I've always wanted a pet.

The woman leaps to her feet and scurries across the room to a pile of papers.

"This is actually so exciting! This'll be the first adoption we've had from the cafe. We just opened a couple weeks ago. I'm the owner, you know? This place has been a dream of mine for a long time. I've been working with cat fostering and adoption for years. This cafe has been an absolute whirlwind. That was your family, right? The birthday party? They were cute! I'm glad I could rent out the whole space to them!" She continues rambling as she returns with a clipboard, pen, and papers, bouncing on her toes as she hands them to me. "Normally, we recommend getting two cats at the same time, so they are well socialized and don't get lonely, but Mercutio doesn't really have a bonded partner."

"Me neither," I joke. "Peas in a pod, huh buddy?"

The cat doesn't respond.

"I'm Bailey, by the way." The woman is all smiles.

"Piper." I gesture to myself.

"Do you live with anyone? A partner, kids, or pets that you might want to get acclimated to the idea of a new cat?"

"Nope. It's just me all alone. My ex was allergic, but he's not a factor anymore." I pause. "Oh, is getting a pet a bad idea if I just had a big breakup?" I ask when my fingers touch the clipboard. For a split second, it's Ant's face that pops into my brain, not Colin. How irritating is that development? The guy who was supposed to stop my obsession with Colin has almost completely replaced him.

"Well, we do have a fostering program. You could always do that, if you aren't sure. There's no chance the allergic person will move back in with you?" she asks.

"No," I say instantly. This time, it's Colin's face that pops into my head. "No, he definitely won't be coming back."

"Well, then I think you'd be the perfect person for a cat like Mercutio." She gestures to the cat in my lap. "Did you have any questions?"

I bark out a nervous laugh. "Not unless you've had someone declare that he's your fated-mate?" I joke, a silly thing to ask a complete stranger.

She blinks, looking a bit surprised. "Yeah, I have, actually."

I gape at her for a moment. "I—are you serious? I don't actually know anyone who's been with a cryptid. Let alone mated to one." I laugh nervously. "It was a cryptid, right? Not just some random weirdo?"

She gives me a bright smile, opening and closing her fist in a way that implies she's still adjusting to a new weight on her finger. "My fiancé is a Bigfoot."

I glance at her hands, there's a giant stone on her ring finger. It's really pretty. She's really pretty, with an adorable smile and wide hips. She seems put together, well adjusted, doing well, running her own business. A life plenty of people would find enviable, someone I might actually get good advice from.

"And he's good? He's fine? He's not creepy or anything?" I laugh nervously at the end, hoping she'll say something I find reassuring.

"Yes. I mean, no, of course not. He's good to me. Really sweet." She shakes her head.

"And he's your...mate?"

She has one of those smiles that are so wide, her face might break. "He is."

I don't say anything for a moment. "I had a one-night stand," I blurt, if anyone is going to help me, it might actually be this complete stranger.

She perches on the bench across from me. "With a cryptid?"

"Yes."

"And he told you that you were his mate?"

"What does that even mean?" I laugh, simultaneously feeling awkward and terrible.

"True love, soul mates, your forever person." She smiles, like she's thinking of the most delicious dessert in the entire world.

My heart skips a little beat. "That sounds..."

"Scary? Terrifying?" Her smile doesn't drop.

"I was going to say, really comforting. To be that sure of something. How do you know? You're a human. Right?" I add with mild suspicion. I don't know all the types of cryptids, let alone what they all look like. Maybe there is a pink-haired Mongolian cat-whisperer or something.

"Yes, I'm human," she laughs before continuing. "Do you already have inexplicably strong feelings for him, find him instantly attractive, and feel ready to ignore basically every self preservation impulse to keep being with him?"

"I... yeah..." I bark out a nervous laugh as I consider. She hit the nail directly on the head. "Yeah, I guess I did feel all of that."

She nods. "From what I've heard, that's what it's like for all humans. It's a bit more obvious for cryptids. Humans evolved with more mating options, so we don't get quite the same intense driving urge to be with a compatible mate when we find one. At least that's the reigning theory on the message boards."

"Message boards?" I ask. "Online?"

"Yeah."

"Could you tell me the names? And could I um... Look you up on there?"

There's something like a twinkle in her eye. "You aren't ready to give up on your cryptid yet?"

"Ugh. I wish it were a bit easier. He said he knew the moment he set eyes on me."

"You just met this guy?"

"Yeah, over the weekend. Things got—intense."

She chews on her bright pink lip for a moment. "If there's someone giving you trouble we, my fiancé really, have a lot of resources at our disposal. Money and manpower both. If you need help, we could—even if that sounds weird because you don't actually know us. Every cryptid I've met has been fully devoted to their mates, but some of them can be really strange and I hate to think your mate would do anything bad to you."

"No!" I insist, surprised by my desire to defend him. "I mean I don't know. He's just—I know I'm being stupid. I should never want to see him again."

"What did he do?" Her face grows serious. "Do you need me to call anyone?"

"No! I'm fine. Fine. I think—" I laugh a little, thinking how ridiculous this is, and all of a sudden, everything comes bubbling out of me in one long stream. "He followed me home, took some of my junk mail, and some of my other garbage. And then he told me he loved me and wanted to be with me forever." A loud laugh breaks through my relief admitting everything out loud. "I think he might be stalking me? He could be outside, right now, waiting for me! And I'm not even sure I'd be angry about it!" I start to laugh so hard that Bailey joins me.

"I'm sorry. It isn't funny," Bailey says in between giggles.

"No, it isn't." I can't stop laughing myself. "I barely know the guy! What am I going to do?"

"What do you want to do?" Bailey asks more soberly.

"I don't know!" I admit loudly.

"Well here, if you want some help figuring it out—" Bailey hands me her business card with her phone number and screen name scribbled on the back. "Call me. Please. If you feel like you need help."

I take the little card gratefully. At least now I have something resembling a plan.

"Remember," she says, with shocking sincerity, "I have muscle on my side. Say the word, and we will do what we need to make sure you are safe." She sounds almost like a mobster offering to do a hit.

By the time I get home it's already starting to get dark. Nights come fast and early this time of year in the Pacific Northwest. It makes sense that a Mothman would settle here. The darker it is, the more likely that he could be following me home. That idea gives me little chills of excitement and not fear, in a way that I find very irritating.

When my ride pulls up outside my apartment, there's a van parked out front. My eighty-seventh surprise for the day.

"Piper Hamilton, right? We're with the storage company, ma'am," a large gargoyle announces as I approach. He's tall and broad, with thick gray skin and large wings folded against his back.

"Storage company?"

"We're here for 'Colin's Stuff', according to our clipboard." He taps one gray finger against his piece of paper. There's a little logo on his shirt with two gargoyles carrying a box and the words 'Stone Solid Storage' underneath.

"Colin's stuff," I repeat slowly.

"We were asked to wait here until you returned. Everything's been paid for. We're supposed to transfer his things to a storage facility. If you could just point us to what you need moved."

"Right, right. Of course I can."

I lead them inside and up the stairs to the second bedroom. Everything remaining from my destroyed relationship is in there. Everything Colin decided wasn't important enough to take to New York with him and he left here for me to deal with. I gesture to the space. There are a couple boxes of clothes and books. His collectibles, the comics that we decided were his, a whole stack of Warhammer miniatures that he never got past the primer coat.

"Take it all. Everything in the room. It's all his." I stand in the hallway, watching as three muscled gargoyles pack up the room, marching everything outside, being careful their wings don't graze my walls.

It doesn't take long to clean out the small room. They load everything into their truck, and in under an hour they are headed away.

And that's the end of Colin. His stuff is out of my apartment, and I flushed him from my body with an insane one-night stand. There's nothing left of him but a few fading memories.

I'm free.

I sink onto the floor of my now empty room and search the internet for the biggest, most obnoxious cat tree I can find.

16
PIPER

Ant doesn't call. Not that I want him to call. Just that he said he would call, and he hasn't. For five days, not that I've been waiting for it, just that I noticed.

I don't see him either. Not anywhere. I spend the first couple of days freaking out and hiding in my apartment, but when nothing happens, I get more adventurous and return to my regular life. I'm not disappointed. That would be silly. I don't want to talk to him, or see him. I just want to get back to normal. Which is exactly what I try to do. By the next Saturday, I'm ready to invite my amazing friends over for dinner just so I don't have to spend another night alone. I make them spinach lasagna. Anam brings two bottles of cheap champagne, and Kelly brings a huge salad. Once the second bottle of champagne is opened, I spill and tell them everything about Ant. Every. Single. Detail.

It's the only thing they want to talk about from that moment forward.

"Ugh, he's so creepy." Kelly shivers, she pours more champagne into the coffee mug she is using in lieu of a flute.

"I guess I've read too many dark romance books, because the stalking sounds kinda hot to me." Anam laughs.

"It's so, definitely, not hot." Kelly puts a reassuring hand on my shoulder, and shoots Anam a look that makes Anam roll her eyes.

"Watching you all the time. He could have seen you doing anything." Anam waggles her eyebrows.

Kelly furrows hers. "Yes, exactly."

"Yeah, exactly." Anam grins wickedly.

Yikes, he might have seen me doing anything. Eating, undressing, fucking.[1] My stomach flips at the idea. I can't believe part of me is in agreement with Anam.

"It's just my stupid luck," I admit. "The first guy I attempt to have a one-night stand with, the best sex I've ever had, is also a stalker?"

"Ooof, girl. The best ever?" Anam's eyes go wide. "I mean, I'm sure you can have more really good sex with other people." She tries to cover for her slip.

"I think you should go to the cops," Kelly says.

I run my fingers across Mercutio's chin. He leans into my hand hard and purrs. After a brief back-and-forth for the adoption, Bailey brought him to my house. He's been the best cuddler and already has far too many toys.

"Go to the cops for what?" I ask. "Because I found a couple pieces of trash at his house? The cops aren't going to DNA test a lip balm when he hasn't threatened me, or tried to hurt me. I haven't even actually seen him following me."

"He's still a monster," Kelly mutters.

"Cryptids aren't monsters," I say, feeling slightly defensive.

---

1 Masturbating furiously when Colin was out of the house because I didn't come while we were fucking.

"No, I mean figuratively a monster, for making you scared to even go outside," she clarifies.

"I'm just so disappointed. We had such a nice time, we were together all weekend, and he was never anything but sweet. Even when I yelled at him. He just kind of accepted it, like he knew exactly what he did wrong." The image of his sad eyes and drooping antennae are embedded in my brain.

"He could be dangerous, Piper."

"Yeah. He could be—" I suck in a ragged breath. "Or I could be overreacting?"

"Girl, no. You reacted totally appropriately. I absolutely would have cussed him out." Anam barely takes a breath before she continues. "Are you going to see him again?"

"Of course she isn't," Kelly says.

"Of course not," I agree much more hesitantly. I catch Anam's eye who gives me a knowing smile.

"Do you want to stay with us for a while?" Kelly asks. "Sleep on the couch?"

"Or stay with me for a couple days?" Anam asks.

Anam is a biologist—a professor on the tenure track at the local university. She's completely dedicated to her job. She lives in a tiny third story walk-up just off campus. If I went there I'd be sleeping on a broken futon covered in research journals.

My other option is staying with Kelly and Jeremy. A happy couple, who are both semi-successful artists. Doing well enough that they don't need secondary jobs, as long as they share a studio apartment that acts as both their apartment and art studio. The only thing separating the couch I'd be sleeping on and their bed would be a thin privacy curtain.

"No. No. It's fine. I can't leave Mercutio alone," I tell them. "And work is slammed right now."

"Are you sure that you're alright all on your own?" Kelly expression is pitying.

"I'm fine," I mutter. "How is the show coming along, Kelly?"

"Fantastic. Amazing. Stressful." She grins. "You are both coming, right?"

"We'll be there with bells on." Anam laughs.

"Because I need to get butts in seats!" Kelly grins.

"There are going to be seats?"

"Absolutely not. You will be aimlessly wandering around a mostly white room, drinking boxed wine, and eating sweaty cheese and crackers."

"And pretending that we could possibly afford to buy one of your very beautiful paintings." Anam rolls her eyes.

"They are very competitively priced." Kelly smirks. "And I promise that when Jeremy and I have made it big you will both get invited to so many more exciting art shows. Bring a date if you can. We need more people, to give the event the appearance of popularity."

"Ugh. No," I mutter. "I am coming alone. I am never dating again."

"Yes, Piper and I are going to become hot old cougars and wear hot pants and date younger men." Anam nods.

"No. No. No. Piper has every excuse to be alone. But Anam you need a boyfriend," Kelly announces, pouring more champagne into both of their makeshift champagne glasses.

"No. Ew. No."

"We all know it's the only way to true happiness." Kelly laughs.

"It's true," I say. "I plan to never have happiness ever again. Anam it's not too late for you."

Anam sighs loudly and rolls her eyes dramatically.

"And the only thing that could possibly make you happier would be a husband." Kelly smirks.

"Eww, no." Anam groans.

"Wouldn't that be just the best!" Kelly continues teasing. "Can't you picture her now, walking down the aisle in a beautiful white dress?!"

"Nooooo!" Anam wails dramatically.

"She would make such a beautiful bride." I nod to Kelly. "Dedicating her heart to one person for the rest of her life."

"Never!" Anam yells jokingly.

"With His and Hers towels in the bathroom!" Kelly says.

"I would rather die!" Anam collapses dramatically onto my living room carpet, keeping her glass of cheap champagne carefully level so she doesn't spill a drop. "I will never allow myself to succumb to the pressures of monogamy!"

My friends hang out, discussing all the random boring parts of life that are fascinating when you talk about them with the right people, until we've finished the second bottle of champagne. When Kelly and Anam finally leave for the night, all that's left is me, the cat, and my frustrated libido.

The apartment feels so empty without anyone here, when the shadows get long at night, it's hard not to think about having someone to live with again.

Once again, it's not Colin's face I'm picturing. I'm thinking about Ant's dark silhouette. Even though I have been doing everything in my power to kick him out of my subconscious. It's hard to even look at certain pieces of media without thinking about him. I can't see Star Trek without thinking about how Geordie is his favorite character, or play Smash Brothers without knowing he always picks Link.[2]

It's hard not to think about him a lot. I haven't managed to orgasm since I left Ant's apartment that weekend. My regular toys haven't really done it for me this week. It shouldn't be a big deal. It's only been a couple days, but I can't manage to get there.

Crap. I am such an idiot.

I can't believe I've lost my orgasm.

I blame Ant, of course.

I've tried every vibrator in my arsenal. I've watched or read every kind of porn I can think of. I've even researched new kinks. Still nothing.

It's not that I'm not horny. I am. I seem to be very horny all of the time. It's just that my parts can't seem to connect with my brain and allow my one brief moment of complete relaxation.

It's embarrassing and frustrating.

So naturally, tonight, after I've consumed several glasses of champagne, I'm feeling antsy. I wash my face, drop my glasses beside my bed, and just as I am about to pull my shirt over my head ,I realize I've left the bedroom curtains wide open, letting in the moonlight.

One week, and I'm already being stupid.

I pull my bedroom curtains closed. There's a blurry figure on the roof across the street, watching me. Just standing stock-still and staring at my apartment.

Crap. It's him. I duck back against the wall, my heart pounding in my chest. It's him. It has to be him. Standing there, watching me. Like the freak he is.

---

2 Ant is convinced that Link is the best character., despite the obvious evidence to the contrary.

"You think I won't call the cops?" I say, even though my windows are closed and I'm sure he can't hear me. "You think I'm too stupid to see you? I'm just going to ignore this? I'm just going to let you watch me? Invade my privacy?"

Why is that idea so hot?

A glance back at the window shows the figure hasn't moved.

Crap, I shouldn't be turned on right now.

"Get a good look, buddy!" I yell to my empty room. I flash my middle finger toward the window. "You gross, peeping tom. You think I'm just going to lie here and be your good little pet? You can watch me, and I won't do anything about it?"

I'm breathing heavily. I reach across the room to grab my glasses and my phone. My hand pauses at the handle to my toy drawer.

Crap, why is this working? The idea that he can see me? That he's watching me?

I shove my glasses up my nose and unlock my phone. I look across the street again and it's not him. It's not anyone. Through the clarity of 20/20 vision, I see the figure isn't a Mothman at all. It's a shadow the moon is casting against a wall.

I take off my glasses to double check.

Yep. Just a shadow. No one is watching me.

Crap, I'm so stupid, and still so oddly turned on.

That's infuriating. I press my hand between my legs, the pressure lighting up those glorious sparks I've been missing, there's a wetness forming too.

If he was out there, right now, he'd see everything. I run my fingers across my clit, it makes me crave more.

What if he was out there? Hunting me. Watching me, waiting for this moment where he gets a brief glimpse of what he really wants to see. Me fucking myself.

I snatch my vibrator from my nightstand.[3] It was my favorite when I was with Colin. The first thing I picked up when he wasn't around to get offended.

He never wanted us to use toys together.

But I don't need a man, I don't need a cryptid, I don't need anyone. I have myself, my fingers, my tools, and my fantasies in my brain.

Screw him. Screw that stupid Mothman. With his perfect dick and the perfect way his tongue attached to me. I don't need him. The memory of him is enough, of his cock filling me, the way his purr seemed to hit every nerve in my body, the way his mouth found that perfect spot.

I come twice on my vibrator. Loud and wet, and I'm proud of myself for not whispering his name. I collapse into my empty bed. The endorphins flooding my brain bring me a brief moment of clarity. I can't keep doing this. I have to stop thinking about him. I have to cut him out of my brain. I can't exist in this weird half-life where I am scared of the only male that makes me come when I think about him.

---

3 Old faithful, because I always blow right on time with this one.

17

PIPER

It's been ten days since I saw Ant, and four since I came on my vibrator thinking about him. I still can't seem to wipe him from my thoughts. I don't know what's wrong with me.

Maybe it's the paranoia of expecting every shadow in the corner of my eye to be him.

Or maybe it's the disappointment from every time I realize it isn't.

Or maybe it's my irritation at my disappointment.

I don't have time to worry about this today, especially when I'm about to host what might be the most important meeting of my career.

The owners of Cryptech want to discuss sponsoring my little non-profit company.

Cryptech is the largest crypto-security company in the country, and Penpoint caught their eye. They are interested in me and my tiny four-person team. Even a small grant or sponsorship from a large company would make a huge difference for us. Cryptech is exactly the kind of partnership that could help us get to the next level.

Penpoint Assist has been advising tech companies on best usability standards for over two years now. Our main focus started with screen reading software, since then we've expanded our specialty to help all kinds of accessibility. It's something I found a passion for growing up with my sister and finding so many apps she couldn't fully access. Most are easy changes that actually make everyday tech easier for everyone to use. Lately there's been an increased interest for tech that will improve usability for cryptids as well.

I didn't realize why Cryptech would care about us until I started googling. The company is run by cryptids.

Magnes Loch, CEO, is a Lake Monster, a human-sized plesiosaur.

Sacha Kwatch, chief financial officer, is a Bigfoot.

Pontius Pleasant, chief technical officer, is the only one I haven't found more information on, and the only one I am really disappointed not to have a decent photo of. He is a famously talented programmer, and a notorious recluse.

Magnes and Sacha are frequently photographed at various social events, and heavily featured on the company website. But there aren't any pictures of Pontius. I assume he's a cryptid too. I wonder if he has wings. I'm scanning their site for the seventeenth time when the door to our tiny office opens.

"Piper Hamilton?" Magnes Loch asks. I'm sure it's him before the introductions even start. With pale green skin and a two-foot-long neck. He's too tall to stand up straight in our cramped basement office. He's wearing a dark green suit that must be custom made. There's a hole for his tail and everything. Maybe he goes to the same tailor Ant does?

No. I am not thinking about Ant.

"Mr. Loch." I smile, and offer him a hand to shake.

"Real pleasure to meet you." He wraps large green fingers around mine and gives an alarmingly disarming grin.

Behind him a Bigfoot steps into our tiny office, looking around with a small frown. We only really have one office space, with four desks crammed into it. Sacha Kwatch, his slicked back hair just barely brushes the ceiling. He must be at least eight feet tall.

"Small space," the Bigfoot says.

"Sacha. Say hello to our newest potential acquisition." Loch gestures to me.

Sacha just nods in my direction. His heavy brows furrowed in concentration. Thick fur covers almost every inch of his visible body.

"I was surprised you wanted to meet here," I admit. "We're operating on a slim budget. A couple of grants and a few clients, having a sponsorship with Cryptech would help us expand into more comfortable quarters."

All three of my employees are in the office today. I feel like we look more impressive when the desks are full, and I wanted everyone to meet.

Kara, who does all of our social media and admin work, has her laptop set up in the tiny corner that barely counts as a desk.

Josh and Lex share a desk at the other end of the room, their laptops set up facing each other. They are rarely both in the office. Most of our work can be done remotely. Josh's canes lean against the wall behind him. It's difficult for him to navigate the tiny office with his walking aids.

I know there's a lot of irony in our offices being less than accessible, but it's the only space that we could reasonably afford, and these issues are part of the reason I am always willing to allow my employees to work from home.

The fourth and final desk in the office is mine. I'm here most days. I prefer having a way to separate my work from my personal life.

But four desks and a narrow walkway in the middle is all the space we have in our tiny office. Not a lot of room for testing or meetings. Not even a quiet room to take a phone call without everyone hearing.

I've done my absolute best to tidy the space for this meeting. There are still large piles of spare tech around the room, overly full drawers I can't quite shove closed, and a precarious stack of mail perched on the edge of my desk[1], threatening to topple over.

I glance past the two cryptids, for a third figure to walk through the door. No one shows up. It's kind of disappointing. I was hoping Pontius would come too. I've admired his work and I was looking forward to meeting him.

"Mr. Pleasant isn't here?" I ask.

Magnes grins widely. "You wanted to meet him as well?"

"I just assumed he'd be with you." I feel a little sheepish, of course I wanted to meet the head programmer of the most famous tech company in the city.

Magnes shakes his head. "Afraid it's just me and Sacha. Pontius is out of town for the season visiting family. He doesn't usually come to these kinds of meetings anyway. He's more like the wizard behind the curtain. Sacha is just our heartless Tinman."

"And Magnes is our brainless Scarecrow," Sacha grumbles. I laugh at his joke, but the Bigfoot is quiet as he examines the room. "Just the four of you?"

"Just the four of us," I agree with a nervous smile. "Getting a larger, more accessible space would be our first priority if you agreed to a sponsorship." I admit as Sacha bumps his shoulder against a storage cabinet, if he spread his arms he could probably touch every corner of the small room.

---

1 Even a tech company can't seem to avoid junk mail.

Magnes nods. "We could certainly make that happen for you."

"If you accomplished everything you've done so far from this insufficient space, I imagine you'd be far more effective in an adequate office." Sacha blows air out of his nose.

"We'd love to expand. Lex has been eager to work on physical interfaces." I gesture to Lex sitting in the corner. "With more space and money, we could invest in injection molding and 3D printers for fabrication. They can probably tell you more about that themselves."

Lex practically leaps to their feet to explain their wildest fabrication dreams. Even though I asked them to keep it relatively realistic, it's great to see them excited about work they are passionate about. There's a lot more boring technical chatter, and to my relief both cryptids seem to be on board. Loch is visibly excited and Kwatch at least seems not to despise us.

"We're excited to work with you, Ms. Hamilton." Sacha's face is still grumpy but his voice is gentle enough. "You can expect to hear from us soon."

"We should put a meeting on the books now." Loch's fingers flying across his phone as he speaks. "We have some free time on Wednesday. If you could meet in our office."

"Oh, that soon?" I ask.

"This is an opportunity we don't want to miss. I expect you'll have a dozen offers any day now." Loch says without looking up, my phone buzzes with a notification, I glance down to see an email arrive in my inbox from the cryptid standing directly in front of me. "I'd like to move on this quickly so we can have the buzz in the news before the holidays really hit."

Kwatch raises an eyebrow in his partner's direction. "You want to do it before Pontius gets back?"

"He won't care, he never gets involved in these kinds of acquisitions anyway." Loch says.

"I can definitely be available," I say, surprised they are offering to move that quickly. I glance between the two males. There's some unspoken communication between them, but I am not going to kick a gift horse in the mouth.

"Excellent. The quicker we can move them into a larger space, the quicker they can expand. Announce new projects, scale up. With our guidance, of course," Loch concludes.

"If that's what you think is best." Sacha gives him a half-hearted shrug. While I'd love for the CFO to have a little more enthusiasm for our cause, I'm willing to accept any level of commitment if it means money and the ability to expand.

"We'll have the details drawn up this week. Bring your lawyer with you, Ms. Hamilton." Magnes is grinning like he just got a new toy for Christmas. "I think we're all excited to move forward with the project."

The Bigfoot shrugs, he really doesn't seem excited.

They give polite goodbyes and leave.

"Holy shit," Josh mutters as the two imposing figures walk out the door. "Holy fucking hell! You did it, Piper!"

The tension drops from my shoulders and I sink into a chair. An old beaten up office chair, with a broken arm and squeaky wheels, and in a few weeks, I'll never have to look at it again. We did it.

Kara is practically bouncing in her seat. "Does this mean I'll have a real desk and not just a folding table?" she asks with a laugh.

"I expected a lot more back-and-forth than that!" Lex laughs, and they're right. But, we aren't a big operation, maybe the cost is nothing for a company like Cryptech. They offered to sign with us the same casual way that I decided to get a muffin with my morning coffee run.

"No more cramped basement office? Or Lex kicking me under the desk?" Josh jokes.

"We'll have leg room, buddy." Lex high fives him over the table. "And resources! A 3D printer, a laser cutter, a painting studio! I'm going to start making a list now!"

"Hold on, we have to make sure the deal is good, that they don't backtrack, or try to undercut our worth or—"

None of my words are getting through the banter in the office. Everyone is too excited, and it's great to see them happy.

"Coffees. Lunch. Whatever you all want, it's on me today," I announce with a laugh, too relieved by everything to pretend I'm not also excited.

"Hell yeah." Josh immediately starts taking lunch orders.

I stare at the email on my phone in disbelief. This could change everything. I could provide really steady paychecks for my employees. Higher wages, hire more people, expand our reach...I'll actually get to see everything I've worked so hard for truly come to fruition.

18

PIPER

I t's been two months. Two full months. Since I saw or spoke to him.

And about fifteen minutes since I last thought about him, he still pops up constantly in my brain. My dark-furred, bright-eyed Mothman.

I try to keep him out of my every thought, every moment, of every day. I'm still constantly looking over my shoulder, wondering if every single shadow might be him—feeling stalked and hunted. Part of me goes warm and liquid at that thought. Sometimes I think too much about it, particularly at night, alone in my bed. I can't seem to orgasm without thinking of him. Which is so silly.

So when I step foot into my office building after New Year's Eve, nursing the second day of my New Year's hangover, I think I'm imagining things when I spot a pair of black wings.

But it's not my imagination. I recognize them as Ant's wings the instant I see them. There's no mistaking him for another Mothman.

But it couldn't be him, right? In my workplace. In my lobby. Of my new building in the Cryptech complex.

He turns and catches my eye, his antennae raise in surprise.

He found me. Again.

The bastard. He stalked me here! At my new workplace.

"Hey!" I yell across the room. "Hey! Ant!"

He holds up his hands in surrender and shakes his head repeatedly while he steps backward into the elevator.

"Oh no you don't, you bastard!" My yelling draws the attention from three coworkers I don't know who are also in the building lobby.

Ant doesn't speak. His hands are held up, palms out in front of him, as I barrel into the elevator after him. He backs into the corner while I shove an angry finger in his chest, not really thinking about it until we are alone, as the doors slide closed behind me.

"What the hell, dude?" I poke him. "What are you thinking?! I told you not to fucking follow me!"

"Piper." His voice shows more surprise than I expect. "What are you doing here?"

"Bull crap!" I announce. "You must think I was born yesterday."

"Why are you here?" He shrinks even further, his antennae flow back against his scalp. I should be scared to be alone in this elevator with a literal monster. Instead I'm noticing how attractive he looks in his suit. It's all black, well-tailored, and somehow doesn't look ridiculous around his neck scarf. He has on a red silk tie, that compliments his eyes and—

None of that matters.

I'm not concerned he would physically hurt me. He could. I know he's strong enough to do just about anything to me. And right now I don't care.

"I can't believe you're here. At my workplace!" I yell.

"Piper, this isn't what you think!"

"Isn't it?" I ask. "Then why are you going to my floor?" I point at the numbers on the elevator wall, only to notice that the top floor is actually what's highlighted. We're traveling past my department's third floor stop, and heading up, up, and more up. To the top floor of the building. "We aren't going to my floor."

I whip my head back around to Ant. He still looks frightened rather than menacing.

"What are you doing here?" I ask.

"That's what I was trying to explain," he says as the elevator doors open. "This is my company."

I glance at the hallway outside. The fancy top floor waiting room, a woman in a sleek blouse, wearing a headset, sits behind a desk. She looks at me strangely.

"Everything alright, Mr. Pleasant?" The woman asks. Her eyes flick between me and Ant as he cowers in the corner of the elevator, one finger still pointed in his face.

"Everything is fine, Tonia," Ant reassures over my head.

Pleasant. Crap. Mr. Pleasant. Pontius Pleasant. Ant. Pleasant.

I look at Ant, and then back at the woman who's expression is somewhere between amusement and concern.

Crap.

I pull back from him instantly.

"Crap. You own Cryptech?" I whisper loudly as the elevator doors close again. "This is your company?"

"Yes. Piper. Why are you here?"

"Like you don't know." I accuse.

"I haven't seen you in months. Do you work here now?"

I shake my head and stab my floor number on the wall, pressing the button repeatedly even though I know it won't do anything. "I can't believe you. Pretending you didn't plan this."

"Please," he says, "I didn't. Please. Can we talk?"

My heart is pounding. My stalker controls my company. He owns my livelihood. He could ruin me. Take everything I've worked so hard for. Tears prick at the corners of my eyes.

"You have until we get back to the third floor," I say. "And then I'm gone. I don't care. I'll break whatever contract I signed. I will ruin my life to get away from you. This is so completely fucked, Ant."

"Piper. Please believe me. I didn't know you'd be here."

"Likely." I mutter as the elevator door closes. I watch Ant's reflection in the doors. "You offered to fund Penpoint just to get closer to me."

Floor number nine.

"No, no, Piper. That isn't it."

Floor number eight.

"Ness and Sacha, they must have signed the contract while I was gone."

Floor number seven.

"Fucking Ness—" his hand clenches into a fist at his side. "I told him I found my fated mate, he must have taken matters into his own hands."

Floor number six.

"I didn't know about this, Piper. I promise."

Floor number five.

I stew in silence.

Floor number four.

"I don't believe you. How could you not know that I was joining the company?"

Floor number three.

"I've been out of town, since November."

"Doing what? Finding another innocent woman to stalk?"

The doors slide open.

"I met my sister," he says.

I freeze, one foot already out of the elevator.

"You don't have a sister," I accuse.

"I'm not sure she is. We just met. She's around my age. She was born near where I grew up."

"You're not sure?" I step back into the elevator and put a hand out to stop the doors from closing.

"We think it's possible. We sent bloodwork to a company, but they don't have enough samples to know if all Mothman blood has the same markers or—" he pauses when the elevator dings, I reach out to stop the elevator from closing again, "—or if the DNA markers actually mean we are related."

"Did you like her?" I ask. I don't care. I shouldn't care. It's stupid to care. Part of me really cares.

"She's nice. She lives in Alberta with her mate."

"Canada?" I ask.

"I just got back. I spent the holidays with her."

"The holidays?" I ask quietly.

"Since Halloween. Since I last saw you. When you asked me to leave you alone."

The elevator dings, and I reach a hand out to stop the doors from closing again.

I chew on the inside of my lip. "I'm glad you got to meet her," I say quietly. This sexy cuddly Mothman has been in my brain for months now. I was terrified that he was around every corner. Waiting for me every night. Now he's standing in front of me, I'm not scared. Just excited. Genuine joy flickers through me before I remember to steel my features.

"I have to go," I mutter.

"Please, don't--" Ant starts to say.

"I have, I need—" I fumble for the words to finish the sentence. "I need to be alone." I shake my head and flee the elevator.

19

PONTIUS

"Piper! Hi!" Bailey appears behind the counter of Rhapsody shortly after I walk in. She's got on a bright pink top and blue jean shorts with little daisies embroidered all over. "Can I get you anything?"

"Decaf, I definitely need decaf," I mutter, still feeling high strung. I'm not sure why I came to the cat café instead of talking to my other friends. Sure, they are busy at their jobs. Anam is teaching, Kelly has her show coming up.

But it is Bay who actually has experience with cryptids. She and I have gotten closer in the past couple months, we've been trading texts and messages online, and if anyone will understand my odd predicament it'll be her.

"Don't normally see you in the middle of the day," she muses, handing me the almond creamer she knows I like best.

"I had to leave work early." I laugh at first, but then I can't help myself. I blurt everything out in one long embarrassing string. "He was there. He bought my company, Bailey. Or, not bought it—he's sponsoring my non-profit."

"Wait. Who did what?"

169

"He could ruin my business, Bay! I've built it from the ground up, and it's going to be ripped from my fingers." My nervous energy has my hand shaking.

"Your mate? You really think he's capable of that?"

"I don't know what he's capable of! He's the head of a huge corporation."

"Oh. Oh no!" Bay's cheeks turn pink. "Wait, you work in tech, don't you? Some kind of programmer?"

"Why?"

Her face gets serious as she walks around the counter into the customer space. "You should really talk to my fiancé."

Confused, I diligently follow her into the cat sanctuary room, where, sitting there in the middle of the floor, is a very large, very familiar, very grumpy Bigfoot. He has a handful of kittens scrambling across him while he cleans out a litter box.

"Sacha?" I squeak without intending to.

He looks up, his big brown eyes finding me.

"Ms. Hamilton?" He acknowledges me with a nod. A kitten in his lap yells loudly for his attention, and he lifts a huge hairy finger to scratch under its chin.

"What are you doing here?" I ask, backing away.

"Sacha is my mate." Excitement flashes through Bailey's eyes as she says it.

"What is going on, Beast?" Sacha asks.

"I was just leaving." I turn for the door.

"Wait! Please!" Bailey steps into my path. "I promise I didn't realize until just now! You never said! I didn't make the connection! But it makes so much sense! You and Pontius are perfect for each other!"

"You can't be serious." I shake my head.

"Beast, what are you talking about?" Sacha frowns in Bailey's direction. Their eyes meet and they silently communicate, the way that really close couples can.

"She's Pontius's mate."

Sacha's eyes narrow, he looks from me to his fiancé and then back again.

"If Pontius had a mate I'd know about it," Sacha disagrees, leaning back on his haunches carefully to not disrupt the kitten pile.

"No he wouldn't," Bailey says to me conspiratorially. "He's completely clueless."

"Who told you? Pleasant?" Sacha asks.

Bailey shakes her head subtly.

"Was it Magnes?" I cross my arms over my chest.

She sighs.

"Ness?" Sacha asks.

"We text sometimes." Bailey shrugs. "He loves the Kardashians."

"Ness knows? And I don't?" Sacha asks.

"Because you're totally clueless," Bailey reiterates.

"You really didn't know about—me?" I demand, searching their faces for any sign of deception.

"We had no idea," Bailey says.

"I wouldn't have allowed your company to become an asset if I'd known." Sacha frowns, while his hand reaches down to pet a kitten clamoring across his lap.

"So it's all what? A coincidence? You expect me to believe that?" I scowl at him.

"I expect that this was all Ness's plan. He led the acquisition, and he loves to meddle in other people's business. I've been stepping away from the company since—" He gestures at Bailey and the cat café in general.

"You're claiming Ant didn't have any part of it?" I grumble.

"I don't think Pontius even knew it was happening," Sacha ponders.

"His signature was on all of the contracts."

"His lawyer's signature was on all of the contracts." Sacha corrects me. "That should have been my first clue something was up. Ness was cagey about the deal but I didn't know this was what he had planned." He scratches a kitten's head with one hand, and the other pulls out his phone to type a message.

"How could Pontius not know?" I bite out. Did he forget about me? Has he not thought about me at all for the past couple months? My nervous feet can't hold still any longer and I start pacing the room.

"He's been in Canada," Bailey says.

I roll my eyes.

"He was visiting family," Sacha agrees.

"He may have found a sister he didn't know he had." Bailey confirms, her face tinged with concern. "He's been searching for family members—"

"I know who he's been looking for," I snap. I cross my arms over my chest and stop pacing the room. "You knew that Pontius was obsessed with me." I accuse Bailey.

"No!" she insists. "I didn't know he was the cryptid you were talking about! I promise. My goodness, I am so sorry, Piper." She reaches for my shoulder. "I should have realized. I wish I'd known. I really do. Pontius can be—odd. I knew he met someone new, but I didn't know any of the details. Ness said you two were 'taking it slow', that Pontius finally found someone who broke the spell Tiffany had him wrapped up in. No idea what he saw in her."

"His ex? I heard about her." I sink into one of the chairs not occupied by a cat. My blood boiling at thought of the things she said to him. "She sounds like a—piece of work."[1]

Bailey's eyes glimmer. "The only thing that snapped Pontius out of her clutches was a woman he met in a bar. Someone who was smart, and kind, and treated him like he was worth being with."

My heart somersaults. "You don't need to make me feel guilty for not being with him." I snap.

"I don't want you to feel guilty!" Bailey holds up her hands in surrender. "Pontius needed you."

"It shouldn't have happened like this. But, Pleasant couldn't help himself." Sacha leans back against one of the benches, his legs stretching long across the floor. "I've been there. It's impossible to stay away from your mate once you find them. It's not his fault."

"Are you blaming me?" I bite back.

"I'm blaming Ness." Sacha rumbles a noise in the back of his throat. "That bastard basically fired me for daring to fuck my assistant—"

Bailey gestures to herself, indicating that she was the assistant. I stifle a giggle even though none of this should be funny.

"And now he's ready to purchase an entire company for Pontius? I'm going to strangle that three-foot neck." Sacha continues grumbling even while a kitten climbs him to settle onto one wide shoulder.

"He won't really hurt him," Bailey tells me with a little smile. "I'm really sorry, Piper." Her face is so completely earnest I could only believe she's telling the truth.

---

1 The other two nod. Everyone in the room knows I wanted to say 'bitch' but held back.

Sacha pauses typing on his phone long enough to actually look at me. "Piper, this will be taken care of. Just please. Don't do anything rash."

"She won't!" Bay announces loudly. "She just needs some time to think. Give her some time to think about it. Right, Piper?"

"What makes you so sure?" I grumble.

"Because you already love him." She grins.

I roll my eyes. "Don't be ridiculous. I barely know the guy."

"Yes, of course," Bailey waves a hand through the air dismissively. "I really am sure that Pontius didn't mean any harm. Not that it negates you being hurt. Just that, he would never hurt you on purpose. You just need to get to know him better. Give him a chance to make it up to you."

"Beast," Sacha starts, there's a warning tone in his deep voice.

"Just go on another date with my stalker?" I grumble.

"No, no. You don't have to date him! I don't care who you date. I'll take you out if you like. To prove it. We can go to a bar. I'll take you to a bar myself and we can find you someone new! I want to be your friend, Piper. I like you! I want to stay friends, please!"

"Alright!" I laugh as her ramble stops. "Obviously, I don't want to quit my job. And yeah, I like you too." I wipe a hand across my face. Bailey has actually been really helpful this whole time. I have been enjoying her friendship, and she got me my cat. Disappointing her sweet face feels like kicking a puppy. I like her. I like Cryptech. I like my job there. I don't want things to change. I don't want more people to abandon me.

"Then let's go out! Like real friends do! I even know a couple really good cryptid bars. You'd like that wouldn't you?"

"That does sounds like fun." I admit. I believe that Sacha or Bailey didn't fully know what was going on, I don't think either of them is capable of pulling some Ocean's Eleven level heist on me. I can give it some time, let Sacha sort it out. Maybe finding someone else to replace Ant would help get him off my mind. I cleared Colin out with Ant after all. Maybe I just need someone new to replace my obsession with the Mothman.

20

PONTIUS

"**H**e's on a conference call," Ness's assistant mentions as I walk directly past her and into his office.

"Don't worry, Teresa. He'll have time for what I need to discuss."

Ness's office is pristine and modern. With sleek furniture and expensive glass finishes.

The Lake Monster twists his long neck toward me. He nods a silent hello and smiles.

I don't smile back, even as he presses a button on his desk that automatically closes the blackout curtains to block the windows lining one long wall of his office. I'm still furious at him, but grateful that he's so considerate. The dim room is much easier on my eyes. The only lighting left is the blue glow of the fish tank embedded in one wall. Ness once told me it reminds him of home.

"We need to talk."

He holds up one finger.

I cross to his desk and press the speaker button on his phone. "I'm afraid Mr. Loch has something more pressing to attend to. He's going to have to leave the call."

Ness's smile falters as he bats my hand away. "Sorry for the interruption. Can we reschedule next week?

Great, thanks," he says to his phone while he glares at me. He doesn't wait for a response before he hangs up.

"The hell, Pontius? First day back from vacation, and you're already barging into my office?"

"Don't try that crap with me, Ness." My wings buzzing with nervous energy. "You hired her!"

"Hired who?" he asks, one smooth eyebrow raising.

"Her! Her! Piper! My mate! The woman who told me she never wanted to see me again."

"Oh, her. Yeah, she's a hottie, got those nerd glasses. Excellent luck there, laddie," Ness says with an irritating smirk.

"You are not to look at her ever again." I hold back a growl in my chest, but I can't stop my wings from flaring. I wouldn't kill him, but I might maim him.

"I didn't hire her."

"What the hell are you talking about? I just ran into her in the elevator!"

"She's not an employee. We just signed a three-year contract to sponsor her non-profit. Penpoint. It's a good company, an excellent investment. You aren't technically her boss, so everything should be totally fine." He makes a wiggly motion with his hand, indicating it's actually a gray area. "Fully on the up-and-up."

"You did what?"

"I'm sure I CCed you on all of it."

"You did not."

"Maybe not, but I definitely told your lawyers." He has the gall to smirk, like this is a positive development. "You put them in charge while you were out of town, remember?"

"Why? Just to try and get me laid?"

"Do I look like someone who would spend that much money just so my friend could get a date." Ness stretches his long neck, and leans back in his chair. I hope he tips over.

"You look like exactly the type of person who would do that."

He smiles broadly this time. "I was doing you a favor."

"It is not a favor! She is furious! She thinks I planned it! That I did this just to be closer to her!"

"She'll get over it." He waves a dismissive hand.

"She won't. You don't understand." I take a deep breath before admitting, "I didn't tell you everything."

"What didn't you tell me?" Ness still grins, clearly not understanding the gravity of the situation.

I sigh and throw myself into one of the sleek leather chairs in his office.

I unload everything. I tell him about the weekend Piper and I spent together. Not the sordid details, not about how she cried, or how good her pussy tasted, or how I came in my pants just from touching her.

I tell him how she left me, and why she left me.

"You stalked her?" Ness asks after my story has trailed to a finish.

"I didn't think of it as stalking."

"Not stalking?" Ness's hand tightens around a pen. He doesn't yell, I'm not sure he's capable of really getting angry, but this is the closest I've ever seen him. "What were you thinking?"

"I wasn't thinking," I admit. "It was just instincts and idiocy."

"Damn straight, it was. You are an idiot. An absolute doofus. An imbecile." Ness seems unable to move on to a new thought.

He puts his face into his hands, like he could wipe away all the stupid things I've told him, before he stands up, crosses his office and opens a cabinet. A fancy shelf automatically rolls out, bottles of alcohol and drink ware clink as it moves. He pours a tall glass of amber liquid and then stares at me.

"No thanks," I say.

"I didn't offer you anything." He keeps staring.

I squirm in the silence between us until I can't help blurting out an attempt at an explanation. "I never expected to see her again."

"You're an imbecile." He downs his entire glass of Scotch in one long-necked gulp. His tone remains even tempered. "A complete and total dumbass. What are we going to do now?"

"Nothing," I say. "I'll leave again. She asked me to leave her alone. I'm going to do that."

"Is that what you want?"

"No! I don't! I want—" I don't know what to say after that. "I love her."

Ness's shoulders slump. "Of course you do. I'm the real idiot here. I thought you just needed to be honest with her. I thought if you got over yourself, asked her out a second time, it would fix everything. Christ, Pontius."

"I told you that it was over! I never expected you to buy her company behind my back!"

"We can still fix this." He pauses, pouring himself a second glass of Scotch while he thinks. "You cannot talk to her. You cannot speak to her. You cannot utter a single word to her. Do you understand?"

"I have been doing that for months."

"It might be best if you work from home. Keep your distance from the office."

"I appreciate you trying to protect her."

"I'm trying to protect you, lad. We can't risk her rejecting you." He lowers himself back into his office chair. "You aren't strong enough."

I want to argue with him, but I think he's right. I don't know what I would do if Piper rejected me.

"We'll start small. You just keep your distance. Give her some space. Let her come to you."

"I don't think she wants to see me again."

"Of course she does, you idiot." Ness argues. "The mating bond has her smitten with you already, or you'd probably be in jail. We still have room to salvage this."

"We?" I ask.

"Yes, you dunce. 'We'. I'm involved now. I signed a contract to get you closer to this woman. You're my family."

"Family?" I ask quietly.

"You are like a brother to me. Hell, I like you better than my own brother. He's a useless lump." He leans back in his chair. "Although you aren't seeming much better right now."

I suck in a breath. Ness, Sacha, and I have been close since we met in college. Eight years building a company together can really tell you a lot about a person. Until recently they were the only people in my life I could call my family.

"We'll get her to be your friend first." Ness cuts himself off with a large sip of his Scotch. "That will create a solid basis for the relationship and you can build from there."

"Friends?" I lean forward, hands on my legs.

"You think you can handle that?" he asks.

"Yes! Yes, I would do anything to have her in my life again!" I say eagerly.

"Alright, if this is going to work, you have to stop acting like such an idiot and do what I say."

"Yes! Of course!" Maybe trusting Ness isn't the best idea, but he's got more experience dating humans than I do. If he says that I need to become friends with Piper, then that's exactly what I'm going to do.

21

PIPER

"**W**ait. He quit?" I ask. For some reason, my heart jumps into my throat.

"He's decided to step away from the company for the time being," Sacha looks pointedly at his business partner. "Completely of his own accord, apparently."

My stomach does a strange squeezing at those words. It's been less than twenty-four hours since I saw Ant in the building. I slept poorly, showed up late to work, then Magnes called and asked me to come to his office.

Magnes's office is that hyper modern style that matches the rest of the Cryptech building. It's irritatingly fashionable. A wall of windows, gray walls, gray floor. Magnes sits behind a glass topped desk. Sacha and I sit across from him. Sacha keeps his arms folded across his chest as he glares at his business partner.

"You're saying he won't be here anymore?" The discomfort bubbles up from my stomach into a nervous laugh.

"He won't." Magnes shakes his large green head.

"Why did he decide to do that?" I demand.

"Pontius called it an 'extended leave'. He said he has personal projects he wants to work on," Magnes says.

"He wanted to make sure you were comfortable. That we could all gain the maximum benefit possible from our companies working together," Sacha adds.

"When will he be back?" I ask.

Magnes shrugs. "He didn't say."

I laugh, feeling uncomfortable. Neither of their expressions change. "You aren't kidding? That's it? He built this company! He poured his entire being into this place, and he just has to leave it behind?" I stand up, feeling like I need to get out of my chair. "Because of me? That's not fair."

Sacha sighs loudly.

Magnes stands up and crosses his office. "Would you like a drink, Ms. Hamilton?"

"No, I don't want a drink." My feet have me pacing the office. "Does he think that's what I want? Him just gone?"

"He's trying to do the right thing." Sacha remains very sensibly seated.

"Well, he's not going to make me the bad guy! I won't let him. I'm not going to be the reason that he abandons everything that he worked so hard to build!" I feel myself ranting as I stab my finger into my own chest, but I don't have the self control to stop myself. "He's not going to blame me."

"No one is blaming you, Ms. Hamilton," Sacha says.

"Because it's your fault." My stabbing finger points toward Magnes.

"Excuse you?" The Lake Monster flinches, although I'm feet away.

"She's not wrong," Sacha mutters.

"There's nothing you can do; he's made up his mind." Magnes opens a cabinet and stares at a row of bottles of alcohol for a moment before he closes the door again with a huff.

"If you don't want to work with us any longer, we understand," Sacha interjects. "We'll cancel the contract, cut you loose, no strings."

I stop in my tracks. "You're punishing me for this?"

"No." Magnes says quickly. "No, and we don't want you to leave!"

Sacha puts a hand up, and Magnes stops talking. "Pontius was very clear. He wants you to do whatever you want, Ms. Hamilton. It was the only thing that he insisted on before he left. You are free to stay, to leave, break the contract, or move your headquarters to another city. We will help with whatever you choose."

"My choice?" I tap my fingers on the table. It isn't really my choice though, is it? It affects my employees. Some of them have been with me since the beginning. They depend on me for their livelihoods. I can't ask them to relocate to another city or go back to those crappy offices or go back to insecure paychecks. I can't stand the idea of disappointing them.

No. This choice is between me and him.

He should have to answer for this. He's forcing my hand, making me the bad guy. Removing himself from my life, just like Colin did.

What I need is to talk to Ant. To yell at him, face-to-face. My employees' opinions matter, but ultimately, I know they are going to choose the higher paychecks, better office spaces, and better benefits. I can't leave Cryptech.

This issue is between me and the Mothman.

"Where is he?" I demand.

"At his home, probably. He rarely leaves it during the day." Sacha sighs loudly. Magnes just continues smirking as I head for the door.

I don't exactly remember where Pontius lives. It takes me a couple hours driving around the waterfront area of town, before I finally stumble on a building that I am sure is his house. From outside, in the daylight, it looks just like a lot of the other industrial buildings. Except for the nerdy little concrete fire flower out front.

The drive gave me plenty of time to compose a long angry rant. When I finally park my car outside his place, I know exactly how I am going to tear into him.

I step onto the sidewalk and freeze. Like the fresh air has knocked some sense into me. This is a terrible idea. Confronting him, alone, in his house. Last time I was here, I was falling in love.

Crap. Not love, something less intense than that.

I shift my keys back and forth in my hands several times. This is silly. I can't be in love with him. I barely, know him. I start toward the front door. Halfway down the sidewalk, I stop myself and head back to my car. Three steps later I stop again and turn back toward his apartment. I repeat this at least three more times, losing track of the exact number.

I just need to walk up to the door. Knock on it. Talk to him. See him again. Confront him. Tell him that he doesn't just get to wash his hands of the situation.

Another car pulls up on the block in front of me.

A human woman climbs out. She's pretty, Black, with close-cropped natural curls and bright red lipstick. She confidently approaches Ant's door.

I duck behind a car and immediately feel ridiculous. She doesn't know me. How could she recognize me?

I don't step out from behind the car.

I peer through the car windows to watch her knock on Ant's front door, and check her phone while waiting for him to answer.

She must know him. Who is she? A date?

Ant appears. He looks adorable, as always, with a video game t-shirt and a pair of loose fitting black pants.

He greets the woman. I can't hear what they are saying, but they smile and hug each other.

Fucking bitch.

Oh, dear. Where did that come from? I close my eyes for a moment, trying to reset my thoughts. She's not a bad person. He's allowed to go out whoever he wants. We aren't dating. I don't even like him. I definitely don't love him. Who cares if he spent an entire weekend giving me mind blowing orgasms like they were Free Comic Book Day issues?

I definitely don't wish this woman was dead. Or maimed. Or hit by a car. Then he'd just have to sit by her hospital bed and nurse her back to health. It would only bring them closer.

I open my eyes. They've disappeared. Crap.

I hurry down the block and around the corner to find them again. Their silhouettes, highlighted by the sun low over the horizon. The frigging golden hour casting them in the perfect amber light. I still can't hear them, but I can clearly read their body language. He leans toward her and she laughs at something he says.

Slut.

Nope. No. Not that.

He's the bastard.

Nope. Not that either. They are fine. They are two consenting adults, and they are allowed to do whatever they want on this fine spring evening. I follow them several more blocks, until they enter a local park, headed for a romantic little gazebo overlooking a duck pond.

I bet he hasn't told her that he has a fated-mate. I wonder if she knows he told me he loved me two months ago. She'd back off then.

Crap.

I have to stop. I turn around to head in the opposite direction. I do not need to follow them. He's not dating Tiffany again. That's all that matters. That woman was genuinely bad for him. This one, she'll be different. Probably. She probably isn't just after his money. She probably won't mistreat him. She probably isn't like Tiffany?

Crap. Is that Tiffany? I never asked what she looked like.

I just have to make sure he's okay. I spin back around and head after them, keeping a respectable distance, hoping they won't notice me. They stop to chat beside a playground. What do they even have to talk about? What could he possibly have in common with her? What could she be saying that makes his face light up and his antennae quirk to the side like they do when he is amused?

Ugh. I have to get out of here.

Two waist-high brown creatures race past me. One spreads little wings, lifting itself a few inches off the ground to take a half-hearted attempt at flying before its feet stumble back to the sidewalk. The figures are yelling incomprehensible baby speak. They are followed by a full-grown Mothwoman in a lavender wrap dress. She pulls a wagon full of toys behind her.

I briefly make eye contact with her, and her mouth arms lift into an awkward smile. Very similar to the face I make when I am expecting an inappropriate comment from a stranger.

Crap. I know I'm being rude by staring at her the way I am. She isn't a spectacle. I return her awkward smile before I turn away and pretend I wasn't watching her.

I've never seen another Mothman before. I know they exist, certainly. But they're rare. She's not much different looking than Ant, slightly different shaped, a little larger, a little rounder, her facial features are slightly more delicate, and the babies, with her are the cutest things.

What a coincidence, to see them in the same park as Ant.

The human woman beside Ant waves in our direction and the Mothwoman waves back. They know each other.

Ant is also looking in this direction.

Crap. He knows I'm here.

"Piper?" He calls.

I try to ignore it, turning my awkward smile away from him.

The two tiny Mothmen crash into the human woman's legs, giving her intense hugs, before they turn and race into the playground area.

It's Ant's family. It has to be.

The two females greet each other warmly with a kiss.

His sister and her mate and two babies. A niece and a nephew maybe?

I can't stop staring. I'm such a jealous idiot. I'm so stupid. I shouldn't be here. This is none of my business. I have to get out of here.

"Piper. Wait," Ant calls as I turn to leave.

I pretend I don't hear him, hurrying back the way I came. I freeze in place as his shadow passes over my head, and then he lands nearly silently in front of me.

"What are you doing here?" he asks.

"Nothing!" I say brightly. "Just going for a walk."

His antennae twist to the side, amused. "Were you following me?"

"I came to speak with you about leaving Cryptech." I roll my shoulders back, trying to appear more confident.

His mouth twists into half of a grin. "You followed me here, from my house," he reiterates.

"I saw you with that woman and—" I pause, and roll my eyes. "I wanted to make sure you weren't wrapped up in another Tiffany situation."

"You followed me to make sure I was safe."

I'm a little annoyed with how pleased he looks.

"Fine. Yes," I snap. "Are you happy? I wanted to make sure you were alright."

"Would you like to meet my sister?" he asks much more quietly. I glance back at the couple and the two tiny mothlings.

"Your sister? And the human woman is her mate?" There's an uncomfortable pit of shame in my stomach. The woman I've been intensely jealous of for the past ten minutes is basically his sister-in-law. "I didn't know they had kids."

"They flew down a few days ago for the adoption. They are staying in town for the rest of the month, until the kids are big enough to make the flight themselves."

"Adoption?" I ask, almost dumbfounded. They are so sweet together, and the kids are adorable. Tiny red eyes, fuzzy brown bodies, and little wings that don't quite work yet. The cutest things I have seen in some time. "I thought Mothmen abandoned their young?"

"Maisie and her mate adopted them as eggs. The twins were left under an abandoned rail bridge. Maisie and Janelle wanted a family. Now, they don't have to grow up alone. The way I did."

My stomach twists. A family.

"They just hatched a few days ago."

"A few days ago!" I can't help laughing. "They are so big."

"They'll be large enough to fend for themselves soon. Mothmen have a shorter childhood, but a longer adolescence. We reach maturity roughly the same age that humans do."

"Oof. They'll be teenagers for two whole decades?" I ask with a smile.

"Something like that." He laughs. "It's just a different development cycle than humans."

"That makes sense, if you need to fend for yourself from birth." I cross my arms while I watch. The two tiny mothlings have already fully thrown themselves onto the playground, clambering over the jungle gym. They couldn't possibly be cuter, it hurts thinking about them truly fending for themselves. The thought of tiny Ant all alone makes my heart squeeze.

"Do you want to meet them?" Ant's voice cuts through my thoughts.

I nod easily. "Okay." I really would.

22
PIPER

I know it's probably a bad idea, but I follow Ant back to the group, and he introduces me to everyone.

Maisie Hill, his sister, is nice. No one is sure if they are actually blood related, but they've decided to embrace the family culture anyway. Her wife, Janelle, offers me a sandwich from their supplies. Their kids, Monty and Helen, are tiny, sweet, and so cute that it borders on annoying the crap out of me. They say 'please', 'thank you', and 'nice to meet you' in near unison, but don't bother pretending to actually be interested in me. They take snacks from their mothers and then race back to the jungle gym.

Ant plays with his niblings, chasing them around, holding them above his head so they can spread their wings and catch the wind. The kids are covered in a light brown fuzz. Maisie explains the fur will get darker as they age and they will be able to fly when their wings mature.

Watching them interact has my ovaries twinging. I've always wanted kids of my own. Or I always thought I would want kids of my own, eventually. Watching him now confirms to my brain I'd be happy even if they were tiny adorable moth creatures that look nothing like me.

193

Not that I am going to raise any kind of child with Ant.

"You came here to see Pontius?" Janelle interrupts my staring.

"I just had a question about our work." I laugh, trying to disguise my real motivation. "He visited you two in Canada?"

"He stayed with us for the holidays." Janelle lounges on a bench beside me. She looks tired, but the kind of satisfied exhaustion that comes with being a new mom.

"All of the holidays?" I specify.

"Just from early November until the new year," Maisie confirms everything I've been told.

"Maisie doesn't have a family. It was nice to watch them connect and talk about their shared experiences," Janelle adds.

"I'm sure that was nice." I feel myself smiling.

"It really meant a lot to Maisie, to have family. That's part of why we jumped at the chance to adopt. It probably wouldn't have happened for us if Pontius wasn't involved." In one hand, Janelle holds a stuffed doll, and in the other, a small, but very important, rock she was given for safekeeping by the littlest mothling. "He's a really solid man. Are you two seeing each other?"

I ignore the question and decide to change the topic. "How did you two meet?"

"Mutual friends introduced us," the Mothwoman steps into the conversation.

"Maisie came into my workplace every day for dinner for a month before she got the guts to actually ask me on a date."

Maisie gives a sheepish smile. "I was a bit obsessed."

"What did you do? Follow her home? Steal all her underwear?" I laugh.

The two women exchange a knowing glance.

"Something like that," Maisie mutters sheepishly.

My eyes widen.

"Maisie! Janelle!" Ant's voice is raised with some concern, followed by a toddler's scream, across the playground.

When I look up, Ant is using his long arms to keep the toddlers, who are invested in having an all-out-brawl, separate. He holds Helen in the air, by the back of her neck scruff, as she flutters her tiny wings ineffectively. Monty is attempting to scale Ant's leg with an impressively loud, but still adorable, growl.

"A little help, please." Ant laughs as the mothlings gnash their teeth, desperately trying to bite each other.

"Coming!" Janelle and Maisie race to him, to scold and console each of the twins in turn.

Ant returns to my side, sinking onto the bench beside me. He's still beaming, despite sighing like the most exhausted person alive.

"They seem really nice," I say quietly.

He nods enthusiastically, watching with bright eyes while the moms wrangle their children. "I'm glad to have found someone I can call family."

My treacherous heart does a somersault.

"I get it," I say without meaning to. "My family are some of the most important people in my life."

He turns to me and smiles, his hands folded in his lap. I fight the urge to reach over and squeeze one. He's so sweet. What harm has he really done? Following me around like a lovesick puppy?

Crap. What is wrong with me?

I steel my emotions, smushing them back down deep where they belong. I am angry at him.

"We need to talk about you leaving Cryptech." I try to school my features.

"Nothing to say." His voice is firm, but his wings shift behind him, betraying his nervousness.

"You can't do this, Ant. You can't just drop your whole life—the thing you care most about—not because of me."

"You're wrong." He shakes his head. "It's not the thing I care most about. Not even close."

I catch his eye and he looks away, toward his sister and her family. I bite my lip. "I'm not going to let you turn me into the bad guy in this situation."

"Who said you were the bad guy?"

"I don't want you wrecking your career, blaming me for things you didn't do or opportunities that you lost." I'm not letting a guy do that to me again.

"I don't blame you for anything," he says.

I don't let his reasonable tone stop me. I had a whole car ride to prepare this speech. Even if it isn't going the way I expected.

"If you left the company because of me then you shouldn't have." I feel my words failing. "If Cryptech only bought Penpoint because you were obsessed with me, then I want to break our contract."

"Piper. No." His voice is so quiet that I can barely hear him. "It had nothing to do with that. You've done incredible work"

I roll my eyes.

"Don't roll your eyes at me." His voice is serious as he turns his full attention toward me, but he's giving me that adorable smile that makes my stomach queasy. "We were already interested in your company. You were on our radar before I ever met you. You've done amazing work. We wanted to be a part of that," Ant explains. "And then I met you, and I ruined everything. I couldn't stop myself."

"Just couldn't stop yourself from fucking me?" I snark, trying desperately to stay mad at him.

He shakes his head. "I thought I was giving you what you wanted. Even that night you said—"

"I know what I said," I snap, without any real malice in my voice. "I know what I said I wanted."

"I thought it was everything I'd be able to give you," he says tentatively. "I never imagined you'd want to be with me for more than one night. I didn't mean to upset you. I was stupid. Following my natural instincts."

"Your instincts are to be a creep?" I shove my glasses up my nose.

"Yes." He sighs like the weight of the world is on his shoulders. "I just wanted to keep you safe. I'm sorry."

"You can't follow someone around like that without telling them. Humans don't stalk the ones we love."

"I know," he says.

"You scared me."

"I know," he repeats. "I didn't mean to frighten you. I just needed to learn as much about you as I could, to convince you to like me."

"Well, I did like you." I squirm, but I can't stop the nervous laugh in my throat. "How much of that personality was fake?"

"None of it." His hands shift in his lap, clenching and unclenching. "I really felt like I could be myself around you."

Crap. He sounds so sincere.

"You really enjoy all that stuff? Movies, video games, and Brendan Fraser in The Mummy?"

"I'd be a fool not to enjoy Brendan Fraser." He smiles. Adorable.

"You weren't lying about any of it?"

"Everything I told you was true. All of my past, my interests. All of that was real. It was just the little things. Your favorite foods. The way you take your coffee. The type of candy you like at the movies." He stops talking, seeming to realize what he's admitting. "I thought it would make you like me."

Crap. I actually believe him. He's a stalker, but he's been honest about it. I don't think he'd lie to me now. Would he? Am I being an idiot? Colin barely remembered that I hated olives on pizza.

"And you really didn't know?" I clarify. "That Loch was offering to sign a contract with Penpoint?"

"I didn't know." Ant says. "Sacha didn't understand the situation either. He never would have agreed. The Bigfoot is completely furious about the whole thing."

I snort half a laugh. "That much has become obvious. You are all just blaming the Lake Monster?"

"Yes," he grumbles. "You asked me to stay away, Piper. I've been attempting that, to the best of my abilities."

I pause. I don't know if I've had a man actually listen to me before. "You know you're famous? I've admired your work for a long time."

"Really?"

"I never knew what you looked like. No one on the internet does. What's that about?"

He shakes his head. "People seem to respond more positively before they know what I look like."

"But parties, conferences, speaking engagements, corporate announcements...Magnes and Sacha are photographed all the time."

"Those events are loud and crowded. Full of noise and smells and bright lights. I can barely handle going to a bar. That's why I bought Moonshine and the Artemis."

"You own the movie theater too?" I groan. "Of course you do. You seem to have a hand in everything cool in this city."

"Only part of the theater." He shrugs. "And a couple other establishments. I wanted there to be places that people like me could go and...feel like they belong."

"You should have just told me all of that. That really would have made me like you," I admit. Sweet. He is sweet and kind and using his money to make sure there are good, inclusive activities in the community.

"It's not all my doing. Cryptech wouldn't be where it is today without Sacha and Ness taking the lead in public spaces. I wouldn't be anything without them. I owe them so much."

I smile softly at that.

Crap. I can't let him do this to me—win me over with a couple quiet words.

"I'm sorry I called you a freak that day that we were fighting," I say quickly. "I feel really bad about it."

"It's okay." His wings flutter before he speaks again. "I wonder if you could forgive me too? For all of the stupid things I did."

"It would be nice if I could, especially if we are going to live in the same city, and work in the same field," I admit. "It'd be better if I weren't worrying all the time. I was looking forward to meeting Pontius Pleasant, who's supposed to be the most talented programmer in the city. It would have been an incredible opportunity to work with you."

"You could still work with me," he suggests.

"I don't know." I shake my head.

"What can I do to make you feel comfortable? Whatever it is, I will do it. Quit my job. Leave the country. Again…" he rushes through the ideas very seriously. For some reason, that makes me laugh, because he did leave the country to get away from me.

"Don't do that." I manage to stop laughing. "You shouldn't uproot your whole life just for me. I don't want that."

His shoulders relax, and his antennae raise. Cute. He's cute. I hate how cute he is.

I take a deep breath. The concept of forgiving him feels much more possible today. Letting him into my life seems preferable to never seeing him again. He's so easy to talk to, and despite my better judgment, I really like him.

"What if we tried to be friends?"

"Just friends?" I ask, slightly surprised. Right, that's the logical thing. Not date him. Not walk back to his place and fuck until I think I might go blind. Be his friend. Take it slow.

"Or even just colleagues? If that's better for you? Polite acquaintances?" He continues, clearly misreading the expression on my face.

"No," I interrupt him with a laugh, to stop him from lowering the relationship status any further. "Friends is good. But you have to level the playing field. You know so much about me. You have to share things with me. And not just the cute stuff, the embarrassing stuff, and the weird stuff."

"I can do that. I will do that." His wings flutter and his voice gets quiet. "But, you already know more about me than almost anyone else."

"Yeah, well! I want to know it all. Okay? I want to be able to blackmail you if I have to. I need to know your embarrassing childhood crushes, what makes you cry, what kind of fanfics you read, all of it. Okay?"

"Tails," he announces.

"What?" I ask confused.

"Tails, Sonics' little fox sidekick. He's probably my most embarrassing childhood crush."

I don't even bother trying to hold back my laugh. "That's a really good one."

"He could fly." Ant smiles.

"What else?" I ask.

"Well, I can tell you about meeting my sister?" There's a bright smile on his face that makes me want to hug him. Touch him.

"Yeah. Okay." I grin.

Crap. I gotta find a way to fix my broken brain. My phone lights up with a text. It's Bailey, saying she's sorry, and offering to buy me an apology drink, yet again.

Maybe I do need to try something new? Get out of my comfort zone and meet people. Maybe one of those cryptid bars she mentioned, might help me move on.

23

PIPER

nt is sweet. He starts texting me little embarrassing facts about himself. When he accidentally says 'You too' after the barista says 'enjoy your drink'. When he flew into a tree branch in front of a group of teenaged gargoyles. When he turned too fast and his wings knocked over a whole table full of drinks at Moonshine.

It's to easy to fall for him all over again.

So when Bailey calls me the next weekend I immediately insist that she take me out to a bar to meet strangers and be my date to Kelly's art show after.

Bailey suggests a cryptid bar called Labyrinth. She warns me it's a bit more intense than Moonshine, but if I want to meet another cryptid, then this is the place to do it.

I am so nervous that I manage to arrive twenty minutes early. The place isn't my usual hang, and I'm not dressed appropriately. I grabbed my favorite dark wash jeans, pink Doc Martens, and a distressed tank top. I feel just trendy enough to hang with Kelly's art crowd, but I don't exactly fit in at Labyrinth. I don't think I'd fit in here no matter what I was wearing.

Labyrinth is a classic nightclub—dim lighting, blaring music, overpriced drinks, and almost nowhere to sit. These places have always made me feel vulnerable, like I am on display.

It doesn't feel safe and cozy like Moonshine does.

I grab a stool at the bar and pull out my phone. I'm so embarrassingly early I can't even text Bailey to see where she is. Instead, I open my reading app. I'm right in the middle of a juicy paranormal historical romance when some women clamber up to the bar beside me, one bumps my shoulder as she releases a loud laugh.

I adjust so the giggling woman isn't in my space.

"Oh my god, sorry," says a beautiful, dark-haired human. She's sitting with a group of women, a blonde human, a female Bigfoot, and a lizard with scaly green skin.

"Not a problem," I say.

"Oh, it's you!" the blonde exclaims. "This is the bitch that Pleasant left me for!" She tells her friends.

I recoil.

"Sorry. I didn't mean that you are a bitch. I don't even know you." She leans forward and puts an overly familiar hand on my forearm. "I mean bitch in a generic 'this woman stole my man' way."

That makes me recognize her. The sexy demon the night I met Ant. She's not a demon at all. She's Ant's ex-girlfriend. Tall, slender, beautiful, with perfect makeup, high heels, and all the other 'hot girl' things I haven't quite managed to get a handle on.

"I'm Tiffany!" she exclaims. "Surely Pontius has mentioned me."

"A little," I admit.

"Oh god, he's not here, is he?" she asks. "Sorry if I am being, like, so awkward. This is Pontius' mate!" She says the last part to her friends.

Tiffany. I am face-to-face with Tiffany. The woman who told Ant that no one would ever be okay with his body. She's a monster. An actual monster.

I stand from my stool, clenching my fists at my side. I'm not sure what I plan to do. Hit her? That's stupid. Insult her? God, she's pretty. What would I say? I guess I could go for an attack on her character or something?

"Oh my god! Look at you! You are so cute!" Tiffany immediately exclaims, looking me up and down.

"I bet you two are perfect together. You got lucky there," Tiffany's friend tells me. "I'd love for a rich cryptid to just pluck me out of obscurity. I bet it's fantastic!"

"I—we—" I fumble for words.

"He'll buy you just about anything you want. I taught him that women love presents." Tiffany laughs. "You can thank me for that."

"I'm not...We're not together."

"Oh, you rejected him? That makes sense. He's kind of a freak." Her face falls briefly before it lights back up. "Is he single again? Maybe I can get him to put a ring on it this time." She waggles her fingers, which are free of any kind of jewelry.

All of her friends laugh.

That's not right. She can't do that. She can't date him. He deserves someone better than a woman who just wants to use him for his money.

"No!" I shout. The women barely acknowledge my outburst, already chatting over me.

Over Tiffany's shoulder I see a familiar pink head walk into the bar. Bailey is finally here, right on time.

"Can I buy you a drink or something?" Tiffany asks. "You can sit with us if you like."

"No, thank you. Have a good evening." I spin on my heels away from them, and am immediately filled with regret.

Crap. That isn't what I wanted to say. I wanted to tell her off. Insult her. Say that Ant is great. He's too good for her. I wanted to tell her she should fuck off to hell.

"Hi." I greet Bailey when I reach her. "Can we go somewhere else?"

She raises one eyebrow and spots the women sitting at the bar behind me. Her eyes go wide with recognition.

"Is that—" she asks.

"Can we just leave?" I shake my head, not wanting to talk about it.

"I'd love to tell her off." Bailey's brows furrow before she catches my expression. "No. No. Of course, let's go." She loops her arm around mine and leads me out of the building.

We end up getting snacks at a convenience store and just eating them while we chat walking down the sidewalk.

"What does rejecting a fated-mate do?" I finally ask, needing to get my curiosity off my chest.

Bailey gives me a sidelong glance, a strained smile pulls across her lips. "Rejection cuts off the mating bond. Completely severs any emotional or physical connection you might have had."

"Completely gone?" The idea brings a well of sadness to my stomach. "That sounds serious."

Bailey nods. "It happened to Ness, you know? Fate usually gets it right but when he met his mate, she was already married to someone else, with one kid and another one on the way. She wanted to stay with her family, she rejected Ness."

"Then it wasn't a big deal?"

"It was a huge deal. They both were in pain for a while. I don't think he's ever really gotten over it."

"Pain?"

"Yeah. Like, physical and emotional." She winces.

I press my lips together in a thin line. I don't want to hurt Ant. Or myself.

"It's really the final option," she says. "I'm not telling you not to do it, but it is serious. You should consider it carefully."

"How do you do it?" I'm nervous even asking.

"From what I understand, you just say it." Bailey shrugs. "I reject you, Pontius. He needs to be around you. You really have to mean it. But you could practice now, if you like."

I shake my head solemnly. That feels too serious, like a risk I don't need to take.

I don't miss the way that Bailey smirks at my refusal. I move our conversation to lighter topics on the twenty-minute walk to the art gallery. The event is on the second floor of an old building, above a cute vintage shop. The space is packed. Kelly is one of three artists being shown today. It's a classic art gallery—white walls, wood floors, super specific lighting that I am sure is supposed to make the art look good, but it doesn't mimic anything I've ever seen in a real home.

Kelly is busy when we first arrive, so Bailey and I circle the room admiring the art. I show her which ones are Kelly's. We pause in front of a large piece of a laughing woman. The woman is covered in reds and oranges, like she's on fire, but also loving it.

"It's gorgeous, isn't it?" I ask Bailey.

"Your friend is really talented," she agrees. "She's got some great stuff." Her eyes track a movement behind me. A second later, I'm enveloped in a side hug.

"So glad to see that someone cool is here!" Anam says. "I need someone to hang out with."

She's wearing a chic black dress and cute strappy heels. Why do I never think to buy cute heels? I'd probably wear them if I had some in my closet.[1]

Anam's eyes catch on Bailey, she leans forward to whisper in my ear. "I thought you weren't bringing a date. Who's the hottie?"

Bay makes a face that implies she heard every word and doesn't mind one bit.

"Anam, this is my friend, Bailey."

"Just a friend?" she asks Bailey conspiratorially.

"I'm actually engaged," Bailey says.

"Oh, you move really quickly." Anam winks and laughs. "And my goodness, look at that rock!" She grabs Bailey's hand in that overfamiliar way that really charismatic people like Anam can pull off. "When is the big day?"

"Two months!" Bailey flashes her engagement ring in the light.

"How do you know Piper then? She can't afford a rock like this."

"This is the cat lady I told you about," I say.

"Oh, I love Mercutio!" Anam exclaims.

Anam and Bay break into a long conversation about animal adoption. Anam might not be ready to commit to a man, but she seems like she might be ready to commit to a kitten.

I leave them to circle the room. Two glasses of white wine later I think I've put in plenty of face time for artwork I could never afford.

---

1 I absolutely wouldn't wear them.

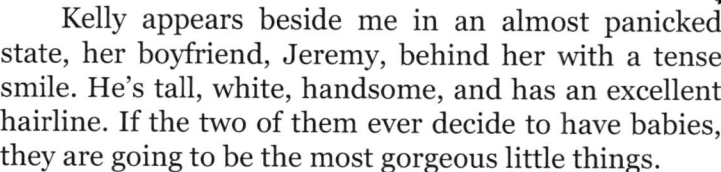

Kelly appears beside me in an almost panicked state, her boyfriend, Jeremy, behind her with a tense smile. He's tall, white, handsome, and has an excellent hairline. If the two of them ever decide to have babies, they are going to be the most gorgeous little things.

Kelly wraps me in a tight hug. "He's here," is the first thing that she whispers into my ear. "I'm so sorry. I have no idea how he found out about it—"

"Hi! Hello! Congrats on the show! Who are you talking about?" I laugh.

I make eye contact with Colin the second the words have left my mouth.

24

PIPER

"Y ou cannot be serious." I mutter into Kelly's ear, who refuses to break the hug. "What is he doing here?

Colin is already walking over to us. What, the crap, is happening?

"I have to go. I'm going to call it a night. I can't handle him right now." I tell Kelly. "Your work is amazing. You are amazing. Congratulations, babe!" I fill the last part in quickly before I practically race for the exit. I see Kelly intercepting Colin as I turn away.

I quickly text my friends that I am leaving on my way out the door. I don't see them, but I'm sure they are entertaining each other. Bailey won't have any trouble getting home on her own.

It got dark while I was attempting to socialize. When my feet hit the slightly damp concrete, the smell of petrichor hits me. It rained while I was inside. The night is cool and wet, I wrap my arms around myself. The light flickers faintly in the distance and a different type of chill hits me. A loose wire in a street light probably. Or it could be...I shove my glasses up my nose, lean against the wall, and scan the shadows of the buildings across the street, searching the rooftops for a Mothman silhouette. There are a few things—fuzzy blotches that could almost maybe be someone. None of it is him.

Crap. I have to stop hoping that I'm going to see him. I told him to stay away, and he's only doing what I asked.

I force my eyes closed and take a deep breath. I'm not exactly sober, but I can't tell if the alcohol or the panic of running into Colin is affecting me more. Between Ant and Colin, I know who I'd rather see right now.

I take a couple more breaths, savoring how blessedly quiet it is out here.

"Piper." A voice pops up in front of me. Without opening my eyes I recognize it. "Can we talk?"

"What are you doing here?" I keep my eyes closed.

"Kelly and Jeremy have been my friends as long as they were yours. The invite was online." Colin's voice is smooth, like he knew this meeting was inevitable. I wish I'd had some indication it would happen.

My eyes finally pop open. "You are supposed to be in New York. Several thousand miles from here."

"The start-up folded a month after I got there." Colin says.

"I'm sorry," I say, even though I don't mean it. "You could have told me you were back."

"I didn't think you'd want to see me."

"I don't." I laugh unexpectedly. Caught off guard by the sound, I laugh again, at my own laugh.

Colin flinches. "Well, you got rid of the rest of my stuff. What was I supposed to do?"

"It's safe and sound in your storage locker!"

He gives me a pitying look, like he thinks I am crazy. "I didn't forget about it. I was coming back for it."

"How would I know? You didn't call or text. You never told me an address for me to ship it." I swallow hard.

"There wasn't room for extra baggage in New York," Colin protests.

"Is that what I am? Extra baggage?" I can't help laughing.

"Of course not, Piper. I just needed a chance to try some of the other things I missed out on while we were together."

"You wanted to fuck other women?"

"I wanted to explore possibilities. And now I'm back. We can start over!"

"Start over?" I must have misheard him.

"I missed you. New York wasn't the same without you." He reaches a hand toward me. I move out of its path.

"I heard you finally got our little project off the ground." He smiles, but it doesn't reach his eyes.

"Our project?"

"Penpoint. You sold it, right?"

"No. I didn't sell it. I found a sponsor who plans to help us expand."

"And now we can expand our lives together." He grins like he's got it all figured out.

"You can't be serious." I step to one side around Colin.

"I never should have left." He moves to block my path. "I love you, Piper."

I laugh, loudly, and this time, I can't seem to stop. How stupid is all of this?

His eyes narrow, and one hand tightens into a fist at his side. He would never hit me, right? I take a step away from him. "You still love me too, don't you?

My stomach flips, but it doesn't take soul searching. I know the truth right away. "No. Colin. I don't."

"Did you ever really love me?"

"Of course I did," I say, but the nerves make a laugh bubble up from deep inside. "And then you left."

"And now I'm back!" He spits out the words, so angry with me.

I suck in a deep breath, not sure how to respond to him. My reaction comes out of me as a loud laugh.

"It's not funny," Colin mutters.

"You showing up, here and now?" I laugh so hard that I feel hot tears welling up into my eyes. "It's basically a dark comedy."

"Piper?" Bailey's figure is suddenly in the well-lit, doorway of the art gallery, "Everything alright?"

Anam and Kelly appear right behind her. They stand just inside the gallery doorway. I don't know where they've been, but I'm glad to see them.

Colin's eyes flick to the small crowd and back to me. "Which one of them are you fucking? Or is it all of them?" He leans in close as he says it.

"You're an idiot," I say, but I can feel my mask breaking and the tears becoming real.

"And what? Now you are going to cry?" he asks. "You always overreact, Piper."

"Please, just stop. I don't want to talk to you." I wipe a tear from my cheek, even though how wrong he is makes me want to scream. I'm not overreacting.

"Enough. You have to go." Anam is suddenly in front of me, stepping between me and Colin, pointing a finger at his chest.

"This is none of your business." He glares at me over Anam's head.

"I'm about to make it my business." Anam puts her arms akimbo. She's barely five feet tall but somehow manages to seem intimidating.

"You do not know me well enough to talk to me like this." Colin says to her.

Colin opens his mouth, but closes it quickly when the other two women step forward. Kelly already has her phone out to dial someone. Ever the reasonable one.

"She doesn't want to talk to you." Bailey crosses her arms, looking not unlike a mafia boss. I think Sacha might have rubbed off on her.

Colin's face is red. He looks ready to scream but his voice comes out deadly calm. "I was leaving anyway. We can talk about this later, Piper." He storms down the sidewalk.

I wipe a tear from under my glasses.

"Are you alright, babe?" Bailey asks. I step away from her arm. I just can't stand to be touched right now.

"He didn't used to be like this." I have to pause and sniff in the middle of my sentence. I don't know why I feel the need to defend him.

"He was always a bit like this." Anam rolls her eyes.

Kelly scowls in her direction.

"I'm sorry, but he was always kind of an ass. And you are better off without him!" Anam throws her hands up in the air.

"No argument there." An awkward little laugh breaking through my tears. "I was so stupid to date him."

"No. You weren't." Kelly says quietly.

"We've all dated the wrong guy before." Bailey pipes up.

"I'm sorry you had to come to my rescue." I try to stop my voice from cracking. "I'm ruining the evening."

They shouldn't have to be here for me.

"Oh, Piper. No, sweetie. You aren't, he did." Bailey shakes her head. "Can we do anything?"

"I'm fine." I smile, although I know it isn't convincing. "I'm okay. I just didn't expect to see him tonight." I end my sentence with a broken sob that turns into a hiccup. I can't help but laughing at the sound.

Anam bites her lip, trying to hide her amusement, and then she hugs me.

"Why don't I give you a ride home?" Bailey offers.

"I can order a ride." I hold up my phone.

"No. Don't be silly. Sacha gave me his driver for the evening. It's pointless if I don't even get drunk tonight." She takes my hand. "And I'm not sending you home in some stranger's car."

I let her take me. She smartly doesn't try to make small talk on our way to my apartment, and she drops me off and waits for me to get inside. I can't help checking the rooftops, one more time, for a familiar shadow again—still nothing. I can't stand the idea of being alone tonight.

25
PONTIUS

Piper: Where are you?

I stare at the message on my phone. My chest squeezes. She's messaging me. She's contacting me!

Me: I'm at home.

Piper: Really? Prove it.

I snap a quick selfie with my apartment visible in the background and send it to her.

Piper: Doesn't prove anything. Take a photo with a spoon on your head.

I grin at the message, walk over to my kitchen, pull a wooden spoon out of the drawer, and take a selfie with it on my head.

Piper: You could have taken that any time. Use a metal spoon.

I grin wider, pull out a metal spoon, and take another selfie for her.

The response dots pop up immediately. My heart flutters. I don't know exactly what this means, but she's speaking to me. We are becoming friends. Me and my mate.

Piper: One spoon on your head and two forks left hand.

Me: My left or your left?

Dots blip past.

Piper: Yours.

Piper: Dummy.

I snicker and do what she requested, sending a fourth selfie.

The dots blink at me for what feels like an hour, so I take the initiative.

Me: Any reason for this quest?

Piper: I thought I saw you earlier tonight.

And then before I can respond...

Piper: Can I call you?

Me: Of course.

"Hello?" I pick up the phone on the first ring, too excited to even pretend to play it cool. Why is she calling me? Why tonight?

"Where were you tonight? For real?" She sniffs into the other end of the phone, and my chest tightens. She is crying. Who hurt her? How can I ruin their lives? Hack into their computers and corrupt all their hard drives? Have all their devices regularly forget their Wi-Fi password so they have to log back in every day?

"I'm at home. I have been all evening. What's wrong, Piper?"

"Okay, okay. Thank you." Her voice cracks.

"Piper, are you alright?" I ask. "Where are you? Are you safe?"

There is another little sniffle on the other end of the phone.

"Please," I add. "Piper. Tell me."

"I'm okay. Everything is fine. I'm...I'm at home. I just thought I saw—" She cuts herself off.

"Saw what?"

"Saw you." She sniffs and then laughs.

"That made you cry?"

"No. That's about someone else," she says very quietly.

"Why are you crying? Who upset you? Are you safe?"

"I ran into Colin."

"Your ex?" My whole body feels hot.

"He's back in town and—"

"And what?" Red fills my vision. I'll kill him. I'll snatch him off the street, fly out to the ocean, and drop him three miles from the shore. "What did he do to you?"

"Nothing," she mutters. "It's okay. I'm safe."

"Then why are you crying?" I release a breath, trying to calm my racing pulse. "Did he make you cry?"

"We just had an argument. He said a few things that upset me." There's a soft noise on the other side of the phone, like blankets being adjusted.

"I'll kill him for you."

She laughs. Is that permission?

"What did he want?"

"It was weird. He wanted the stuff he left in my apartment back," she says, "but he put that in storage months ago."

"Ah."

"What?"

"That's my fault," I admit.

"Ant, what the crap are you talking about?" She laughs.

"I put his things in storage."

"What?"

"I sent the storage company to your house. I've been paying for temperature-controlled storage for his things. I didn't like that it was in your home, bothering you." I pause. There's only silence on the other end of the line. "I did have a key sent to him in New York."

There's a sharp intake of breath on the other end of the phone. I've ruined everything. She's going to tell me off; insult me.

Her laughter breaks through the phone speaker. That loud, open-throated, full-body laugh that makes me want to bury myself in her.

"Ant. That is absolutely hilarious." She presses the words out through her gasping giggles.

"I was worried you would be mad," I admit.

"No. No." Her laughing finally subsides. "Fuck him," she says quietly, but I can almost hear the embarrassment in her voice. I can imagine the pink creeping up her cheeks.

"Fuck him," I respond, certain she can hear the smile in my own voice. "Are you really okay?"

"I'm fine. It's fine. My friends took care of him. It was kind of embarrassing. Anam and Bailey had to step in."

"That's not embarrassing, your friends care about you."

"Hmph," she disagrees.

"Don't roll your eyes at me," I growl.

"You can't even see me." She laughs lightly. I love the sound.

"Are Anam and Bailey still there?"

"No. I'm alone. I think."

"You think?"

"I kinda thought I saw you tonight. Watching me."

"I'm not. I haven't."

"It's okay. I kinda..." Her voice trails off to nothing.

"Kind of what?" I swallow hard.

"It made me feel a little better. The idea that you cared."

"I do care. I can be there in five minutes—"

"No. Maybe. Crap. No!" she repeats with a gorgeous little laugh. "I don't want you here. But, it's nice to hear your voice."

"It's nice to hear yours too," I say. "I really am sorry."

"For what?" she asks idly.

"That I upset you, before, when I followed you. I didn't consider it stalking. But it was wrong of me. I'm sorry if I scared you."

"I know you are." She's quiet, her breathing growing more even.

"I caved to my baser Mothman instincts. I shouldn't have let them win."

She takes a deep breath, so I continue.

"I just wanted to know more about you. To know who you were and what you were doing. To know everything about you. But, I haven't followed you anywhere since you told me to stop after our first weekend together."

"Never?" she sounds incredulous. "Not even once?"

"No. Of course not."

"Huh." She laughs. "I guess I'm not used to men respecting my boundaries."

"I'm sorry for that too, Piper." I pause so I can listen to her gentle breathing. She sounds much calmer now. "Do you feel better? Is there anything else I can do for you?"

"Will you just—" Her voice is strained. "Will you talk to me for a little while?"

"Of course. What do you want me to say?"

"What have you been doing lately?" The noise on the other end of the phone is like her rolling over.

"I've kept myself busy with work. And my sister's family." Anything that distracts me from thinking about her. "The mothlings are heading back to Canada next week. Sacha and Bailey invited me to their wedding, but I don't know if I'm going to go."

"What?" she asks. "Why not?"

"It's going to be loud and crowded," I say. "I'm not sure they even want me there."

"Of course they want you there."

"I just don't know if I'll be comfortable."

"You're going to regret it if you don't go. You should go, take a date."

"Who would I take?" It's a stupid question. I'm not going to take anyone but her. "No one would want to go with me."

I hear her shifting on the other end of the phone until a string of questions comes out of her in a rush.

"You haven't been dating anyone else? You don't have anyone to take?"

"If I said yes, would you come over and try to stop me?"

She grunts in irritation.

"No, I haven't been dating."

"Just promise me you won't get back with Tiffany." There's a sneer in her voice.

"Why are you thinking about Tiffany?"

"I met her today. Ant, she was just awful. You can do better than that. You deserve someone who—"

I swallow hard. "Someone who what?"

"Respects you."

My chest squeezes. "Thank you, Piper. For respecting me."

There's a long pause before she talks again. "Would you like me to go with you?"

"We can go anywhere you like," I joke.

"To the wedding. I could go with you, if it will help you feel comfortable."

My stomach does a swoop.

"If the crowd is too big, or it's too bright, or too noisy, we can leave," she assures me. "We'll bring your sunglasses and earplugs if you want, and—"

I cannot stop smiling. "You'd do that for me?"

"Of course," she says with a little laugh. "Why wouldn't I? We're friends."

"Right. Of course. We're friends," I repeat. The word stabs at me, but Ness was right. This small contact is so much better than never speaking to her, or seeing her.

"Yes, friends," she mutters. I hear her shifting in the bed. Alone. Curled under her covers. Warm and soft.

I cannot stop the purr caught in my throat.

"Hmph." She makes a strange noise on the other side of the phone.

"What are you doing right now?" I ask.

"Just lying in bed. Trying to sleep," she replies. "I can't sleep when you purr like that." Her voice goes breathy.

"Do you want me to stop?"

"God no."

I settle into my office chair, making the noise again, letting my chest rumble.

"I could listen to that sound all day. It's almost like ASMR, but—" she murmurs, on the edge of sleep, or maybe something else.

My rumble deepens, and she releases a small gasp. Yes. That is what I wanted to hear, she's far from sleep.

I pause my purr. "But what?"

She groans.

"What?" I pester, leaning forward in my chair. I can feel she's about to say something amazing.

"Ugh. It's hot, alright? It's sexy! It's really really nice to listen to," she grumbles.

I'm grinning as I let another purr rumble through my chest for her. I hear her sigh and shift on her bed. I rub my palm across my heated groin. A growing need to touch myself.

She makes a strangled noise.

"Is something wrong?"

"Ant. I don't want you to think this means anything."

"What would it mean?" I ask, cupping my own slit. My cock strains behind it, longing to emerge.

"I just wondered if you would help me with something."

"What's that, my flame?"

"I... haven't been able to come since we were together," she confesses. I suck in a breath.

"That must be really frustrating." A small part of me preens at her admission.

"It is. Believe me. I've tried. A lot. The only times I have was—" She stops herself from speaking.

I need to hear the end of this sentence so badly. "Was when?"

"When I pretended you were outside my window. Watching me."

Fuck. My dick shoots out in one fast swoop, into my waiting grip. Another purr rumbles deep in my chest, I couldn't stop the noise now if I tried. She makes another soft moan on her side of the phone.

"Fuck, baby girl. That's hot."

She lets out one of her sexy little giggles.

"I can help you," I tell her. "If that's what you need right now. Friends help each other with things, right?"

"Right," she agrees easily.

"What are you wearing?"

"Nothing," she mutters. "I mean, clothes of course."

"A shirt?" I ask.

"Tank top."

I reward her with a louder purr.

"No bra," she murmurs. I can picture her now, spread across the bed. The slopes of her full breasts, her nipples puckering at the thin fabric of the shirt. Fuck. One hand tracing lazily across her stomach down to—

"Underwear?" The rumble settles deep in my chest.

"Big baggy granny panties," she says, but I hear the giggle in her voice.

"That's a lie," I say, slowly stroking my cock.

"It is," she admits with a little laugh. "I'm Pooh Bearing it. No bottoms. Completely bare down there."

I reward her with a deep loud purr and feel justified when I hear her breath hitch.

"Piper," I whisper her name.

"Ant?" she whispers back.

"Are you wet?"

"I don't know." She giggles.

"Why don't you touch yourself and find out?" I resume the warm purr.

She's quiet for a long moment. I worry that I pushed her too far until her voice comes back a little strained.

"Yeah. I'm really wet."

"I bet you are," I whisper. "Are you touching yourself for me?"

"Ant," she says just my name, and my whole body lights up.

"Do you think you could come for me now?"

She makes a soft noise that I can only interpret as an agreement.

"Would you put a couple fingers into that wet pussy?" I purr. She lets out a soft moan. My fist pumps furiously along my shaft. "Will you stroke yourself, for me? Play with your clit?"

She doesn't say anything for a long moment. I just sit with her, letting her listen to my continuous purring. Waiting to find out what else she needs from me.

There's a little whimper on the other end of the phone. So quiet that I barely hear it. It's gorgeous. Not the same noises that she made when she was with me. It's different when you are touching yourself. There's no surprises, nothing to tease or make you gasp.

"How are you doing, beautiful?" I ask. "Are you close? What do you need?"

"I don't know—" She makes more quiet needy noises that make me squeeze my cock harder. "I don't know what I need, Ant."

"What if I was outside your window right now? Looking at you? Watching you put your hands between your legs. If I could see your dark nipples through your tank top. The way your mouth hangs open, those plump lips gasping and begging for me."

"Ant. Please."

I don't think either of us knows what she's begging for. "I'm outside watching, while I stroke myself, my big long dick, wishing you were wrapped around it. Maybe if you are a good girl, and come for me, I'll fly across the street, open your window, sneak into your room, and fuck you into that mattress."

"Yes. Yes. Ant." She's gasping now, her voice strained and broken.

"Come for me, baby girl." I purr deep and long, my own pleasure half forgotten. At this point, all I can think about is her needs. Her desires. "You are going to come for me as many times as you can, and then, I'll be at your side, using you, taking your body. Making it mine. Sliding into you and filling you up with my cum."

"Fuck. Fuck. Fuck." She's whispering, her voice shattered and broken. I hear when she falls apart. The break in her gasps let me know she's reaching her climax. I speed up my own strokes, trying to meet her. "Fuck. I—"

A strangled noise that contains my name spills through the phone, and a breath later, my own cum splashes across the bottom of my desk.

"Wow. Ant. That was—did you?" She doesn't finish her question, and she doesn't need to. Her breathing slows to a more regular pace, but all of her words remain monosyllabic.

"Yes." I purr for her, wishing it was my hand, or my mouth, or my cock that made her come. I'm okay if it's just my voice.

"Oh my god, Ant. I really needed that."

"Any time, beautiful."

"Oh yeah?" She laughs. It's such a perfect sound, I love hearing it from her.

"Yes. You need to fix this orgasm problem. Human women are already having tragically few orgasms. If you need to call me to get off, that's okay."

She laughs again. "I wish it were that simple."

"It can be," I tell her. "If you want it to be. At least until you figure out how to come without me."

I hate even saying that, but I mean it. As long as she's happy. I'd rather she call me and break my heart every day than turn to another male.

"Okay," she says quietly. "Maybe I'll take you up on that."

26

PIPER

as it stupid to have phone sex with the guy I'm trying to avoid? Maybe.

Do I regret it? No.

I just can't help it when he purrs like that or says my name in the middle of a dirty little epithet. I try to just pretend it never happened. Even when I pass him at work and remember his offer to help me come again.

Ant doesn't mention it. I almost wonder if it didn't mean anything to him. Except that I constantly catch him staring at me.

We start texting more often—trading memes about our favorite Zelda games and playlists full of nerdy songs. He offers to kill Colin for me at least once per week. I laugh them off, but I'm not completely sure he's joking.

One Thursday, we happen to meet in the hallway at work and end up having lunch together. When I complain that my schedule has made work hours last late into the evening, Ant starts asking me every night if I've eaten. If I say no, or don't answer quickly enough, a green curry from Thai Me Down arrives at my front door. The first time it happens, I almost cry with appreciation. The fourth time I tell him I have too many leftovers already.

He sends egg rolls as an apology.

A couple of weeks later I finally go back to Moonshine. It's really nice to return to my favorite little bar. Anam, Kelly, and Bailey meet me for a drink one Saturday night. I'm nervous at first but then I spot Ant across the room and wave. He stops by to say a quick hello, then pays all of our tabs without telling us.

I have to stop sending him links to things I find online and think are cool, because those things start to show up at my front door too. A woman only needs one Snorlax-shaped bean bag chair.

> Me: Why did you buy this for me?

> Ant: Is it the wrong one? Do you want me to send it back?

> Me: No! I love him!

> Ant: Good! As long as you are happy.

He's sweet and kind and a bit obsessive. The same guy that I spent a whole weekend falling for. My brain catches on a memory of something Tiffany said.

> Me: You don't have to buy me things.

> Ant: I like buying you things.

> Me: Okay. But it isn't necessary to get me to like you. We're friends. Right?

> Ant: Yes, of course we're friends!

> Me: I like my friends. I don't need bribes.

Friends with benefits, I guess. We did agree to remain friends, but an evil little inkling hits me. I chew on a thumbnail, plotting my next move.

> Me: Let's practice, then. I'll send you a link to something that I think is really cool, and you won't get it for me.

> Ant: I won't?

> Me: Promise that you won't.

> Ant: Yes. I promise.

> Me: Okay, whatever you do, don't buy me this.

I already know the perfect item. I send him a link to a sexy little lingerie set. It's yellow mesh, with little daisies embroidered in very strategic places.

The little dots pop up. I grin, watching him try to decide what response to type. I break the silence myself.

> Me: Don't order it.

I end up chewing my thumbnail down to the quick while I nervously watch his dots blinking before he replies.

> Ant: It would look really good on you, though.

> Me: Yes. It would.

Ant: But, what will you wear if I don't?

I snicker to my empty bedroom.

Me: I guess I'll be wearing nothing at all?

The dots appear instantly. This time, I don't wait for him to decide how to reply.

Me: Good night! I'm heading to bed.

I put my phone on silent and bury it in my nightstand drawer before I even see if he writes back.

Everything seems really great, sweet, easy, simple. We haven't done anything but flirt since the evening we had phone sex. Until one Monday I'm called into Loch's office for a meeting. It's not uncommon for us to discuss the company prospects, so I'm not suspicious until I arrive at his office. The curtains are drawn and the lights are turned down low.

It's not the way that Loch usually operates. I bite the inside of my cheek when I spot Ant standing in the corner. We have reached a quiet complacency at work, no public displays of affection. But, I don't know how much the other two board members in the room know about our relationship. Sacha and Loch are wearing the same serious expression.

"Thank you for coming, Ms. Hamilton. I hope you don't mind the lights. Pontius has a hard time with—"

"I know." I swallow hard. Has he told his friends that we've been getting closer? That we had phone sex, and flirt regularly? "It gives him headaches."

Loch glances at Ant but speaks to me. "Would you like to take a seat, Ms. Hamilton?"

"I don't want you to worry about anything we ask you today," Sacha says.

I settle into the chair. If they start discussing our relationship, I'm going to squash Ant like a bug. "Why would I worry?"

"We've already spoken with our lawyers," he continues. "Please know, we'll believe whatever you say on this matter."

"What does that mean?" I purposely do not look at Ant. I might actually kill him.

"Cryptech received a letter this morning pertaining to your company," Loch says.

"A letter?" This throws me for a loop. "About what?"

"It accused you of using stolen code."

I laugh very loudly, but the other faces in the room stay serious. My chuckling slows to a stop.

"Who would even say something like that?" I demand.

"Colin Thompson." Loch taps a folder spread open on his desk.

I'm on my feet, reaching for the paper before Loch's finished saying the name. "What did that motherfucker do? I swear to god. I'll kill him." I stop myself, resting both palms against the cool glass surface. "I'm sorry. That was hyperbole, obviously. I don't wish him any harm. If that matters. Legally, I mean." A nervous laugh bubbles up. I feel like I might actually be sick to my stomach.

Sacha gives half of a grin. "It's okay. Believe me, we understand your frustration, Ms. Hamilton."

My phone buzzes in my pocket. I ignore it.

"Do you know Colin?" Loch asks.

"I didn't take anything from him. He's never touched my freaking code." I manage to pull away from the desk, but I'm too nervous to sit back down. "He's an ex-boyfriend."

"Would he ever have had access to your computer?" Ant asks from the corner of the room.

I wince a little at the sound of his voice. It's the first thing he's said since I walked in the room. I want him either much further away from me or much much closer.

"No, of course not," I snap. "I mean, yes, technically, when we lived together. My laptop was in our apartment all the time and—" My gaze flicks between the males in the room. "But he never even touched it! I never touched anything!"

"He knew your passwords?" Ant speaks again. I finally look at him. Really look at him, nearly invisible in the dark corner in a black suit. His bright red eyes mark his location. "He could have gotten on your computer without you knowing?"

"Well—sure. Technically, yes, probably." Crap. I'm nervous saying this in front of the Mothman. I don't want him to think anything is going on between me and Colin. "But he didn't!"

"Do you know why he might be choosing to retaliate now?" Loch turns the papers on his desk around so they are the correct orientation for me to read.

"He—" I pause to look at Ant before I pick up the stack of papers and leaf through them while I pace the room. I should have told him everything the night it happened. Now it seems like I was trying to hide it.

"He—what?" Ant's voice hits a low tone.

"I ran into him a couple weeks ago. He asked if I would take him back. Like, romantically." I try to ignore my impulse to look at Ant again, waiting for any kind of response from the other two males in the room. Searching for an indication that they know what occurred that weekend. But if Ant does kiss and tell, then these two men are excellent at keeping it out of their expression.

"You turned him down?" Sacha asks.

"Yes! Of course, I fucking turned him down! I never want to see that ass—" I stop myself, that awkward nervous laugh boiling out of me in place of the rage. "I'm sorry, I'm sorry."

"Piper. It's okay. They believe you," Ant says. "We believe you. We just need to know any facts you think would help in this situation."

"I don't know," I say. "Yes, he's a programmer too, but we never worked on projects together." I can't stop my feet from pacing the room. "Sure, we tried working on things together a couple times, but they never panned out. Never got out of the planning stages really." I flip back and forth between the pages of the document, so frustrated that the words start to go wobbly as my eyes fill with tears.

Fuck him. Fuck Colin. Of course he would do something like this. He's an asshole. Who's bad in bed. And he's going to try and fuck up my life because what? Because he left me and I wouldn't take him back?

"Piper." Ant's voice is right beside me. When I finally look up from the folder he's standing between me and the other two Cryptids. His beautiful wings spread enough that I'm blocked from Loch and Sacha's vision. "It's alright. We'll take care of it. We can make it all go away."

"No. It's my fault," I manage to say, "I'll fix it myself."

The Mothman shakes his head, one of his hands raises tentatively to stroke his knuckle along my arm.

"Sor—ry," I say again. This time my voice cracks, and I turn my head away, trying to hide the tears from them. How embarrassing to cry at work. In front of everyone.

"Loch and I will talk to the lawyers." Sacha's voice is already near the door.

"Take a moment. We'll let you know anything important we find out." Loch lumbers after him.

Ant stays where he is. His hand drops to his side. His large red eyes are soft.

"Would you like to be alone?" he asks. "Can I get you any—"

I don't let him finish. I throw myself into him, pressing my face into the soft vanilla scent of his shirt and letting it muffle my sob.

"Piper?" His question is quiet.

"Hug me, you idiot."

His arms circle me, holding me close. Pressing me against him. Solid and comforting, I manage to choke out a ragged calming breath.

"There, there, my girl," Ant murmurs. "We'll get this all sorted out. You don't have to do this alone."

I want to protest that I am not his girl, but one of Ant's hands strokes along my back, and then he begins to purr. The gentle rhythmic vibrations have me pushing myself further into him.

All of that helps. Soon, I'm breathing much easier all wrapped up in him. I'd almost forgotten how easy it is to be in his arms. I could let him hold me like this for hours.

My phone buzzes in my pocket again. I ignore it. Whoever it is can wait.

27

PONTIUS

deepen my purr, and she practically melts into my grasp until I am almost taking her full weight in my arms. I take advantage of how close she is to suck in her scent. I can't stand seeing her upset like this. I would do anything to fix it.

She turns her face to the ground. She's breathing heavily, and I can smell her growing arousal.

"Are you feeling better?" I ask. "What can I do?"

"Nothing," she mutters.

"I want you to have everything you want, Piper. I would give you anything you asked for."

"I don't like asking for things." She shakes her head.

"Then let me give you the entire world."

I dip my face closer to her bright red hair, to smell her better.

Her hands go to my arms, grabbing my biceps firmly. She enjoys touching me. She smells so good, warm, and welcoming. I remember the way her cunt tasted. The nectar she made for me. I can smell it dripping from her now. Just being in my arms is enough for her.

I feel the same way. I've missed holding her. The mating bond has my cock straining at my seam every time

I smell her. I need her. I want to make her feel better.

I dip my head down, letting my antennae caress her face. She's so soft, so sweet, so warm. An unintentional purr rumbles through my chest.

She makes an unmistakable moan beneath me.

"Are you still having trouble coming, Piper?" My voice comes out rough.

"We shouldn't," she whispers, but her fingers clutch me close.

"But, you're going to let me, aren't you?" I ask. "You are going to be a good girl, and come on my fingers?"

"Ant." Her voice sweet and needy.

I kiss her, long and hard. It's the first time I've done it in months. The first time we've physically been this close since our first nights together. She kisses me back instantly, eager and hungry and tasting slightly of tears. She's missed me too, I can feel it in her mouth.

I slip a hand down to her waist, tugging at the button on her pants until I can open them and slip my hand inside. I need to touch her. To feel her. To make her come.

She gasps and presses her face against my chest as my hand drags along the outside of her underwear. The fabric damp against my fingers.

"Wet for me already, baby girl?" I ask, moving my palm up and down her mound, using my fingers to press the fabric between her lips.

She fucking whimpers. Such a pathetic needy noise in the back of her throat. I back her into Ness's desk, so I can prop her ass against it, providing me a better angle to give her pleasure, to enjoy the way she clings to my arms and arches into my body. No woman has ever been like this for me. So hungry, so easy, so malleable.

All of my partners have felt hard, almost robotic, but Piper is different. I feel needed. Wanted. Like she would do anything for me. Every part of me worries I am taking advantage of her, being wanted like this. She's like a drug. It feels like I could do anything I wanted to her. I've had years to dream of things I want to do with a mate. I love bringing her pleasure and I'd do anything to keep pleasuring her. She could ask me to move the moon and I would, just to hear her say my name the way she does.

Her hips roll again, and I dip down to kiss her, claiming her mouth with mine, teasing and sucking her tongue. Pouring all of my desire into her, desperate to feel just how much she means to me.

I slip my hand up to the top of her underwear, tracing my fingers along the textured edge. The lace trim temptation under my fingers. I pause, wanting to keep going, but not sure how to ask.

"Ant," she murmurs my name again—my name, mine—on her perfect lips. The next word out of her mouth has me ready to do anything for her. "Please."

"Fuck, baby girl, you don't need to beg me."

I slip my hand into her underwear, seeking out her wet lips, then moving down until I can press a finger into her. She moans into my chest. I let myself play for a moment, discovering what noises I can pull out of her, looking for ways to make her whimper and moan and gasp. Her hips tilt so she can grind hard against my hand, desperate for a release. I rumble another purr through my chest for her. She whines quietly. I cannot bear to bury the sound with my mouth again, so I latch my tongue onto her sensitive neck, and I grip her thigh with my idle hand. Wrapping it around my hip and tilting her leg to give me better access. She cries out as her head tips back, and her hips change to an erratic rhythm, until I finally feel her body clenching around me as she orgasms.

Her hands cling desperately to me. I catch her before she comes down from her orgasm, rubbing my thumb across her clit and pressing against her until she comes again with a small yelp. Her inner walls spasming and milking my fingers, and she finally slumps forward, boneless and easy against my shoulder. Completely relaxed after quick and dirty stress relief. I purr deep in my chest, I gave her something at least—something she really needed. Really wanted.

I pull my hand out, and she watches me with half-glazed eyes while I put my wet fingers into my mouth and suck her sweet nectar from my knuckles. I missed the way she tasted, salty and tart. I could never get enough of this. She chuckles, and her hand sweeps up to cup my cheek, her hand cradling my mouth arms. She doesn't say anything, but I enjoy the way she watches me.

The silence is broken by a printer warming up in the distance.

"Oh crap!" She whisper-yells and then slaps a hand over her mouth.

"What is it?" I brush a red curl out of her face. What if she's changed her mind about what we just did?

"I completely forgot we are in an office and people can hear what we are doing." Her words are muffled by the hand that she still has covering her mouth. "They absolutely know that I'm in here fucking my boss."

"I don't mind people knowing that you are mine." I stroke my fingers through her hair. Her phone vibrates, indicating a message. And then another message. And then three more in quick succession.

"Ant. I don't belong to—" She stops herself from talking when her phone buzzes again, pulling away from me gently. "Let me go." Her voice tinged with irritation.

I move, so she can climb to her feet, but I don't take my hands off her completely, letting one rest on her shoulder. She rearranges her clothing and takes a deep breath as she pulls out her phone.

"Oh no." Her eyes go wide, staring at the screen. "Ant. I have to go. My sister is—in the hospital."

"Is everything alright?" My wings splay out behind me. I've only had a sister for a few months, and already I can't imagine what I would do if something happened to her.

"She's pregnant. She's having the baby." Her face contorts, her voice getting louder the longer she talks. "She's early. It shouldn't be happening yet. She wasn't due for another two weeks. Oh my goodness, I'm terrible. I should be there. I should be there for her. It's her first kid. She's my baby sister."

Her fingers fly across her phone in a rapid flurry, her feet already taking her around the room in a nervous pace.

"She's at St. Augustine. It's all the way across town." She gnaws at the corner of her thumb. "I should go. I should go right now." She's muttering without any real concern if I hear her. "This time of day, rush hour, it'll take me almost an hour to get there—"

"You shouldn't be driving right now," I say.

"Well, I don't have much of an option, do I?" she snaps.

"Let me take you. I can fly you there."

Her eyes dart up from her phone. "You'd do that?"

"Of course!" My hands flex at my sides, eager to touch her. "Anything for—a friend."

She gives me a worried smile and turns back to

her phone. Her fingers resume typing before she finally looks back up at me.

"Okay. We have to go right now, though."

"Alright." I nod, and her shoulders finally relax a fraction. My perfect mate. I will keep her safe and happy.

28
PIPER

I t's only a few short minutes until Ant has me wrapped in his arms as we fly above the packed city streets. He is traveling much faster than the last time he carried me. We are easily overcoming the rush hour traffic. The harsh spring air hits my cheeks and I press my face into his neck ruffle, breathing in his calming vanilla scent.

Everything will be fine. I know. It will be fine. Penny is healthy and young. She'll be okay. She has to be.

I just didn't expect this now, today, and I ignored the texts so I could get finger banged in the office. I am such an idiot.

I squeeze Ant just a little bit harder and his arms tighten around me in return. Somehow, he seems to know exactly what I need to feel better. A hug, or an orgasm on someone else's desk.

When we get to the hospital, I regret having to leave his arms. I try to ignore that feeling. I don't have time to think about how I'm probably falling in love with this Mothman. Right now, I am focused on my sister and her baby.

"Mom!" I run to hug her first. Then my dad the second I spot them in the waiting room. "Mom, how are they? Is Penny okay? The baby?"

"Oh sweetie, she's fine. She's just a little early," Mom reassures me. "Michael is with Penny. She's doing great. Everything is okay."

I nod, taking a deep breath to push back my tears.

"Michael will let us know any new information, but they aren't having more people in the room right now," Dad finishes.

"Who's your escort?" Mom asks in a voice that isn't nearly low enough for Ant not to hear.

The Mothman is standing near the door, his antennae low against his head, shielding out some of the harsh hospital lighting. His shoulders are high near his ears. A very strained smile plastered on his strange features. In his dark, tailored suit, and purple tie, with Tetris patterned socks peeking out of his pant legs, he looks handsome. I barely had time to notice just how handsome he looks before now.

"He's a friend, Mom. He gave me a ride to the hospital."

"Just a friend?" she asks with a sly smile. "Invite him over here."

"Mom. We're here for Penny."

"Penny is fine, dear. Introduce us to your gentleman friend."

I glance over my shoulder at Ant. He stands patient and firm near the door.

"Hello, dear!" Mom waves at him over my shoulder.

"Mom, please don't." I roll my eyes, but Mom coos and motions him over.

Ant sheepishly approaches us. I'd be scared to disobey her right now as well. Her red hair may be fading to gray, she may barely reach five foot two, but she has the air of a woman capable of browbeating you into doing whatever she asks.

I don't really mind my family meeting Ant, until my father shakes his hand and I'm reminded where those long dark fingers were less than an hour ago.

I laugh at the thought, and then have to put my hand over my mouth to stop it from continuing. Mom shoots me a glare that promises consequences if I don't contain myself.

I manage to squash down the noise. Thirty minutes pass and my brother shows up. Twenty minutes after that, when it is obvious that my mother is getting on my nerves, Ant volunteers the two of us for a snack run. He walks me to the vending machine, where he immediately spends way too much money.

"I told you." I take a third bag of chips from his hands. "I already like you. You don't have to buy me things."

"Yes, but this is so your family will like me," he says with a boyish grin.

"My mother clearly adores you," I point out. "And Dad will love you if you bring up your vintage game collection. Paul will just be happy that there's another man in the family. And Penny, well, Penny will like you if you like Penny. And you'll like Penny. She's the most likable person I've ever known."

"Very important information." Ant leans toward me to whisper conspiratorially into my ear, making my heart do a cute little somersault. "What I've learned here is, you want your family to like me."

"You just said you wanted them to like you!" I protest with a laugh.

"Yes, but it's important to you that they like me." He leans just a little bit closer, and I think, for a moment, that he's going to kiss me again, in the middle of this hospital, in front of the vending machines. It shouldn't be romantic at all. But we are well past the friendship stage, or even the friends with benefits stage. I like him more with every passing moment.

"Piper?" Mom calls as she rounds the corner. Ant smoothly turns away from me, handing my mother a bag of chips as he makes his way back to my family.

"He seems really nice." Mom takes one of the bottles of water from my armload.

"He can be."

"How long have you two been together?"

"He's just a friend."

She shakes her head like she's disagreeing with me. "No. He's really into you. Mother's have an intuition about this. You can trust me."

I bite my lip to stop from laughing. This isn't something I need a mother's intuition for. "We are keeping it firmly in the friend category, for now."

"For now," Mom repeats the phrase very seriously as she opens her bottle of water. "How does he feel about kids? Have you asked him?"

"Mom!" I scold her quietly as we return to our group, Ant is chatting very friendly with my father and my brother. Maybe I shouldn't be encouraging this. Not if I'm unsure about the relationship.

Am I unsure? I think I'm unsure about being unsure.

Ant smiles at me. I get a little more sure.

Penny, has an uncomplicated delivery. Except for the slightly early labor, everything goes as smoothly as it could. A bouncing baby girl is born. Presley has ten fingers and ten toes, and is the most beautiful thing I've ever seen in my life.

I get to hold her for a moment that is entirely too brief. She's tiny and perfect. She smells so good—exactly the way that new babies do. It's a moment that is only overshadowed by the memories of holding my other nieces the days they were born. Getting to meet her when she's brand new is incomparable. A chance to hold her and whisper that I will love her forever, even if she grows up and becomes something terrible like a used car salesman, or a meter maid.

I want one. Just like her. Even if it becomes a televangelist.

I wonder what would happen if I had a baby with Ant. Would an egg come out? Or something else? Human? Or adorable little mothlings like his niblings?

When visiting hours are over, and we are finally forced to leave my tiny, perfect niece, we step into an unexpectedly drizzly evening. Without a word, Ant removes his suit jacket and drapes it around me. When the fabric hits my shoulders, I realize it wouldn't matter what our offspring might look like. I am sure that I would enjoy having them.

29
PIPER

nt flies me home in the dark. Floating above the streetlights, the darkness surrounds us. I trust him completely to navigate, not just because I know his night vision is excellent. I know he would do anything to keep me safe. By the time we get to my front stoop, my damp hair has gone from 'frizzy' to sticking to my skin.

Ant sets me down gently. I'm still wrapped in his jacket. My stomach sinks as his hands release me. I don't want him to leave.

"Are you okay?" he asks.

I nod. "I'm happy. So glad I got to meet Presley. I'm just relieved everything went so well. Thank you, for everything. For all of it."

"What are friends for?" he asks.

I laugh. His expression doesn't change. It wasn't a joke.

Right, we are just friends. Crap. Even after he fingered me in Loch's office? Even after he met my parents? Even though I'm falling in love with him? Does he not realize?

"Piper." He moves his wings to guard me better from the rain. "Would you like me to stay?"

His voice is so low that I can barely hear him. I avoid the urge to lean in closer. Instead, I wrap my arms a little tighter around myself.

"Stay?" I ask hopefully. He'll barely fit into my tiny bed. Is that where he's planning to spend the night?

"Across the street." He gestures to the rooftop opposite my bedroom window. I laugh again and his antennae tilt toward me.

"Oh," I laugh lightly. "I thought I saw you there once before. Looking through my window. But I think it was just an air conditioner." I end the sentence with another laugh.

"I do bear a striking resemblance to a large metal box." He smiles. "Would you feel better with someone watching over you tonight?"

I'd feel better with him in my bed. "I don't want you to stand outside in the cold rain."

"I don't want your ex bothering you again." His voice hits a dark tone.

"He won't." I don't even convince myself with that sentence. "Maybe stay, just for a little while, until I fall asleep?"

His wings shake in the rain, throwing water droplets everywhere. His shirt is soaked through, plastered to his body. "As you wish."

And in a blink, he swoops away. There's nothing in front of me but a memory of him. Was that a Princess Bride reference? Was he trying to say...

I retreat into my apartment, determined not to think about him standing in the cold rain. Watching me.

I shower until I feel warm again, holding my head under the spray and letting the heat of the water sink into my bones. I move to my bedroom and toss the towel onto a hook on the back of my door. Then I freeze. My curtains are wide open.

Crap. What is wrong with me? I've got to remember to close my curtains. Even if the idea of him seeing me is a bit exciting.

Is he still there? I start to reach for the towel and stop myself. A glance at the window shows that there is a shadow. A figure standing on top of the building across the street, watching me with a pair of glowing red eyes, drinking in my naked body.

I swallow hard, then cross to the window, still naked, and reach up to the lock, very pointedly unlatch the window, and crack it open. The noise of the rain is more prominent in my bedroom now. I stretch my arms high over my head. Putting my body on display.

Ant's shadow doesn't move.

I spread myself across the bed and reach for my vibrator. I'm just going to do what I would do any night of the week, I justify to myself. Any time I couldn't sleep, I'd pull out Old Faithful, turn her on, slip her between my thighs, and find that perfect spot with just the right setting that makes my whole body light up. I allow my thoughts to drift to dark fur, wide-spread wings, and a deep purr. I tilt my hips, increasing the speed.

I know he can see me. He can look if he wants. My big beautiful Mothman.

The sound of the rain gets louder, and there's a creak of wood and plastic. I chance to open my eyes, just as Ant slips into my bedroom.

The sight of him steals my breath. So tall he barely fits into my room. His wings cannot spread all the way open, and the tops of them almost brush the ceiling. Water drips across my dark carpet and second hand furniture. His suit is gone. He's wet and naked, just like me.

"Piper, what do you think you are doing?" His voice hits a low register that sends chills through me.

I groan at the sound of him. He stalks across the room, like a predator. The feeling of him in my room, wanting me, is oddly soothing.

His large hand lands on top of mine, his fingers wrap around my whole hand, guiding the tool between my legs.

"What do you think you are doing?" he repeats. "Showing off like this? Showing off my sweet pussy?" He moves his wrist, tilting the vibrator to angle it slightly differently. I am already so close, so primed and ready. "Anyone could have seen you. Anyone could have crept in here."

I'm fighting the urge to giggle, and the noise comes out more like a moan instead.

Ant releases a low purr and moves so that more of his body is over top of mine, bracing one hand above me on the headboard.

"You greedy woman. You want all the fun for yourself. Who said that you could show off like this? Those tempting tits. Those luscious thighs. If you wanted to come, all you had to do was call me. If you wanted me in your bedroom, in your cunt, all you had to do was say something."

"Something." I manage to blurt out with a little giggle.

He smirks, and leans back to take me in. My view of him is highlighted by the streetlight through my window.

I shiver. He doesn't touch me anywhere except my wrist that controls the vibrator. He tilts it slightly in one direction, and then the other, changing the pressure until I gasp under him. Something inside me is scared to touch him, to move without instruction. I just wait, letting him take control.

A low purr rumbles through his chest. The noise does something to me every time. My bed creaks as Ant shifts his weight until he is completely over me.

That's when I come. The tightness spreads through my body, my mouth releasing a gaspy little shudder, and my legs clenching together. I start to pull my hand away, but his grip around my wrist tightens.

"Was that it? Do you think that's all you are going to give me?" He moves his hands and my vibrator. "You haven't even said my name. You haven't even told me who you belong to. Say my name, darling. Tell me who is in charge of your pleasure."

"Ant," I breathe.

"Who's pussy is this?" He grins.

"Yours," I choke out.

"And do you think you can come again? For me." He moves my vibrator in a tiny circle, keeping the sensation on my clit, and I gasp. His smile is so wide.

I nod eagerly. Even while his hand works at making me squirm.

"Good girl," he murmurs. "I hope you are ready to work for it."

Then, the vibrator is gone.

"Hey!" I protest with a laugh.

"Laugh all you want, pretty girl. I'm not going anywhere," he growls. "I'm here just for you, and when you are finished, I am going to take what's mine. I'm going to use that perfect pussy anyway I like. Now stick your ass in the air for me."

I laugh again but nod eagerly, and then with deft hands he flips me over. One hand presses gently on my shoulder blades, while the other massages along the curve of my ass until he dips between my thighs, grazing across my pussy with each gentle stroke of my leg.

"Be a good girl for me, Piper. You are going to fuck my fingers until you make yourself come, and then I am going to fill you with my cock."

I shift on the bed, moving my ass up into the air.

"There's my good girl." He slips his fingers easily into my wet pussy, curving inside me to stroke my walls. His thumb moves to graze my clit.

"Now, use me, Piper," he growls. "Grind that sweet pussy on my hand and make yourself cum."

It's so easy to do what he says now, turn off my brain and let him be in control. I move my hips backward against him until the pressure and the roughness of his hand send a delightful spark through me.

"Feel how wet you get for me? How easy it is for me to use you?" He purrs and that only sets me off more.

I can't see him, but I can hear the grin in his voice. I grind my hips against him, the solid comfort of his fingers. He's so good, so warm and solid. I lose myself in the feeling. Letting my thoughts fade and my body take control, slowly at first, and picking up pace as the feelings roll through me. His fingers pound into me, while I moan and drool and mutter his name into the pillows in between profanities. I come at least once, in a powerful flash through my body, but I don't let it stop me, continuing to fuck his hand with aggressive enthusiasm until I can barely breathe.

He finally pulls his hand away with a little growl, leaving a void inside me. I can barely moan in protest before he is wrapping his hands around my hips, jerking them up and back so he can wrap his claspers around me, holding me in place while his aedeagus begins a slow powerful penetration. Filling, and twisting, and pushing his thick heat into me.

"Fuck, Piper." He groans my name over and over while he takes me. His hand wraps around the back of

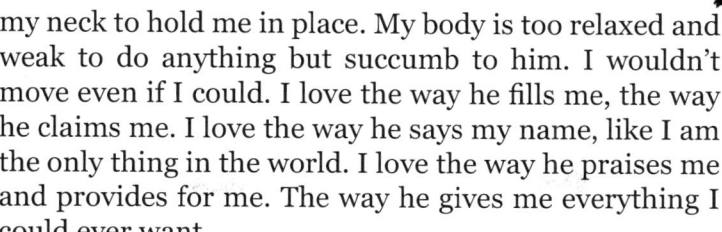
my neck to hold me in place. My body is too relaxed and weak to do anything but succumb to him. I wouldn't move even if I could. I love the way he fills me, the way he claims me. I love the way he says my name, like I am the only thing in the world. I love the way he praises me and provides for me. The way he gives me everything I could ever want.

He comes with a rolling shudder that fills me with heat.

This time, I feel tears prick at the corners of my eyes before he's even pulled out.

I roll into the pillow, trying to hide my face from him.

But Ant's hands wrap around my chin and pull me to look at him.

"My flame," he whispers. His face contorts with concern, his fingers wiping at the corners of my eyes. "What stupid thing have I done wrong this time?"

I shake my head, not wanting to admit I'm only overwhelmed by my own emotions. "It's nothing. I'm tired of being mad at you. I don't want to pretend anymore."

"What are you pretending?"

"That we are just friends. I want—to be more than just friends."

"More than friends?" he asks. "Like what?"

"Like—" I pause, feeling a long strain of conflicting emotions. Everything has gotten so indefinably complicated—the texting, the sex, the presents, the feelings of guilt, like I am taking advantage of his kindness.

"Like—best friends?" he asks with a gentle chuckle.

"Ugh." I push him away playfully.

He grabs my hand and pulls it to his mouth, pressing a little kiss to my knuckles. "What do you want?"

"Just hold me? Please."

"That was never optional." He rolls onto his side so that his wings drape over the edge of my bed, and tucks me into his arms. I push my face into his chest, breathing in his vanilla scent, and letting my fingers play along his wiry muscles. His arms stroke along my back and his gentle purr hits my ears. "What if we went to the wedding next weekend together?"

"Aren't we already going together?" I ask.

"What if I bring my girlfriend?"

"Girlfriend?"

"Yes." He chuckles.

"Do you want to call and ask her?" I tease.

He tugs my face to look at him again. "I think I am asking her right now."

My heart is beating so hard I'm almost embarrassed. I'm sure he can hear it—that he knows exactly how excited and nervous I am right now.

"I can come." I nod.

"Good. I want everyone to see us, together. As a couple." He presses his face to the top of my head. "You were never *just* a friend to me, Piper."

30

PONTIUS

"**Y**ou look beautiful," I say the moment that I think she can hear my words. The sun is low over the horizon and the spring air is crisp and fresh. Clear skies and the perfect weather for Bailey and Sacha's outdoor wedding. I adjust my sunglasses that keep out the fading rays of daylight. I'll be able to walk around comfortably without them once the sun has set.

Piper's face lights up at the compliment as she steps out of her Uber. Her bright red curls are pinned up with little ringlets hanging around her face. She's wearing a pretty yellow dress that highlights her freckled skin and shows off her amazing curves. I cannot wait to take her back to my place and see what's under the dress.

"Thanks." Her cheeks pinken, and she looks at her feet, where the dust of the gravel parking lot settles onto her heeled sandals. "You look nice too," she blurts without looking up.

"Did your shoes tell you that?" I ask.

She glances up with a little scowl between her brows. I take the opportunity to lean in and kiss her. She's mine now. I know it, she admits it, and I'm going to kiss her every chance I get.

"My mom bought me this dress," she tells me when I come up for air. "It's the only thing in my closet nice enough to wear to a fancy wedding like this."

"I could've bought you something new," I offer. "Something you actually want to wear."

The loose curls around her face bounce when she shakes her head. "I'd rather you bought me a new video game, or a new costume for the Renaissance festival, or a VHS copy of Tammy and the T-Rex."

"I can get you all of those things, my flame."

"But you won't, right?" she teases. "You aren't going to buy me every little thing that I ask for."

"I can never buy you anything?" My antennae droop a little. I know what she's said, but it makes me happy to shower her with things that she loves.

"I guess you could put those items into your notes app under a list called 'Presents to Buy Piper for Her Birthday, which is August 3rd'."

"I will be doing that." I grin. She will have the greatest birthday, full of anything and everything she could ever ask for. There are going to be many years for me to shower her with gifts and presents. "Are you ready?"

I reach for her hand, she nods and intertwines her fingers with mine, her eyes shine with the kind of admiration that makes me nervous to disappoint her. It's like the first night we met all over again. We're here tonight, as a couple, and this time everyone will know we are together.

I rarely go to large events. The crowds make me nervous, and the noise gives me a headache, but I couldn't miss this wedding, not when Sacha's been such a huge part of my life for so long. He's my family. I want to be here for him.

With Piper at my side, everything seems a little bit easier; a little more possible. She's so good to me. So kind and accommodating. I want to be good for her in return. Other than buying her things, I'm not entirely sure what that entails.

She smiles up at me, her skin glowy in the afternoon light.

I rest my hand gently on her back.

There. That's boyfriend stuff.

We follow a short trail through tall trees that takes us to the small clearing where the ceremony is taking place. The forest keeps the area shaded and temperate. The crowd isn't small. Humans and cryptids intermingle in every direction, with a lot of Bigfoots in attendance.

Piper finds us seats near the side, away from the majority of the crowd. She makes a point to check if I'm comfortable or overstimulated before we sit down. I casually slip my hand into hers, intertwining our fingers. She clasps my hand tightly and pulls it into her lap.

Yes. This is all definitely boyfriend stuff.

The wedding is perfect. The ceremony starts just before dusk. Bailey wears an elaborate gown covered in embroidered flowers and vines. She fits into the setting perfectly. Sacha cannot take his eyes off his bride the moment she appears.

I've never been to a human wedding before. I know a lot of the customs from TV and movies, but this is the first I've ever attended in person. It's better than I expected. Especially with Piper at my side.

Piper leans against my arm during the ceremony, a wide smile on her face. I wonder if she would want a large wedding like this. I know she has a big family. Would she want them to celebrate with us?

The couple says their vows under an arch of bent tree limbs and vines. Both of them cry. Piper cries even while she smiles. I would cry too, if I had tear ducts, and when Sacha bends down to kiss his new wife, the whole crowd cheers.

This is when we learn that Bigfoots are not quiet partiers. It's not long before food, alcohol, and music appear in excess. A party truly indicative of just how much people love Bailey and Sacha.

"Fancy seeing you here." Ness sidles up beside me.

"I wouldn't miss Sacha's wedding," I say defensively.

"I was speaking to your lovely mate." Ness smirks.

My wings flair before settling back against my shoulders.

"You look beautiful tonight, Ms. Hamilton. Have the two of you finally decided to kiss and make up?" Ness asks.

"Is it any of your business?" Piper's fingers squeeze mine, and she releases an exacerbated sigh.

"Well, you have me to thank for it!" Ness laughs. "It was my meddling that got you here. My advice got you together. My desk where you hooked up."

"Magnes, if you weren't responsible for my employment, I'd call you an ass," Piper mutters.

"I can call him an ass for you," I suggest seriously.

"Would you, darling? It would be very inconvenient for me to lose my job."

"Ness, you're an ass," I announce, and Piper tucks herself closer to me with a wide grin.

Ness laughs, loud and full-throated this time. "You kids enjoy your night!" Then he leans in close to my ear. "I'm glad she finally got you out of the house." Before he turns to find his date—a young woman that I've never seen before and will probably never see again.

The Bigfoots have really started partying. There is a bonfire surrounded by a half-nude dance party and a drum circle. In the shadows beyond are activities that appear to be games and wrestling. The music is a loud, pounding pulse that I can practically feel in my sternum.

Piper watches everything with wide excited eyes.

My heart wants to pull her out into the crowd and grind my body against hers to the beat of the music, but even my earplugs aren't enough to make me comfortable when the volume is this high.

"Are you alright?" Piper seems to sense my discomfort.

I shrug. I know she wants to stay, and I want her to have a nice time.

"Do you want to leave?" she asks. "We can go if you want."

I watch the shadows dance across her face for a moment. Her eyes can't help traveling to the dancing and the merriment.

"I think I'll just step away for a moment." I gesture to a dark path into the woods. "You go and have fun."

"You're sure?" She bites her lip. "You don't want me to come with you?"

I shake my head. "Please. I want you to enjoy yourself. We can meet up in a little while."

She grins. "Alright. If I don't see you in twenty minutes, I'll come find you."

"Take your time." I bend down to kiss her, slipping my tongue briefly into her mouth before I pull back. She tastes like honey.

She steps away from me. My body is cold where her touch left me, but I'm confident she'll be back soon enough; at her place, by my side.

31

PIPER

head into the crowd to make the rounds and say hi to my friends and colleagues. The party is wild, full of strangers and large bodies bumping into each other. Bigfoots play drums and sing in loud guttural voices to a tune that changes and flows, but never really seems to end.

There's something really special about getting lost in a large crowd. The way no one pays attention to you in the press of bodies especially, with pounding music that is so loud you can feel it in every bone.

A hand lands on my shoulder.

"Oh my god! You look amazing!" Bailey throws her arms around me. She's clearly had a few glasses of champagne.

"Me?" I ask with a laugh. "Girl, you look amazing!"

Her dress is layers and layers of cream and white tulle, with tiny flowers and leaves sewn all over it. She looks like a freaking fairy princess. Exactly the type of person who could marry a Bigfoot.

"Can you believe all of this?" she gestures to the wild, intense group of Bigfoots around us. "This is all my family now." She laughs, hugs me again, and kisses me on the cheek. "I'm so glad you are in my life, Piper, and now we are going to be like sisters!"

"Sisters?" I ask.

"Sacha, Ness, and Pontius are basically brothers! And when you two get married, it'll be like we are sisters." She's grinning wild.

"Married? Me?" I ask, not even sure that she can hear me over the music.

"Oh, please tell me you are gonna marry him! Or don't marry him. It doesn't matter! You are here with him! You guys are together now, and it's so great, isn't it? I bet it's great, and I'm sure that sex with a Mothman is nothing like sex with a Bigfoot, but I bet it's still the best you've ever had, isn't it? You know what? Don't answer that. I really don't need any details. Pontius is basically my brother now. I do not need to hear details." She nods emphatically.

"You are drunk," I say with a laugh.

"What?" she yells over the music.

"YOU'RE DRUNK!" I yell much louder.

"YOU HAVE TO COME WITH ME! I NEED YOUR HELP!" She grabs my hands and pulls me after her.

"My help?"

"BRIDE PRIVILEGE! I AM THE BRIDE! YOU HAVE TO COME WITH ME!" She is still yelling even though the music is getting quieter as we leave the bonfire and·drum circle behind.

She leads me down a short forest trail to a little tent decorated with chairs, rugs, pillows, and fairy lights. It's an adorable makeshift bridal suite. There are six other women there. I'm introduced to them all in quick succession and immediately forget everyone's names.

"Drink this." Bailey hands me a glass of champagne.

"And wear this." A woman, Margot, I think, hands me a long white robe.

"What is this?" I ask with a nervous laugh, taking both items. The champagne flute is easy enough to understand, but the robe confuses me. It's silky, edged with lace, but otherwise looks like a bathrobe you could find in any random store.

"Running of the bride," Margot announces. "Love your dress, by the way."

"It's Bigfoot tradition," Bailey adds.

The other women laugh. They all seem to be familiar with each other.

"What does that mean?" I set the glass of champagne to the side, alcohol doesn't seem like a great idea right now.

"Don't worry, it's totally safe." Bailey giggles in a way that isn't very reassuring. "We're going to have so much fun!"

"That doesn't really clarify anything." I laugh.

"You're a decoy," says a woman lounging in an Adirondack chair.

"I still don't understand."

"Put on the robe. When we tell you to run, you run. We're just here to distract Sacha. He has to prove he's worthy of Bailey by chasing and catching his new wife."

"Come here!" A skinny Black woman holds out a flower crown for me. It's not nearly as elaborate as Bailey's. Her's has crystals, large blooms, and bright colors, the one I am handed is made of simple fake daisies.

"I don't think anyone is going to mistake us for each other." I laugh, slipping the white robe over my dress, like the other women are wearing theirs, and placing the crown on my head. I don't compare to Bailey's gorgeous dress or her bright pink hair shining under her fancy flower crown.

"It's just for fun! You all look perfect! Thank you for being here for me!" Bailey tosses back her own glass of champagne and slips her feet into a pair of running shoes. "Come on! Come on! Let's get back to the party!"

She exits the tent, headed back toward the bonfire. The other women follow, so I bring up the rear. The music is still raging, when the other women start dancing I'm happy to join in.[1] Somewhere in the distance, someone blows a loud horn. The drums quiet. My ears are left ringing in the near silence.

"It's time! It's time!" Bailey squeals, grabbing my hands.

"BAILEY!" Sacha's voice comes from far away, near the edge of the forest. "WHERE IS SHE?"

Bailey squeals again and ducks down low in the crowd.

"Is... everything alright?" I ask her.

"Cover me!" she mouths.

She pushes her way through the crowd that parts easily for her. When we get to the edge of the dance party she grabs my hand again.

"Run!" she yells between her giggles and takes off toward the surrounding woods, dragging me behind her until I stumble in my shoes and slip out of her grasp.

I glance behind us. The other women are running too, but in all different directions. Their white robes stand out in the darkness, like fleeting ghosts of distraction.

"WIFE!" Sacha's roar is audible, even from across the field. His gaze focuses on the direction Bailey ran—the path that leads directly past me and only me. He charges in my direction. I duck down the path in the woods that Bailey took. I can't run in these shoes or in

---

1 I'm always ready to make a bit of a fool of myself in the name of good fun.

the near darkness. Somewhere in the distance, I hear Bailey laughing. She has the right footwear. She knows where she is going. She presumably does regular cardio. I'm a panting sweaty mess, and I'm barely inside the tree line, already feeling hopelessly lost.

A roar echoes through the forest.

I freeze in the middle of the path and turn to find a Bigfoot in a tuxedo charging toward me, his pupils blown wide. I'm pretty sure I scream. I don't think Sacha would hurt me, but he's still absolutely terrifying.

A shadow scoops one strong arm around my middle and pulls me sideways off the trail.

Sacha doesn't even pause as he runs past us. Charging forward, very nearly on all fours, toward the white blur that is Bailey's wedding dress in the woods.

My heart is pounding. I grip the arm around my middle and lean back against a familiar chest. I would know this vanilla scent anywhere. Ant presses his face into the top of my head.

I can still see the pale shadow of Bailey's dress when Sacha catches up with her. She laughs as he scoops her up and throws her over his shoulder like a sack of potatoes. She doesn't struggle, just kicks her feet in the air and squeals as he carries her into the darkness.

The arm around my middle tightens.

"Are you alright?" The husky voice in my ear heats my body, his chest warm against my back.

"Yeah. I'm great," I mutter, adrenaline and arousal mixing in my stomach. I'm still breathing hard, but I'm not sure it's from the running anymore. I choke out a nervous laugh. "I gotta start working out."

"What are you wearing?" Ant chuckles. His hand strokes along the wispy white lace of the robe the women gave me.

"It was for the Running of the Brides."

"What is that?"

"What just happened, I think." I laugh.

"Does it—happen at all human weddings?"

I don't have to see his face to know it's an earnest question. "None I've been to before. Apparently it's a Bigfoot tradition."

His chest presses into my back as he releases a long sigh. "So, you won't want me to chase you through the woods on our wedding day?"

My heart skips several beats. "Ant! You are not asking me to marry you right now!"

"Here in the woods? On a beautiful romantic evening?" His hands trace up and down my arms. "No. I would never."

"Good." I laugh. "When you do ask, I want to be embarrassed. Really put on the spot. In public! With a huge audience and a lot of societal pressure to say yes!"

He chuckles and presses a light kiss to my shoulder.

"Are you feeling better?" I ask, leaning back into him. "Getting away from the noise?"

"I am much better now." His hands sneak under the robe to fan his fingers over my stomach. It makes my heart flutter in time with the music I can still faintly hear from the distant party. I can barely hear the drums, so I know it's probably still loud for him.

He dips down to kiss my neck, making me giggle when the heat of his breath tickles my skin.

Goaded by the noise, he explores a little further, slipping his long narrow tongue down my neck and across my chest. His hands pull the shoulder of the robe down until we let the whole thing fall to the forest floor. My dress is lower cut than most things in my closet. It can make me feel exposed, but there are acres of bare skin for him to explore, and I let him.

One of his hands creeps a little lower, tugging at my dress until he finds the slit along the side of my leg. His hand sliding easily under the fabric to grab my bare thigh.

"I really like this dress," he murmurs into my skin.

I chuckle.

"Will you do me a favor?"

"Depends on what you're about to ask," I tease.

"Will you dance with me?" It's such a simple request. Like the night we met.

"Yeah, I like that idea."

"You like the idea very much," he jokes. "I can smell it on you." His hand tightens around me before his arms leave me completely.

I spin around and find him removing his pants.

"Moving a little quick there, aren't we, buster?" I cross my arms under my chest, but I do admire his long legs while he disrobes.

He shakes his head with a grin, dropping his pants, jacket, and shirt in a pile on the ground. His wings spread wide behind him, flapping freely and catching the moonlight in their spectrum.

"Do you feel safe with me?" he asks me seriously.

"With you? My stalker? The guy who crept into my bedroom window to fuck me last week?" I joke, putting my hands on his bare chest.

His hand catches under my chin, tilting my face up to look at him. The sincerity in his smile squeezes my heart. "I don't want you to be scared."

I shake my head. "I feel very safe right now."

"We are going to dance, but I want to be sure you are secure."

"Secure?" I ask.

He nods, wraps a hand around my waist, pulls me in close, then lifts me slightly from the ground, so we are face to face, and his claspers unfold to wrap around my hips, holding me firmly in place, flush against him.

I gasp at the feeling. It isn't technically sexual, but the action sends a flush through my whole body. My feet dangle above the ground, and I can barely move.

"How do you feel now?" His voice is a little heated.

"Very secure." I laugh and loop my arms around his neck.

The leaves on the ground move with a few powerful gusts of his wings before we lift off. We're flying, again.

I laugh. He grins and lifts us a little higher, until we are lost in the limbs of the trees.

Like every other time he's carried me, I know that, logically, there should be fear in my brain, but all wrapped up in him all I feel is safe. There's no chance of being hurt or falling. I know I'll be taken care of, I know he has me.

A gentle rumble echoes through his chest to the same beat as the faint music in the background.

"Now, would you like to dance?" he asks.

I glance up into his eyes, where he's studying me, a contemplative tilt in his antennae.

"Up here?" I ask.

A smile breaks across his face. "Yes."

He waits for me to nod.

My stomach drops as he lifts us even higher. He twists as he flies, swooping us through the air in time to the music, our bodies warm where they are pressed together. I sigh against his chest. The night air is just a little chilly. I almost regret leaving my bridal robe on the ground. Until Ant's hand finds that slit in my dress again. His hand explores my backside this time, my body getting warmer the more he touches me.

Finally, something seems to occur to him. He leans in close to my ear. "You are not wearing any underwear."

"In this dress? I get panty line." I squeal when his hands move to squeeze my mostly naked ass. "Hey. You aren't wearing anything at all!" I point out.

"I'm not." He grins, perfect and strange, his antennae dipping to touch the top of my head.

I move my arms around his neck, tugging his face down to mine so I can press our mouths together.

His tongue dips down into me, building up the heat. I dig my fingers into his mane. There's nothing under me but empty air. There's nothing but him. His hot mouth, his hand on my breast, the purr in his chest, and his warm vanilla scent. I could spend forever in this moment.

He adjusts our position slightly. I realize he's raised my skirt, and his aedeagus presses forward, just a little.

"Ant, someone could see us," I murmur, not making any real move to stop him. We're over the trees, not far enough from the wedding to truly be alone.

"And my little voyeur wouldn't want anyone to see us, would she? You wouldn't want anyone to hear you coming on my cock?" He laughs. "I'm going to fuck you up here, in the air. I'm going to make that pretty cunt cry for me."

I giggle, slightly appalled at the way that being with him makes me want to drop every inhibition I have. I want to give him everything. I don't give a crap who knows that we are fucking up here.

His aedeagus slips along my lips, but he doesn't enter me yet. Instead, he teases the head of his cock against my clit.

I let out a little moan, which he captures with another kiss while his cock continues to play with me, circling my clit and teasing me until I am whimpering his name and squirming to be filled, to be satisfied, to get fucked.

"Ant, I need—" I whisper.

"What do you need, baby girl? You need my cock inside you?"

"Yes." I gasp when he teases my opening, slipping in only partially before sliding back out.

"You need me to fill you up? To take you? Claim your tight little cunt here above the forest, where a whole group of people could hear the way I make you scream?"

"Yes. Yes," I whisper. He dips into me with each agreement. Going a little deeper, a little further, every time until he is filling me completely and my body feels like it might shatter from the pressure.

The first time his aedeagus pulses I break into a thousand pieces, so grateful that he is there to hold me, to literally keep me afloat. Fireworks flash behind my eyes, and I have to throw my face into his collar.

He purrs for me, just for me.

"Fuck yes, good girl," he mutters in my ear, but I can hear the strain in his voice.

"Just do it, Ant. Just use me. Come for me, daddy."

He releases a noise unlike anything I've heard him make before. A screech that no human could ever create. His fingers bury deep into my hair, pulling it tight enough that light pain lances through my scalp. It's like something inside him snaps. His mandibles wrap around my neck, holding me still while his tongue invades my mouth.

His aedeagus slips out of me, leaving a cool void in its absence. I whimper just before it slams back into me, fast and hard. He does this again and again. Fucking me almost like he's lost his humanity.

With our chests pressed tight together and his legs tangled with mine, he feels wholly inhuman and powerful. It feels like every part of him is vibrating, coursing through me, holding me captive. Pinned to him, with my arms trapped at my side, and exposing my body. I'm completely at his mercy. I couldn't move even if I wanted to. Totally vulnerable while he slams his dick in and out of my body.

I'm probably already crying when I come the second time, his grunting body locked to mine when he finally buries himself deep, and with a final terrifying push that makes me jerk my head back from him.

"Mine," he hisses, shuddering as he comes. I feel it filling me, hot splashing against my walls. "Mine," he repeats, shuddering as aftershock roll through him several times before he slowly pulls out of me. The cool breeze highlights where his cum is dripping down the inside of my leg, marking me.

I'm panting, and when I finally start to come back to earth I realize we are very high above the earth. Probably a hundred feet above the treetops, judging by the tiny people below us. The view is beautiful, but looking down pitches my stomach.

"Ant. We are too high." I grab a handful of his fur and press my face into his chest.

"What?" He sounds unaware of his surroundings. "Oh, shit. I am sorry, my flame. Do not worry. I have you."

His arms circle me, tender and sweet. My stomach leaps again, the way it moves when an elevator descends. He is whispering comforting compliments the entire trip, not stopping his sweet ministrations until his feet touch the ground.

His claspers release my hips, but he doesn't set me down.

"Ant?" I murmur tentatively as he rearranges me in his arms. I honestly don't know if I could walk right now.

"You are coming home with me, back to my nest," he whispers into my ear. He holds me with one hand while the other collects the items we left on the forest floor.

I don't protest. He flies me to his house. I haven't been inside it since the first time we met, but everything feels the same. There's a pile of children's toys in the corner of his living room, and hanging by the front door is a familiar painting. It's beautiful—a woman surrounded by flames. I know it wasn't there before because it's Kelly's painting. One from her show.

"You bought this?" I ask.

"Of course," he calls from across the apartment as he throws his armful of clothing into his hamper.

"Why?"

"Besides the obvious, I wanted to support your friend."

"What's the obvious part?" I ask.

He looks at me strangely. "Because it's a painting of you."

"No," I protest. The painting is of a force of nature. That's not me in my knock off Chuck Taylors and the hair that was only half dry when I left the house.

His hand scoops up my chin. He is suddenly very close. "Yes, my flame."

I catch his bright red gaze and feel my cheeks heat.

"You are a force to be reckoned with. Passionate, intelligent, driven, beautiful. I love you, Piper." He smiles when he says it. Like it's the easiest four words in the world.

I laugh awkwardly. Really awkwardly. Right in his face. He doesn't even flinch. If anything, his smile gets a little wider. Stupid. He is so stupid, and patient, and nice.

"Yes. Well..." I say, my face so very hot now. "You are pretty cool too. And I—love you too."

"Do you mean it?" He moves just a little closer. "You don't need to say it if you don't mean it."

"Yes. Yes. Of course I mean it. You are great! Sexy! Smart! Good dick! Nice to kids! Nice to me! You are the complete package! The perfect mate! I love you!" I declare, throwing my hands into the air with a laugh. "Are you happy?"

"Very happy, my flame." He dips in to kiss me, and soon, we are spread across his bed again. We bang two and a half times, before we finally succumb to sleep, curled together in a nest of blankets. I don't remember ever feeling this satisfied or this safe.

32

PIPER

Ant flies me home in the morning, I'd rather stay in bed with him, but I have to feed Mercutio and get some work done even on a Sunday.

It's so early when he places me on my steps that the sun isn't even properly out yet. I fumble to unlock my door, still a bit dick drunk and pleasantly exhausted by the evening we shared. I pause at the threshold to watch Ant's silhouette flit up into the sky. We're meeting later for dinner, and more sex, if I'm lucky. Gosh, he's amazing. Having him in my life again feels so right.

When I step into my entry Mercutio yells at me from the top of the steps.

"Hello, baby boy!" I call. He doesn't move from his comfort crouch at the top of the steps. I start to drop my things beside the door but pause. Something is wrong. Something feels off.

There's a noise in the kitchen. I nearly leap out of my skin. Someone is here? Who the fuck is in my house? I ball my keys in my fist so the prongs are between my fingers like Wolverine's claws. It's probably just my landlord. He's supposed to notify me before he comes in though.[1] Except it's so early that seems highly unlikely.

[1] But we've all had a landlord break that rule, haven't we?

Is something wrong with my apartment? Maybe there was a gas leak, or a plumbing emergency or a—

Colin appears in the kitchen. Crap.

"How did you get in here?" I call down the hallway.

"I have a key." He grins like he's proud of himself.

"Get out of my house."

"It's our house, Piper." His voice soaked with mock concern. "Don't I have every right to be here?"

"Your name isn't on the lease anymore. Get out."

"Where have you been this morning?" He takes a step forward and stumbles into the kitchen door frame.

"Are you drunk?" I ask, finally noticing the mostly empty bottle of rum in his fist. He's still on a bender from last night.

"I called your mom yesterday. She says you're fucking the guy who bought your company." His words wobble when his body does. Mom definitely didn't know that for sure, but she also definitely didn't use those exact words.

"It's none of your business." I realize I should not be engaging him and step out of his path to the door. "I need you to leave."

Colin stumbles a few feet toward me, stopping to steady himself on the staircase banister. At the movement Mercutio abandons his spot at the top of the stairs to flee into my bedroom. His favorite hiding spot is under my bed.

"You are just trying to bang your way to the top." Colin points an angry finger at me. I flinch even though he's several feet away.

"Then I guess I'll be getting a raise any day now." I know I shouldn't be taking the bait, but I can't help myself. "Get out."

"You were with him, weren't you?"

"Fine, I'll be the one who leaves." I reach for the doorknob and pause, thinking of Mercutio. I can't leave him here at Colin's mercy.

I turn back around, finding Colin right in front of me. So close that I can smell the booze on his breath. I used to think he was cute. Tall, trim, sandy blond hair. It's strange what love can do to you, because now all I see is how ugly anger has made his features.

"Just tell me where you've been. Admit, out loud, that you've been fucking someone else." Colin repeats.

"Yes. I was fucking someone else!" I throw my hands into the air. I know it isn't going to help.

"You're a whore." There's venom in his voice.

"Yeah, but I'm not your whore." I roll my eyes and realize it was the wrong thing to say because Colin's face starts to turn a dark splotchy red.

Crap. I am such an idiot.

I duck around him, bounding up the stairs to my bedroom to grab Mercutio's carrier, my laptop, and a couple changes of clothing.

"What are you doing?" Colin follows me into the bedroom. His figure fills the doorway. Crap. He is blocking the only exit.

"I'm leaving. I'm taking my cat and my work. If you want the apartment so bad, you can have it." I bend down to check under the bed for Mercutio. He is huddled in the dark corner and makes a plaintive meow when he sees my face. Poor baby.

A shadow covers my bedroom window. I look to it and wince.

Ant is on the other side of the glass. Hovering in front of my second story window. The flap of his wings occasionally blocking out the early morning light. Watching me and Colin, together, in my bedroom.

"Open the window, Piper." Ant's voice hits a dangerously low octave.

Crap, crap, crap. I hurry to the window, unlatch it, and shove it open as far as it will go.

"Ant. This isn't what it looks like," I say hurriedly.

"You aren't being harassed by your ex-boyfriend? A man who's currently suing you and shouldn't be in your house?"

"Oh!" I laugh nervously and glance behind me. Colin is staring at the window with pure ire. "I guess it's exactly what it looks like."

"Are you alright, my flame?" Ant doesn't take his eyes off of Colin. "I know I shouldn't have been, but I was watching from across the street."

I shake my head. I couldn't be more grateful for his voyeuristic tendencies right now. "I'm fine. I'm just packing some stuff so I can leave and come to your place. I gotta grab Mercutio," I say tentatively, like I think he might say no.

"Yes, my love, go and pack. You will come back to our nest," Ant says, like it's the most obvious thing in the world. "You shouldn't be here." Ant glares at Colin.

"You're the one who shouldn't be here!" Colin is yelling now. I wince, thinking back to all the times I let him yell at me like that. Why did I put up with him? Why did I let him treat me like that? "This is him? This is the freak you are with now?"

"Leave or I will contact the authorities," Ant threatens.

Colin laughs. It isn't a fun sound. He storms toward me. "Do you think they'll believe a monster over a human?"

I glance between the two men, human and Mothman, my heart racing. "You can't talk to him like that," I insist.

"I knew it. I always knew it. You always liked those weird cartoons and all those little fantasy movies a little too much. Beauty and the Beast, Robin Hood where he was a fox, Tim Curry in Legend. It's all falling into place now."

"What are you talking about?"[2] I roll my eyes.

"You're a monster fucker."

I start to laugh. I step past Colin, but he grabs my arm to stop me.

"Don't touch me!" I yell, shoving his shoulder with one hand as I jerk my other arm out of his grip.

Drunk Colin stumbles two steps backward toward the open window, catching himself on the sill.

"If I am a monster. Perhaps I should start acting like one," Ant growls.

A dark hand reaches into my bedroom, wraps around Colin's shirt, and then he's is gone. Jerked through the open window.

---

2 I know exactly what he's talking about, but I'm not going to admit it.

33

PONTIUS

I cannot kill him. I will not kill him. Piper would not like it if I killed him.

Beneath me Colin screams. His wrists are wrapped in my dark claws while his legs dangle, helpless and hilarious, in the empty air above Piper's building.

"Let me go! Let me go!" Colin yells. He has been screaming so loudly that I decide to take us a little higher, so we won't bother any of her neighbors.

"If I drop you from this height, you will die." I'm not sure if Colin can hear me, but when his mouth snaps closed, I assume he understood enough. "Piper wouldn't want me to kill anyone."

I'm fairly certain she wouldn't, at least. It's not the only thing that stops me from dropping him, but it's the main thing. I squint into the distance. The sun is starting to creep over the horizon, the brightness will sting my eyes in about an hour. I'm not sure what to do with Colin now.

It was stupid to grab him. I couldn't let him stand there, berating and frightening my mate. Even remembering it now has my blood boiling. I should've had a plan when I pulled him through her bedroom window. Now, I'm left holding him with no clue what to do.

My phone buzzes. I'm a bit surprised that it is working this high in the air. I transfer all of Colin's weight to one arm, and drop one of his wrists.

He screams, using both hands to cling to my arm. I use my newly freed hand to pull my phone from my pocket.

I'm not surprised to see Piper's name on my screen. I punch the green answer button.

"Hello, my flame."

"Ant! Where are you? Are you alright? What is happening?"

"I am perfectly fine. I'm about eighty feet above your apartment. I just wanted to talk to Colin alone, to give him a chance to cool off. I promise that I will not kill him."

There's a short pause on the other end of the line before she laughs. "Ant, please don't kill him."

"I won't!" I protest with a grin. "I promise you right now, that I won't. Killing him is the furthest thing from my mind."

She laughs again. "It's just that the more you protest, the more it feels like you might kill him."

"I don't know what you are talking about. I said I'm not going to kill him. Even though it would be very easy for me to just drop him right now and let gravity do all the work," I tease. I glance down at the man, who is now attempting to cling to my arm with both hands. "Why would I say I wasn't going to kill him, if I was just planning on killing him?"

"An alibi?" she jokes.

"Hmmm, not a terrible idea."

"What is he doing?"

I look down at Colin, whose eyes are squeezed shut. His lips are moving silently. "I think he might be praying?" I offer.

She laughs again. I love it. "What are you going to do with him?"

"I'd love to drop him in a lake."

"Oh dear. That would absolutely ruin his hair," she teases. "You know there's that duck pond in the park near your place."

It will be our place soon enough. After this morning, I am never going to let Piper out of my sight again. "Colin seems like the kind of guy who loves ducks."

"I don't want to begin this relationship by ordering you around. But, if you wanted to cool him off—"

"Ducks are super cool," I say, already flying in that direction. Colin screams and begins flailing again. "I had better go, my flame, before I drop my cargo."

My intelligent lovely mate is so full of great ideas. I am going to marry her one day. It's something I hadn't really considered possible before but after attending Sacha's wedding, I know I need it to happen. White dress. Ceremony. Food and drinks. All the people we love coming together. Ours will be at night, and the music will be quieter. Maybe even a silent disco.

By the time I have come to this conclusion, I'm hovering over the duck pond.

As I get lower to the water, Colin's tirade changes, from pleading for his life, to a long string of curses and insults.

He definitely isn't looking forward to a dip in the water.

"I'll sue you! I'll tell the news about this! I'll have it all over the internet. Reporters will be knocking at your door! I'll ruin you!" He's ranting, but it's pointless.

About a foot above the pond, I drop him.

The park is empty right now, so no one notices the very loud splash noise. Or his flailing. He disappears below the surface for a very brief period of time, then his head pops back up, and after some fumbling, he stands. The water comes up to his chest.

"You can swim, right?" I ask, hovering a couple feet above the water. "I definitely should have asked before."

"You idiot!" He's yelling, which means he's not drowning. So I'm pretty sure he'll be fine. "I'm calling the cops!" He pulls a waterlogged phone from his pocket, and his face falls.

"And tell them what? That you got drunk and fell into a lake?"

He scowls. "You can't drop people into ponds and get away with it."

"You can't break into someone's apartment and get away with it."

His face blanches. "I didn't—I—"

"The apartment of your ex-girlfriend, whom you've filed a lawsuit against, and very publicly threatened."

"You attacked me!"

"What would you expect from a monster?" I hunch toward him, spreading my wings as wide as possible to make a large imposing figure. For once, I'm very glad to be perceived as a monster.

"You—you—tried to murder me!"

"We both know if I wanted to murder you, that you'd already be dead." I grin, trying to make it wide and weird—the kind of smile Tiffany always said was unsettling, the one that's terrified so many people.

"Are you threatening me?" Colin looks like he's trying not to piss himself. Too bad he's in the lake, and I will never know if he did.

"Step foot in Piper's apartment again and find out." I chuckle. "I will gladly use every resource at my disposal to be sure she never has to see you again. And I am a rich moth, with many resources."

"You wouldn't bankrupt yourself," he scoffs.

"I'd spend time in prison for her." I laugh, because it's true.

Colin's eyes widen. It's not quite a threat.

My phone buzzes in my pocket.

"Settle your lawsuit with Cryptech, and you will walk away from this, or wade away from it, through about twelve feet of duck shit." I gesture to the pond. "But you will never see Piper, or speak to her, ever again."

I pull my phone back out. It's Piper's face again on my screen. My heart swells when I see her picture.

"Is everything alright, my flame?" I ask as I answer the call.

"Mercutio and I just pulled up outside your place," she says. "But I don't have a key—"

"We will rectify that immediately." I'm en route as the words leave my mouth. Leaving Colin, standing in the middle of the pond, surrounded by various water fowl. Although the water is plenty foul with just him in it.

Piper is waiting for me outside my apartment—cat carrier in one hand and a duffle bag in the other.

Her face lights up when she sees me. "Are you alright?" she calls, when I am still quite far away from her. When I land in the parking spot in front of my building, her eyes search me like I may have an invisible injury.

"I'm fine, my flame."

As soon as the words are out of my mouth, she rushes me, throwing her arms around my middle. "I can't believe you did that." Her voice muffled by my chest.

"You won't see him again."

"Did you—?" she asks quietly.

"Kill him?" I joke.

"Leave him in the duck pond?" She laughs.

"He is probably wading through two feet of duck poop right now."

She giggles and pulls back to look me in the eyes as she says it. "You didn't have to do that for me."

"I didn't do it just for you," I murmur, helping her collect her things from her car. "I did it for me. I am tired of being called a monster. I may as well act like one."

"You aren't a monster." She follows me inside, finding a quiet corner to set Mercutio's carrier down.

She grins, before opening the door of the carrier. She makes a few encouraging noises and eventually the cat's large ginger head emerges.

We watch together as Mercutio sniffs the air and then slinks carefully to a dark corner.

"Is he comfortable?" I ask as the cat curls into a fluffy ball.

"He'll be fine," Piper says. "He's a cat. He just needs a little while to get situated before he'll feel safe."

"He can have as much time to get acclimated as he needs," I say. "You both can."

"You really don't mind us staying here?" She laughs, but I hear the nerves in her voice.

"Of course not." I step behind her to wrap a comforting arm around her waist and pull her against me. "You are mine now, my flame. My mate. Mine."

"Yours?" she scoffs quietly.

"You're denying it?" I snicker.

"What if I am?" she taunts.

"You are testing me," I growl. "You know, I think I enjoyed being a bit of a monster today."

"I think I liked it too." She giggles and leans back into my chest.

"Maybe we can find another way to indulge those baser instincts, my flame?" I chuckle, swiping her hair slowly away from her neck to tease my fingers along her nape.

"I don't belong to you." She makes a soft noise and presses her ass back against me.

"You are mine. Admit it." I kiss along her neck until she gasps and squirms, but taking no real attempt to get away from me.

"Make me," she teases.

"You are mine. You have always been mine." With a growl, I press her front against the wall as I slip my hands up her thighs until her dress is lifted above her waist. But I don't touch her pussy, not yet. She makes a quiet noise that might be my name. I purr for her, grinding my hips into her ass, taking that easy control that she allows me. I love the way she opens up for me, letting me do anything to her, for her. My aedeagus strains at my seam, ready to show her who she belongs to. As soon as she admits it. I shove my pants down to my ankles and urge her legs open so the smell of her pussy, wet and ready, is free to permeate the air. I lift her into exactly the right position, she gasps against the wall as her feet leave the ground. I grab her with my claspers, holding that plump, freckled ass against my groin.

Now she's exactly the right height for my aedeagus to protrude and finally stroke her underwear, pushing it aside so I can reach her wet cunt.

"Ant!" she yelps at the sudden feeling.

"Are you telling me who you belong to?" I chuckle in her ear.

She laughs, but I quiet it with another swipe of my cock.

"Who does this cunt belong to?"

"You," she whispers, clearly still reticent to admit it.

I snicker as my dick moves along her, swiping up and down her lips, coating myself in her juices. Moving my hand to her face, I cup her chin, run my thumb along her lips, then plunge it between her teeth and into her mouth. She wraps her tongue around me and sucks with a soft moan.

"Whose mouth is this?" I pull my wet thumb away, teasing her neck with my breath when I ask.

"Yours," she admits.

"And this?" I ask, dipping a hand into her dress to find her nipple with two saliva covered fingers.

"My boob?" she asks with a laugh. "Yours. They can both be yours."

"The heart, under the boobs." I purr, massaging her nipple. She giggles. So cute, so sweet, so kind.

"Yours, it's all yours," she says with a little gasp as I finally sink my cock into her hot cunt.

"Good girl," I growl and fuck her slow and hard against the wall until I get to finish inside her tight heat.

We collapse on the couch together, sweaty and satisfied. She's mine now. Finally. Safe in my arms. My sweet beautiful mate.

Epilogue
PIPER

"There you are, Mercutio!" I praise the large orange cat as he emerges from one of the shelves that Ant has installed along the high ceilings of his apartment. I open a can of cat food. Mercutio yells at me a few times as he makes his way along the custom shelves and down to the little shelf where we feed him.

It's only taken Ant a couple months to fill his home with every cat toy, scratching post, and pet bed that he could find on the internet. He's spared no expense, making every single inch of his home cat-friendly. The cherry on the cake was a cat walk installed high in the ceiling, with bridges and carpeted shelves and cute places for him to hide. We've already started talking to Bailey about fostering some kittens. It'd be great for Mercutio to have some friends now that there's so much room for them in his home.

Our home.

The final moving boxes in my car make it official. My lease isn't quite up on my apartment. But after two months of keeping my stuff in two separate places, I finally pulled the cord and asked to move in. Ant, of course, agreed immediately.

I am a bit sad to leave an apartment I really loved,

but I'm exchanging it for a mate I love even more. Ant did not fit in that apartment. He could barely spread his wings in my bedroom, and we really need space for him to spread his wings in the bedroom.

The bedroom is one of the few places that we haven't cooled down.

Work is going well. It's busy, without being too stressful. Teaming up with Cryptech has been a godsend for resources, we've doubled my employee roster, hiring three new people over the summer.

Things also got significantly more chill with Colin.

Ant told me everything that happened between the two of them at the duck pond. I'm only a little surprised that Colin dropped his lawsuit against me. He's always been a bit of a chicken, so of course he ran the moment that he was truly threatened. He left town, yet again. This time to Chicago, or Los Angeles, or Atlanta, it could be the fucking moon, for all I care. He's gone. Out of my life. Hopefully, I never have to see him again.

For his sake, I hope that Ant never sees him again either.

I'm grateful to Ant for all of that. I probably could have fixed it myself eventually, but it's nice to occasionally let someone else take care of me for once.

"Is that the last of your stuff?" Ant asks as he walks into the house and drops his work bag at the front door.

"That's the last of it!" I grin, taking him in. He's wearing his work suit—a custom Brooks Brothers. It's a deep violet. He looks so handsome, a proper business-man. He kicks off his shoes at the door, revealing socks covered in a Triforce pattern, showing that nerdy side I love so much, lurking beneath. "All of my boxes are here, and they are unpacked! You are living with me, for real. Regret it?" I tease.

"Never," he says, but there's hesitation in his eyes.

"Something wrong?" I ask. He's been excited for me to move in for weeks now, there must be something else upsetting him.

"Nothing, it's just—" He sighs, like the weight of the entire world is on his shoulders. "They found another abandoned Mothman egg. Alone, in an empty factory, a couple hours west of here."

"Oh no!" I cross the room so I can wrap my arms tight around him. "I mean, I'm glad they found it. Is it okay? I can't believe they are still being left to fend for themselves."

"It's okay. Safe." Ant shakes his head sadly, "Some cryptids are still stuck in their ways. I'm sure it would have grown up safely all by itself."

"Of course, but it will be better if it has someone taking care of it, right?"

"That's the thing—" Ant stops talking in a way that makes me nervous.

"Does it not have anywhere to go?" I look around the apartment in a mild panic. "We have room here, don't we? Do you think we could take care of it? We might need to build some privacy walls. Would you be alright with something like that?"

His shoulders sag with relief. "I am so glad you suggested it. I was nervous to ask."

"You really want to?" I can't help how excited that makes me. I bounce on my feet. "Adopt them?"

"It's just one."

"Well, that's where we'll start, obviously."

Ant grins broadly and swoops me into a hug, burying his face in my neck and lifting me from the ground to spin me in a full circle. "I am so glad you feel this way, my flame."

I laugh, wrapping my arms around his neck. "Don't get too excited just yet! We have a lot of work to do. This place isn't exactly baby proof. How long do we have?"

"How long?"

"Until the egg hatches."

"About two weeks."

"Two weeks!" I gasp, tapping his shoulders until he sets me back on my feet. "That's so soon! I've got the NJD Project to finish next week at work, but it's going to take a lot of effort to get this place baby ready." I'm already pacing out some of my nervous energy.

"What if—" Ant pauses, seeming uncertain again.

"What if?" I wait for him to finish his thought.

"What if I took some time off work?" Ant suggests very quietly.

There is a tiny pleading smile on his face.

"You want to do that? Really?" I ask. "It's something you want and not just something you are doing for me?"

"I've been thinking about it for a while. Since I got back from my sister's in Canada. I've been running myself ragged the past couple of years. Sacha only works part time these days. I figure if it's good enough for a Bigfoot, then it's good enough for me."

"Okay," I agree instantly.

"Okay?"

"I mean, okay, as in, of course. Yes! Whatever you want to do." I grab his hands, pulling them to my face so I can kiss his knuckles. "I would love to bring a baby into our family. If you are happy taking some time off work, then I guess I'm prepared to be the breadwinner for a while."

"You wouldn't be the breadwinner. I have plenty of

savings that we can dip into. Moonshine and the Artemis also bring in some money." Ant laughs.

"Alright, alright, enough bragging," I joke. "I liked you before I knew you were rich, remember?"

"If I remember correctly, for a while, you didn't like me at all," he teases, wrapping his hands around my waist. His warm palms spread heat across my body. "Then you found out I was rich, and then you liked me again."

"You're right." I pretend to ponder. "Actually, I think it was the money that brought me back to you." I lean into his grasp.

He growls low in the back of his throat. and squeezes me tight. I squeal in reaction. His growl becomes a purr as he dips down to kiss me again. His light touches still send sparks through every little nerve in my body.

"As long as you are mine now, my flame, I do not mind how you got here."

"Me neither," I mutter, already willing to lose myself in him again.

THANK YOU

Thanks so much for reading! I wouldn't be anywhere without people reading my books. A big fat thank you to the many people who helped me get this thing where it is today, with support, encouragement, and so very many comma adjustments: Meghan, the Wifey Coven, and my very own personal Carney.

I mostly write about big soft cinnamon-roll monsters falling into gross gushy love. I hope we can all find the perfect hairy beast to curl up next to at night, who will make us tea, read us a good book, and rip our enemies in half if we ask them to very nicely.

If you enjoyed Moth Manager please consider leaving me a review! And then check out the other stuff I've written.

⊙ INSTAGRAM.COM/LUNACANTRIP

◼ FACEBOOK.COM/LUNACANTRIP

♪ TIKTOK.COM/@LUNACANTRIP

ALSO BY LUNA CANTRIP

The adventures of the Cryptid Billionaires will continue with at least two more books, so don't worry, you'll get to see Mr. Loch fall in love as well and if you haven't yet you can read Sacha and Bailey's story in Bigfoot Boss.

Bigfoot Boss

A grumpy Bigfoot billionaire, his awkward human assistant, and a half million dollar date...

Bailey isn't good at stuff, she's used to trying new things and failing repeatedly, but she's determined that new job is going to last, she's willing to do anything to make sure it does.

Even if it means dating her stern cryptid boss.

Sacha Kwatch has spent years convincing society he's more than a monster, he's a responsible businessman. But when a beautiful woman walks into his office his mating bond snaps into place awakening his most primal urges.

He needs her. So he offers her the one thing she needs in return, money.

Bailey knows it's ridiculous to date your boss, but who turns down half a million dollars? She's determined to get her money but the more time she spends with Sacha the more she begins to think she might be able to trust his declarations of love. Is it ridiculous to think she can have her payday, and eat it too?

Cryptid Billionaires is a series of low-angst high-steam standalone romances centered around employees at the tech company Cryptech, each book features a love story for a different kind of cryptid with a guaranteed happily ever after

https://books2read.com/u/47JWd7

I Saw Krampus Kissing Ms. Claus

Being Ms. Claus kinda sucks. During my favorite holiday of the year the only thing anyone cares about is what my brother Santa is doing.

But when the famous Christmas Eve ride is threatened, it's up to me to fix it. And the only person who can help me solve the mystery is the little boy who used to pull my pigtails when I was a kid.

But Krampus isn't such a little boy any more.

He's all grown up into a seven-foot tall demon, with a penchant for punishment, and this year he has his sights set on more than just Santa's naughty list.

He wants me.

Will being thrown together light a yule log of romance? Or will meeting under the mistletoe be the distraction that destroys Christmas?

https://books2read.com/u/47JWd7

Printed in Dunstable, United Kingdom